WIZARDBORN

WIZARDBORN

WORLD'S FIRST WIZARD™ SERIES BOOK 03

AARON D. SCHNEIDER
MICHAEL ANDERLE

LMBPN

DISRUPTIVE IMAGINATION

LMBPN Publishing
PMB 196, 2540 South Maryland Pkwy
Las Vegas, NV 89109

First US edition, November 2020
ebook ISBN: 978-1-64971-299-8
Paperback ISBN: 978-1-64971-300-1

THE WIZARDBORN TEAM

Thanks to our Beta Team:

Kelly O'Donnell, Jim Caplan, Larry Omans, Rachel Beckford

Thanks to our JIT Team:

Diane L. Smith
Micky Cocker
Jeff Goode
John Ashmore
Paul Westman

If I've missed anyone, please let me know!

Editor
SkyHunter Editing Team

Yeah, I burned like a witch in a Puritan town
It lit me
It was a good dream
—*Lit Me Up*, Brand New

No course was open to me save to leap, with eyes self-bound,
into the yawning abyss of the future.
—*Vathek*, William Beckford

Blood-Curdling Story

That story is creepy,
It's waily, it's weepy,
It's screechy and screamy
Right up to the end.
It's spooky, it's crawly,
It's grizzly, it's gory,
It's the awfulest story
(Please tell it again).

—*Falling Up*, Shel Silverstein

I devoutly dedicate this book to my wife, my darling, my dueling partner, and the peg o' my heart. Nothing I've ever done of consequence has always been with your love and support. Love you, babe.

PROLOGUE: FIDITE NEMINI

Of all the tragedies that had strutted their hour upon the stage of the Bolshoi Theatre, none were as heartbreaking as the sight of the theatre as the warlords shuffled in. It had been nearly two decades since the premiere theatre of Moscow, perhaps of all of Eastern Europe, had opened for a show, but in the meantime, the Bolshoi had been ill-used.

The Bolshoi had not been afforded the dignity of a placid, dusty decrepitude as the Russian Empire crumbled. There had been meetings held in its concert hall, some public and others more clandestine. There had been vandalism, some more artistic than the rest, with scrawled tragic poetry sharing sections of the wall and floor with crude, anatomically impossible pictograms. There had been treasures and decor and furnishings ransacked for reasons ranging from posterity to fuel for the hearth. There was even evidence of creatures having taken shelter in the place from the feces-encrusted roost in the blackened chandelier to the nesting pile of detritus from which rodent eyes gleamed.

Larger but no less feral occupants had been cleared out along with most of their filth in preparation for the meeting.

The roof was still intact, though for the past few years, a

growing stain had spread like a seasonally swelling inkblot worked in beige and brown. With that had come damp that had crept and wept across the walls and balconies until they were woolly with molds and other less easily classifiable forms of life. The only place that could accommodate the meeting was the central floor. Most of the seats were in disarray, having been destroyed or gnawed by scavengers, and in places, the carpet had been stripped away, leaving the bare boards. Such bare spots near the occupied orchestra pit had seen even the boards gnawed to splinters, and through those jagged gaps on the unsound floor could be glimpsed the dark and glistening depth of the stygian basement.

To avoid plummeting into the depths, what seats could be salvaged had been dragged into the center of the hall. Here they formed a three-quarter ring, and to this ring came warlords, commanders of armies, patriots, and murderers. Each man had left his contingent of soldierly bandits without, having been permitted only one attendant at the meeting. Some had chosen their attendant as a tool of intimidation, being escorted by hard-handed and cold-eyed killers, while others were accompanied by men whose skills were strictly secretarial.

They fell into separate but roughly equal camps as their attendants shuffled their seats to one side or another. The two tribes eyed each other warily, one band muttering imprecations against "traitorous Whites," while the other hissed and spat at the "godless Reds." After the opposing congregations were seated, some time was spent in muted choruses of denouncement, but it never reached beyond that.

Finally, realizing that they'd been whispering amongst themselves for some time, a spokesman emerged from each faction. For the Reds, it was a bushy-haired man with spectacles on his prominent nose and a mustachioed goatee around thick lips. Apparently no one had bothered to tell him he looked positively Mephistophelian, or perhaps that was the point. For the Whites, it was a tall, long-featured man with a dark mustache whose crisp uniform accentuated his thin, straight figure.

The men eyed each other, the Red speaker seemingly intent on boring holes through the other man with his piercing stare, while the White viewed his opponent as something to be brushed off his brightly polished boots.

"So why did you call us here, Trotsky?" the White asked in a drawling voice pitched to express how little he cared. "Did you want us to see one more thing this rebellion has cost us?"

To illustrate the point, however mildly spoken, the White swept an arm to indicate the putrefying balconies and the verminous orchestra pit.

"Trying to remind us how great this revolution of yours is?"

For a moment, Trotsky bristled so fiercely that his bushy hair began to quiver, but with a supreme effort, he quelled his obvious wrath. One hand rose and very carefully adjusted the glasses across the bridge of his nose, while the other gripped the front lapel of his overcoat with affronted dignity.

"The losses of this war weigh on us all," the Red said, stiffly at first, but warming to the speech as he went. "But the reason I called us all here has nothing to do with the past and everything to do with the future."

Rustling among the Whites was greeted by indignant glares from the Reds, but no one contested the point.

"By now, I'm sure you've all heard what has happened with Stalin," Trotsky continued, ignoring the leers and unsympathetic comments from the Whites with his dignity intact. "I'm sure you've also heard about the construction project in Petrograd."

There were more muttered exclamations, but these were far less energetic and far more uncertain. They'd been too busy waging war on the members of the opposite faction and occasionally each other, but word had still reached them, though not with its meaning understood. Yes, they'd heard, but even if they believed, the information did not lend itself to understanding.

After all, why would anyone waste valuable resources on building anything in a blasted pit like the fallen capital of the Russian Empire?

"I thought you said this meeting was about the future?" the White asked, a lazy smile making a half-hearted attempt at mimicking his mustache. The Whites around him nodded and chuckled deep in their chests. "Do you plan to delay until the winter snows fall and collapse the ceiling on us all?"

Trotsky sniffed but did not take the bait, turning slightly instead to make it clear he was addressing all present.

"We have good reason to believe both of these incidents were the direct result of German meddling in Russian affairs. In the face of our great nation falling under the control of the black-coated heathens, it seemed to be high time we came to some sort of understanding."

The Red turned sharply to his counterpart and arched an eyebrow.

"Does that serve as an explanation, Wrangel?" he hissed. He rocked back a little on his heels as he hooked his thumbs in the pockets of his greatcoat.

Wrangel, who was much taller than Trotsky and seemed even more so given his gaunt frame, glared down his nose at the Red and seemed prepared to say something particularly unkind. Finally, his shoulders bowed a little more, and his gaze became distant. His chin rose and fell slowly, to the obvious consternation of several of his fellow whites.

"You may be a godless little Jew, but you aren't wrong," Wrangel declared with a retiring sigh. "The Germans and their legions of treacherous conscripts are circling like wolves."

Many of the whites nodded gravely along with their ad hoc champion, but a few clearly did not appreciate his sudden commiseration with the Reds.

A stout officer sputtered beneath an outward-sweeping mustache that looked ready to engage a bull horn to whiskers.

"My intelligence reports say Stalin cooperated with the Germans," he declared, shooting a narrowed glare at the Reds before angrily turning to scowl at Wrangel. "How do we know this isn't some ploy by the communist vermin to get us to lower our guard?"

"Because leaving the scattered corpses of our armies in the Caucasus Mountains is a pretty stupid way to win the war, Yudenich," Trotsky rebuked before Wrangel could reply. "Stalin took more of our strength than any of us cares to admit, and it was irrevocably broken in Georgia."

Yudenich's mustache writhed as though ready to strike, but Trotsky glared through his spectacles undaunted.

"If you have intelligence about Stalin and the Germans, it must corroborate what I am saying," the smaller man snapped before turning back to Wrangel. "We can keep suspecting and killing each other, but it will only be that much easier for the blackcoats to come along and pick us apart if we do that."

Again, Wrangel looked as though nothing would please him more than to sneer in the Red's face, but an absolute weight bore down on him, and he could only nod.

"I would see you all dead in a ditch, but not if it means those savages become our new masters," he said, turning to his constituents with a measuring eye. "I don't think any true Russian would want such a thing."

The emphatic phrasing combined with the tall man's relentless stare cowed the other Whites, even Yudenich. Some muttered similar sentiments of wishing ignominious death on communists, but not if it meant German boots on their throats. Most nodded silently.

Satisfied, Wrangel turned to regard Trotsky coolly but without challenge.

"I assume you have something in mind?"

Trotsky nodded again as he and all the Reds stared in shock. For all their wild hopes, none had thought the Whites would be won over so easily. Many had declared days ago that the royalist snobs would rather see Russia in ashes before they worked with the Bolsheviks. It seemed that Trotsky's statement that their country was already in ashes had been more successful than even he had dared to hope.

"Well," Trotsky said, wiping off his glasses pensively to buy time, "the first thing we need to do is secure our western borders and co-opt the supplies headed to Petrograd. I'm sure we could all make use of what is being funneled there."

Several heads on both sides nodded in unison before noticing and stopping with juvenile alarm.

"Do you know what is being built there?" Wrangel asked, a frown spreading across his face.

From above them, a deep, velvety voice reached down to brush every man's ear like a descending silken noose.

"The future," the voice said, and every man present looked upward at the royal box in the center of the theatre's back wall.

Standing over them like an emperor grinning down into an arena was a tall, powerfully built young man. He was brutally beautiful, his pulchritude accentuated by ink scrawled across his skin. The tattoos were displayed by his half-open shirt and rolled sleeves, and he held his silver suit coat over his shoulder like a regal cloak.

"The future of warfare and therefore the future of mankind is being built in Petrograd," the newcomer declared, managing to meet the eye of every upturned face without deigning to move an inch. "A future you are going to help build."

Several voices cried out at once to know the man's identity, and some of the attendants drew pistols and pointed them at the royal box. Trotsky and Wrangel exchanged concerned looks before turning to regard the man standing above them. Despite several weapons aimed at him, he didn't seem concerned, and that alone gave the two leaders pause.

"You seem quite confident about our cooperation," Trotsky

called to the man, his tone flat and neutral. "Yet, none of us seems to know who you are. A rather odd way to begin a partnership, don't you think?"

The stranger looked down at the Red spokesman and displayed a wolfish smile.

"I'm not sure I said anything about cooperation. Did I?"

The first canister rolled across the floor then, releasing jets of orange-yellow vapor as it went.

Horror robbed most of the men of the first few vital seconds, and panic stole the rest. Hurried shots scored and pitted the balcony beside the stranger or punched dusty holes in the ceiling. The man didn't budge an inch, his fingers not even tightening on the crumbling scrollwork beneath them.

Those who hadn't wasted time shooting or succumbing to fear had run for the exits, but that proved as ineffectual as the other options when brutes in gas masks emerged like specters from the thickening fog, clubs and canisters in hand. A few hard strokes and the runners were sent stumbling back with broken jaws and flattened noses.

More canisters with brilliant hissing contrails spun into the gathering until the main floor was thick with yellow fog. Men screamed and more shots were fired wildly, but they only bit into walls and the moldering seats. The armed men stood, breath rasping through their protective gas masks, and watched the figures inside the murky cloud contort and spasm as their screams grew fainter.

There was a splintering crash, and a biblical wave of chittering rodents rushed out of the fog. Some still bore the gas on their fur like tarnished motes of gold. Many of them collapsed spasming, while others, frenzied with pain, bit and tore at their brethren, but all were carried along in the verminous tide that sought to escape the poison. Even as high boots shuffled away from the coming torrent of rodents, the eyes of the masked men swept up to the man still watching the scene below. In a second, it seemed, all made the same decision.

Better to face the plague of rats than face their master's wrath.

Fortunately, the dying vermin were more interested in escape than vengeance and so flowed past the men in a stream of squirming bodies. Most did not make it more than a few bounds through the doors before they succumbed.

In the distraction of the rats, the guards hadn't noticed a single figure lurching through the fog toward them. One hand held a handkerchief to his mouth, while the other groped before him as he staggered forward. He was unrecognizable beneath a web of swollen and broken blood vessels squirming beneath his skin. Rivulets of dark blood seeped freely from his eyes and nose and smeared the handkerchief, further concealing his visage. A thick, horrid gagging sound issued from deep in his throat, and it was that which drew the guards' attention.

The nearest man noticed too late as the groping hand grasped his hand, in which he carried a cudgel. Fingers turned to claws, and the handkerchief was abandoned as the dying man raked arm, shoulder, and face. The guard managed to beat his attacker back with a desperate punch and several savage blows, but not before the mask had been torn off his face. The poisonous fog was thin enough at the edge of the hall that its vapors could be seen sliding up the unfortunate man's nostrils even as he cursed his dying attacker. Dark eyes wild with panic, he looked upward and saw with absolute horror his master's eye upon him.

"Oh, my dear Ilyah." The tattooed chieftain sighed with heavy resignation, then gave a slow nod.

A desperate gibbering moan escaped Ilyah's lips as he dropped his club and tried to force the mask back into place, but the others closed in around him. He screamed and tried to find a face to plead with, but behind the flat, reflective eyes and rasping respirators were monsters beyond reason or pity. With single-minded implacability, they drove him deeper into the fog as he wailed and begged. When he tried to push past them, one of them kicked him hard between the legs so his body came off the ground. Gasping and mewling, he reached out, but a cudgel swept down and broke his arm at the wrist. Then his comrades retreated to the rear of the hall, boots crunching on the bodies of dead rats, and resumed their vigil.

Ilyah's screams were swallowed by the choking fumes within a few moments.

Soon there was only the grating breath of the masked guards and the vapors congealing into small clouds that settled across the hall floor. Jutting from the saffron murk were the tortured forms of the dead warlords and their attendants, strewn across and between the upturned seats. Behind them was a jagged hole in the floor near the orchestra pit where one of the wretches had crashed through the rat-gnawed floor and now lay broken in the darkness beneath the Bolshoi's hall.

The man in the royal box, his mouth bowed into a frown and shoulders hunched, looked at the scene and shook his head.

"Does it have to be such a gruesome process?" he demanded with a tremor in his voice that he couldn't quite hide.

From the dark recesses of the box came a whistling, grinding chuckle.

"Roland, if I didn't know any better, I'd say you felt bad for them," commented a voice as agonizing as the laugh. "I thought you hated these men, boy. Instead of complaining, shouldn't you be thanking me for the gift?"

Roland kept sweeping his eyes from one side of the hall to the next, desperate to avoid the bulging, ruptured eyes that all seemed to stare up at him. How could their blind looks seem so accusing?

"I wanted them dead, Zlydzen; that's simple enough," he said with a shrug, then flapped his hand. "But no man deserves this, much less what you are going to do next."

The chuckle returned like a teapot singing with its belly full of boiling gravel.

"Oh, humans, so sentimental," Zlydzen burbled as he ambled out of the box's shadow. "I'm making use of what would have been wasted otherwise."

Roland snorted and spat but didn't say anything.

In one swollen hand, the dwarrow held an arcane device like a bronze tuning fork that had sprouted branches and leaves of metal. Upon the leaves were inscribed odd, spiraling symbols which made the eyes ache and the stomach knot if they were stared at for more than a second. Shuffling to the rail, which he could peek over, he held out the device and began to rotate it in a tight little circle.

The engraved leaves began to flutter and sent up a whistling chorus, then the branches started to turn with a dull thrum. The whistle and thrum sharpened and deepened respectively, and the air thickened with a pressure that had nothing to do with the toxic gas

The first of the rat corpses swelled and popped. Quick spasms wracked the little bodies as odd engorgements strained and burst. One or two managed to lurch upward in ungainly hops, but they all became gory blooms on the floor within moments.

Beyond the dead rodents, the clouds of poison began to recede, drawn inward by those who were better able to absorb the noxious burden. The men, their bodies deformed by toxic swellings, squirmed, shuddered, and as the noisome device reached its crescendo, rose unsteadily to their feet.

THESE PICTURES

Milo felt a bead of sweat travel down the side of his scarred cheek to race along his jaw before it broke free of his chin. The dot of perspiration fell on the photograph in his hands.

He idly swept away the offending moisture with his thumb, but he supposed it didn't matter. There were plenty of other photographs, and they all told the same damning story.

"We would appreciate an explanation," stated the man sitting across the table from Milo. From its liver-spotted dome to its collar-pinched throat, General Erich Ludendorff's face looked to be carved from a single tube of flesh, with the barest attention given to his wrinkled features. The wizard thought they could barely be called features, more like sags and ripples around peculiar little orifices.

Yet this simulacrum of a human form slumped in front of him had been the most powerful man in the German Empire since the death of Field Marshal von Hindenburg a few years ago, and he wanted Milo to explain something he hadn't known about until the moment they'd shoved a folder full of photographs into his hand. Now he had dozens of grainy photographs from the valley surrounding Shatili, all of which depicted a large number of corpses displaying gruesome yet imaginative methods of elim-ination.

One of them showed two men who'd simultaneously rammed pistols into each other's mouths and pulled the trigger. These unfortunate gunmen lay under a trio of corpses, one of which was a burly man who'd spitted a smaller man on each knife-equipped fist before every bit of his skull above the lower jaw had been blown off.

If Milo hadn't been where he was, he might have believed that this was some kind of macabre farce of battlefield photography, a set of staged photos that went too far in their quest to artistically portray the horrors of war. All the men were wearing the same uniform.

"This looks to be a goodly number of Soviet soldiers all dead near Shatili, sir," Milo said cautiously, feeling another drop of sweat slalom down his face. "As to how they all got into this state, I'm not sure I can answer."

General Ludendorff's frown deepened within his slab-like face, and from beneath a mass of sagging wrinkles, two eyes burrowed into Milo relentlessly. One speckled hand, claw-like despite the general's flabby features, tapped a hooked nail upon a piece of paper in front of him. Ludendorff's eyes never left him as he spoke, punctuating each word with a tap.

"It states here in your debrief that you placed countermea-sures at Shatili to thwart the Reds," he growled thickly, his voice all the more ferocious given his frailty. "Your report states the countermeasures were non-conventional misdirection."

Milo nodded mutely, though there was no question in Ludendorff's voice. For his part, he wasn't sure how much he was supposed to say. Colonel Jorge had made it clear early on that the general staff was finicky about openly calling things magic or blatantly confessing to working with and against monsters. The one thing Milo did not want to do right now was to offend their touchy sensibilities, but he had a growing premonition that it would become unavoidable.

He couldn't know for certain, but he was a wizard, after all.

"After you left these countermeasures in place in the pursuit of your renegade plot to capture Stalin," the general continued, his finger still tapping, "the Soviet forces moved into the area. When they investigated the fortress complex, something occurred that caused an army of several thousand men to begin fighting among themselves."

Milo dared a look down at the photograph. That did seem to be the case, but he imagined stating that would not do him any favors with the general. He'd ceased to tap as he leaned forward to let his rheumy eyes burrow deeper into the wizard.

"This infighting also left us with no witnesses since every single one of the soldiers was dead or fled. Even their vehicles and materiel were subjected to this violence, destroyed by their owners. In effect, what we have here is the utter destruction of an enemy force on a scale never before seen."

Milo stared back as his chin rose and fell. He managed to keep his mouth from hanging open, but that was about all his dignity could afford at this point.

"The question then seems clear," Ludendorff said, still frowning and boring his eyes into Milo's soul. "Did your non-conventional countermeasures do this? Are those photographs evidence of the magical boobytrap you set?"

Milo stifled a wince as some along the sides of the long table muttered and hissed. He had nearly forgotten about them under Ludendorff's scrutiny, but at the blatant mention of the supernatural, they intruded on the wizard's attention as they officiously preened ruffled feathers. To his credit, the general didn't pay them any heed.

Milo tried to weigh his words carefully, but every one felt jagged and top-heavy on his tongue.

"I would be lying if I didn't acknowledge the part my, er, non-conventional means played, sir," Milo said, wondering why he suddenly found it so hard to say the word "magic." "But I would also be lying if I didn't say that I have no idea how they achieved that result."

Ursine grumbles and less subtle noises of indignation came from thick, bewhiskered mouths around the room. Milo had thought the ghulish court in Ifreedahm over a year ago sounded dangerous with all their viperish whispers, but he would take a snakebite over a bear mauling most days.

"So, these were not the countermeasures you planned?" Ludendorff probed, inclining his head ever so slightly to the pictures in Milo's hands.

"No, sir," Milo said with a shake of his head he hoped would seem earnest rather than frantic. "The, um, countermeasures were supposed to misdirect and disable communications to confuse Stalin's forces and buy us more time to escape with him."

The magus held the photographs in front of him as though touching them made him queasy, which wasn't far from the truth.

"This was never my intention," he said, honestly, bearing up under the general's gaze.

Milo recognized that there were nuances to the statement he'd made, but the complexity of it didn't bother him. He knew at the bottom of his heart that he didn't have a problem with those men dying on principle. If it had been a case of him versus one of them, he'd have ended this or that soldier with a bullet or magical fire or a handy rock and not given it a second thought. He expected that any of them would have done the same, perhaps doubly so because most of them were under the influence of a dwarrow's magic.

His disgust was for the scale and the necessity. First, scale because though he was no great philosopher or statistician, he imagined death on the scale of thousands having farther-reaching consequences than he was comfortable with. He supposed generals and statesmen could send men to die in droves at a word, but the wizard wasn't one of those. Second, necessity because while war was a bloody business, such utter destruction of life was gratuitous. Enemies surrendered and materiel was captured; the bloody business wasn't reduced to complete extermination.

At least, that was how it should have been to Milo's reckoning.

"So, you are suggesting that this outcome," Ludendorff asked as he sank back with a wheeze, "was an accident? A magical mishap?"

The grousing about the mention of magic nearly drowned out Milo's answer of "yes," but when it registered, the room subsequently filled with throaty snarls and wet growls. He wondered if Goldilocks had heard similar sounds when she woke up from her pilfered nap.

Ludendorff sat quietly for a moment, shriveled talons resting on the table, eyes sunk into the folds of his face. Had the lights in the room been dimmer, he might have looked like a wizened idol carved from stone. The expression on his sagging face didn't change as he began to speak, but despite that, every voice in the room quieted when the calm, phlegmy voice emerged.

"I would like you to think very hard before you answer this next question," the general warned, still holding his pose. "Speaking as the only expert we possess on such things, could there be any possible explanation for why these countermeasures malfunctioned so grotesquely?"

Lie, Milo thought instantly, and unbidden, a very convincing, very intricate collection of rubbish sprang to mind. It would be easy because as Ludendorff had already noted, Milo knew more about magic, or its practical applications at least, than any other person in the Empire or the world for that matter. He could mention anything he'd learned in Ifreedahm or the Marquis's court and fabricate a befuddling and engaging lie right there on the spot. After all, not that long ago, lying had been second nature to him in his ill-fated attempt to be a professional criminal.

But damn it all, he wasn't that person anymore, at least not entirely, and he wasn't about to sit there with a folder full of death in his hands and twist things to try to save his skin. He wanted to—oh dear God, he desperately wanted to—but some swelling, festering sense of decency wouldn't let him.

So instead of lying, he opened the folder full of carnage again and perused the horrors as his mouth gave voice to his mind's musings.

"I'd rigged a series of unstable soul wells to collapse when disrupted," he explained as he flipped between the photographs, searching for inspiration among the black and white splashes of blood and entrails. "The shades inside the soul wells were old spiteful things from around the fortress, the sort of resonances folklore might call poltergeists or other disrupting spirits. Once set loose, I expected they'd frighten some of the soldiers and wreak havoc with their wireless communications, and maybe cause engines to stall and machines to misbehave."

There were more mutters and rumbles, but Milo snuck a peek in time to see Ludendorff quiet them with a wave of one vulture-like hand. He felt the gaze settling on him, but it seemed more intrigued than hostile, and that steadied Milo. He looked at the photos again, and something caught the corner of his eye and dragged his attention back to one photograph.

A smile, wide to the point of splitting, stretched across the face of a corpse. The dead man had spitted two men who had gutted him as they died. Something about the scene seemed familiar, and not just the two impaled men.

It was the smile, he decided as he stared.

"The shades were powerful but unfocused," he continued as he flicked through the other photographs, unsure of what he was looking for. "Without magical will to channel them, they would have exhausted themselves quickly since unfocused actions waste huge amounts of their essence. They needed a receptacle."

There!

He found the same smile on another face, just as wide and somehow disturbingly similar even though it was clear this was another body with another cause of death. Scanning the body, he saw that its hands were drenched in gore so that it was hard to see them clearly in the black and white photograph, while it was easy to see that the legs were gone below the knee. As he studied the maniacal grin straining the features, he thought it was almost like the man's face had been forced to adopt features that were not his own.

Something twisted in his stomach, and he wondered at his choice to leave his cane outside with Ambrose. He could have mentally conferenced what was becoming a theory with Imrah, though right now, he feared she would confirm his growing dread.

"The shades would have been looking for a receptacle for their essence, something they could latch on to," he carried on, then words failed him and his mouth went dry as he flipped through more photographs. "But without a magical focus or will to anchor them, they would have been butting up against the natural barrier that all living souls create."

Milo stared at another photo.

In this one, a dead soldier lay flat on the ground, his head turned to the left. His arms were extended out to either side, and his fingers were buried in the backs of the men on either side of him. Dark splashes of blood ran up to the shoulder of his uniform. Half of his face was pressed into the dirt and there was a fist-sized hole through his back, but Milo could still see the gaping grin.

Again the features seemed pressed out of their natural shape to create a maniacal mask.

"Shades are echoes," Milo said, his voice and thoughts in

danger of being lost amongst the growing clamor of German oaths and denouncements. "They might act like thinking spirits, but they are pieces of what they once were. They have a set of patterns, and they can't do anything except repeat them."

Milo remembered what Rihyani had told him about the kind of mental degradation those manipulated by Zlydzen would undergo over time. Could that damage have been spiritual as well? She had talked about them being hollowed-out shells, but what if it was more than their thoughts that had been scraped clean?

"Damn it all!" Ludendorff barked, then gave several rattling coughs. The room quieted as all eyes, even Milo's, turned to watch the crumbling titan struggle to regain his breath.

"I'll have the room cleared if that happens again," the general said in a wheezing growl as his watery, red-rimmed eyes swept the chamber. Several of the faces staring back at him raised chins and puffed out chests defiantly, but none was so bold as to say anything.

"You seemed to be reaching for some discovery," Ludendorff said as he turned his gaze back to Milo. "I suggest you come to it quickly."

Milo nodded, but he felt like there was a boulder in his stomach and that burdensome lump was also chained to his tongue, which didn't want to verbalize what he now realized must be the truth.

He started to speak, but his voice failed him. He told himself that not saying it didn't make it not true, but somehow in his very foundations, he knew it *did* make it more true.

Especially for him.

"I think the shades possessed the soldiers," Milo said, the words coming out in a bitter and caustic rush. "The long-term magic the Soviets were under left them vulnerable. Left them open somehow, and the malicious shades leaped at the chance."

How many of the wicked things had he bound up in those soul wells? Hundreds, at least.

"The shades became violent upon possessing the soldiers," Milo continued, tasting bile and iron at the back of his throat. "Hundreds of men turned on their comrades, and after they were put down, the shades sprang out of the corpses to possess new men. Those shades that ran out of living targets would have destroyed anything within reach. Nothing was left because the shades wouldn't have left anything alive or in one piece."

The silence in the room was so complete that Milo might have thought he'd gone deaf if not for the hammer of his heart in his chest and the rasp of his breath.

Ludendorff's face was a pensive facade again, and none dared to disturb his considerations.

"I confess that I am not well versed in all of Jorge's reports on such matters," the general said at last, his words slow and measured, "but I think I have the rudiments of what you have explained. You unwittingly exterminated a host of magically vulnerable soldiers using a conjured army of ghosts."

It wasn't a question, but Milo nodded anyway, the movement weighed down by his powerful guilt.

"Yes, General." Milo sighed, then found he couldn't manage to keep his head up. "Yes, sir."

Ludendorff raised one claw to scratch his chin.

"This will take some time to discuss," he said, his voice flat, betraying nothing. "I think it would be best if you allowed the general staff to consider the gravity of all of this. Unprecedented times, but we need to carefully consider the possible responses to this situation."

The way the general said the last word made the wizard raise his head from where it hung miserably between his bowed shoulders. The black coat across them seemed heavier than ever.

Milo could read nothing in the dying warhorse's expression. As he looked around the room, he wished he could say the same of the faces staring at him. Many of them were fighting to hide it, though some doing better than others, but he could smell the truth despite their posturing. They were scared.

A few years ago, that might have made him proud—cocky, even—but now Milo was wise enough to know the truth.

What men like these were afraid of, they destroyed.

THESE STAINS

Ambrose was waiting for him in the entryway of the general staff offices. The big man had been forbidden to enter, though the instruction wouldn't have stopped him except for Milo's nodded acquiescence.

The bodyguard studied Milo's expression but didn't bother to ask how it had gone. Without a word, they left the general staff building and stepped into the late afternoon sunshine of Berlin. The chill of fall was in the air despite the sun, and Milo told himself that was why he shivered and drew his surcoat tighter.

"We free for the rest of the day, or do they want you back later?" Ambrose asked from his position at Milo's shoulder.

The magus shrugged as he looked up and down the street, marveling at the economic bustle of the city. As long as one didn't look too closely at the posters on the walls, one could forget there was a war going on as one walked the streets. People went about their business and seemed untroubled by the incredible violence being done in their name and on their behalf.

The violence that Milo had accidentally become a master of.

"I need a smoke," he grumbled, ineffectually patting the extra-dimensional pockets worked into his ensorcelled coat. He knew there was no tobacco, but he was unable to think of anything else to do.

He patted around, staring blindly at the street until Ambrose produced the precious carcinogen and some rolling papers.

"Thanks," Milo muttered as his fingers began the automatic process of feeding his addiction.

Ambrose eyed him with obvious concern but didn't comment until Milo had returned the cigarette materials.

"So, that bad then?"

Milo nicked his thumb and snapped a flame into reality with a miniscule necromantic ritual. He lit the cigarette and then snapped again to dismiss the flame. He took a long toke and then pinched the paper-rolled tobacco between his forefinger and scarred thumb.

"Let's go for a walk," the wizard announced, with a sour look over his shoulder at the general staff offices looming behind them. Without further preamble, Milo hung the cigarette from his lip and took off down the street, head down and hands shoved into his pockets.

"We headed anywhere in particular?" the big man asked as he stutter-stepped to catch up with Milo's long strides.

"No," the magus muttered flatly around the cigarette between his teeth.

"Then can you take this thing?" Ambrose grumbled, holding out the eagle-skull cane he'd kept tucked under his arm. "I think the witch is trying to whine at me, but it keeps coming across as whispers that make my ears twitch."

Milo snatched the cane without slowing his pace. A second later, his steps were being announced by the rap of the metal-capped tip on the pavement. A second after that, a cold, jagged voice raked through the avenues of his thoughts like a biting north wind.

This fetish is a work of necromist mastery and supreme masonic artisanry and is powered by one of the most necromantically talented ghuls in the history of that storied people. It is not a walking stick!

Despite himself, Milo smiled as the cane connected again with a sharp tap.

We can't have the silly humans knowing that, Milo thought back. *Now shush before you blow your cover.*

"Giving you what-for, is she?" Ambrose asked as he moved to stay shoulder to shoulder with Milo, who nodded through a rush of blue-gray smoke.

"She doesn't appreciate her disguise," Milo murmured as they crossed a street and merged into the broader flow of foot traffic.

For some time, there was no conversation. Milo was unable to say anything, and Ambrose seemed determined to give him as much space as he desired on the matter. They moved through the commercialized city center past the post office buildings, trolley stations, and shops. Some people gave them an uncomfortably wide berth, while others nodded respectfully or smiled at their uniforms as they passed. A trio of young men in business suits threw them jaunty salutes as they passed, but it all slid off of Milo's mind as he valiantly fought a futile battle to shake off the memories of the photographs in the file.

You are troubled, Imrah noted. *What has happened?*

A bitter, snarling smile curled one side of Milo's mouth at the question.

My booby trap for the Soviets worked too well, he thought, then very carefully allowed the cane-bound spirit to peer into his memories of the general staff meeting.

Imrah's failure to make an icy retort at what she saw made his heart drop inside him. He expected her to ridicule him for being a sentimental human and act as though this kind of carnage was typical. After all, hadn't she been the one to set loose a demonic tide of all-consuming slime? Surely, she would brush this off callously, and he could push back in a ferocious bid to save his humanity.

But no flippant dismissal came, and for some time, he thought she wouldn't say anything. As they rounded a street corner and he stood pretending to decide where to go next, he felt the cold thoughts, but they were gentler than ever before, accompanied by a wintry sigh.

You couldn't have known, she said softly. *This wasn't your fault.*

Milo laughed out loud at that.

Tell that to thousands of dead soldiers, he retorted.

If they were so worn down by Zlydzen's magical propaganda, they were beyond any hope of saving.

The words sounded definitive in his mind, but perversely, that only convinced him of their falseness. Imrah was lying to spare his feelings. Maybe her discorporation had left her soft.

I guess we'll never know, Milo replied, then clamped down on his thoughts and cut himself off from her voice. He felt a frosty whisper at the back of his mind, but he shrugged it aside like a windborne shiver.

"Think we can go in there?" Ambrose asked, reminding Milo that he couldn't shut himself off from contact with everything else. He wasn't that powerful—not yet, at least.

Milo blinked and followed the big man's pointing finger. Two streets down from where they stood, twin steeples thrust into the blue belly of the clear autumn sky.

"A church?" Milo asked with a raised eyebrow as he flicked the stubby cigarette into the gutter.

Ambrose looked taken aback at the question and an unfamiliar nervous look came into his eyes, but his head seemed to bob up and down of its own volition.

"I'd like to light a candle or two and..." The big man swallowed roughly and looked at the steeples.

"And what?" Milo asked, coolly ignoring the obvious discomfort his friend was experiencing. He wasn't being gentle or kind; at the moment, human decency hardly seemed worth the effort.

"And, er, pray for you," Ambrose said, refusing to pull his gaze

away from the steeples. "You and me both, for the days ahead. I've got a feeling we're going to need it."

The wizard stared at his bodyguard, a vast heap of scarred muscle complete with twinkling green eyes and an impressive mustache, and snorted as if he'd heard a child tell a rather feeble joke.

"Need it, huh?" Milo said, but Ambrose remained on point like a bird dog, still staring at the church.

Milo looked at the steeples and felt pugnacious energy flowing through him. It was the same spirit that surged through him when pressures mounted at the orphanage and he'd taken to the streets with Roland and the crew. He'd look down the dark, dirty streets of Dresden the same way he was looking at the steeples as the first tinge of dusk slid into the heavens.

He was looking for a fight.

"Sure," he said, a razor-edged smile creeping across his face. "Why not pay our respects to the second estate?"

Ambrose sensed the sharpness in Milo's words and turned to him with a quizzical frown, but the magus was already springing across the street, heedless of traffic.

On a weekday afternoon, the Church of Saint Nicholas, *De Niko-laikirche*, proved to be singularly unfulfilling for Milo's combative intentions. For one, there was hardly anyone in the building, and secondly, those who were present seemed hardly worth the time.

Apart from some vague notions about vandalizing the austere building, there seemed little to engage even his most juvenile aspirations.

Milo wasn't sure what he'd been expecting when he'd swept through the double doors, but a quiet gothic hall full of empty chairs with a few aged parishioners shuffling around votive candles was not it. The doddering ancients didn't even look up from their observances at his entry, though whether because of failed hearing or religious rapture, he didn't know.

As he stood flummoxed and fuming at his thwarted aims of transgressive catharsis, Ambrose shuffled past him to deposit a few coins in a box. Milo tried to recover with a snide remark about throwing good money after bad idolaters, but Ambrose had taken a votive candle off a waiting tray and was headed away. The wizard was left at the head of the sanctuary with nothing but his thoughts and Imrah's sullen silence.

In an act even pettier than the impetus which had driven him into the church, he rapped the cane tip sharply on the floor with his first step. No one, not even the fetish-bound ghul, rose to the bait.

Muttering curses and blasphemies he barely understood, Milo walked a few steps down the aisle between the empty chairs, deflated and defeated. He'd hoped for a chance to sneer at a priest's unctuous manner or disrupt the preening of church-goers, but the scenes and figures he'd concocted on his way over were absent. No, oily, fork-tongued ministers, no fat, blustery men in nice suits, no puckered, frowning women in over-elaborate frocks were present, just a few old men in workmen's dusty coveralls and one old woman, her bowed head covered by a scarf that couldn't quite contain a copious mass of brittle gray locks.

Milo supposed he could saunter over to where one of the workmen knelt with hands clasped and start pulling faces or whispering obscenities, but he wanted to struggle, not abuse.

He wanted to shake off the gory chains that had bound and burdened him in the general staff meeting, but he couldn't do that by teasing and taunting a bent old man with gnarled hands clasped in prayer. He wanted to purge himself through struggle, to rage against an enemy, to remind himself he was bloodied and unbowed, even if it was in the theoretical realm.

But to blast some wiry-haired old woman made him the

abuser, the monster, and he had enough of that burden sitting between his shoulders already.

The urge to kick one of the small wooden chairs down the aisle was suddenly so strong he sat down crookedly before his legs betrayed him. The chair creaked loud enough that Milo couldn't help wincing and looking around, but no one seemed to notice. This inattention of the patrons combined with his anger at his childishness gnawed at him with long, sharp teeth. The magus hung his head, anger, guilt, and fear writhing inside him like wrestling serpents.

With burning eyes, he swung a sidelong look at the crucified Christ.

"I hate you," Milo spat under his breath, feeling the venom slide freely back into himself even as the words slid between his lips. "I hate you so much."

"What was that, young man?" asked a soft, cracked voice behind him.

Milo jumped and nearly toppled out of his chair as he twisted around to see that the old woman had somehow crept up on him. Despite her shuffling gait, every step was silent. The magus in Milo instantly suspected magic, yet as she came closer, he saw that it was consummate skill and no doubt a lifetime of practice that enchanted the worn creature who stared at him with expectant, watery eyes.

"Uh," Milo began pathetically as he realized he hadn't answered her, "I'm sorry. I was just..."

Staring at the frail being in front of him robbed Milo of the last vestiges of his self-indulgent rage. He was hollow and black inside, but he couldn't bring himself to fight with such a vulnerable creature.

"Just praying," he lied, smiling weakly up at her as he folded his hands over the eagle-topped cane, which now felt paganly garish as he sat there.

"Hmmm," the old woman said, clearly unconvinced. Milo held

her gaze like all good liars, daring her to challenge him with the sincerity of his expression. The elder did not; to his horror, she did something much worse. With joints so stiff he could almost hear them give creaks of protest, the old woman settled into a seat near him.

Milo balked, suddenly experiencing social anxiety unlike anything he'd known since childhood. The woman seemed to sense it and took pity on him. She sat there in silence, letting the shock of her proximity settle and still, while the light of the setting sun shifted across the sanctuary. A shaft of dusk's ruby light fell across her, and for a moment, Milo felt as though he saw her not as an age-bent creature but as a woman in her winter years but still very much alive. The scarlet light played across her features, and whether from a trick of illumination or imagination, he thought he could see more of her than the patina of age.

There were stripes of darker hair amidst her dry locks, iron and silver, and in her wrinkled face, her eyes, while dimmed with years, were sharp chips of emerald. He saw a strong Roman nose, a clean jawline, shoulders accustomed to heavy burdens, a wide, nurturing bosom, and hands hard with work but still femininely tapered. Age and all its cruel cares and infirmities couldn't hide these things, not fully. Milo saw a fierce but faithful woman looking at him with knowing eyes.

For a moment they considered each other, disciple and blasphemer, the magus Milo felt a mad thought caper through his mind:

Perhaps I'd have been safer with her if I'd stayed angry.

Almost as though she could hear his thoughts, a slow smile broke across the old woman's face. Green eyes flashing with hidden humor, she shifted stiffly to look at the crucifix over the altar.

"Sometimes I am angry at him too," she said quietly, one arthritic, ravaged hand rising shakily to a simple locket hanging from her throat.

Milo narrowed his eyes at that, a hard, shadowy place within calling for him to spring up and wait for Ambrose outside. Tension rippled through his legs as almost without thought, his body began to obey. He looked around for his bodyguard and spied a broad uniformed back standing in front of a wax-dribbled stand, a single lit candle shining.

He thought about willing Ambrose to look up so he could gesture that he was going outside, but the big man's head was bowed, and he felt the intrusion would have been sacrilege. Milo realized he'd have to get up and walk over there, but that would mean blatantly walking past the old woman, and somehow that would be even more awful than the conversation she seemed determined to have with him.

Milo sank back into his chair, running his fingers over the contours of the eagle skull as the devout elder waited patiently.

"You ever get him to answer?" Milo finally asked, not caring how sharply the question came out. "To answer for the ways he's wronged you?"

She nodded, another knowing smile, reflective, not mocking, danced across her face.

"Sometimes, but not always." She sighed, the breath carrying ages with it. "Sometimes I learn about hidden gifts, sometimes I see the bigger picture, and sometimes I know him better for it."

Her fingers toyed clumsily with the locket as she turned to look at the crucifix again.

"Sometimes I have my Gethsemanes and my wildernesses."

A tremor began in her shoulders. She stilled it with obvious effort and gestured with her free hand.

"But then, so did he."

Milo blinked, his mind struggling to recall what she referenced. He remembered there was something about a garden, not that first one with snakes and nudity, but one about sweating blood and unwanted cups before an arrest. In the wilds, hadn't there been a devil?

They were the pieces picked up from the times he was forced to attend services by the orphanage and the prattling of some self-important priest who harried the unwary in the streets of Dresden.

The fullness of the reference was lost on him, but he felt he understood enough, and it galled him.

"That's not answering, that's rationalizing." Milo snorted. "He leaves us to suffer and squirm in the mud and then expects us to find excuses for him amidst the torments. That's why I am not just angry at him. That's why I hate him."

He expected righteous indignation at his proclamation, flared nostrils and curled lips. Instead, her hand let go of the locket, and she turned back to look at him, her wrinkles deepening with concern.

"How has His creation tormented you?" she asked, her tone curious and without accusation. "What has hurt you?"

Milo's awakening antagonism once again found itself thwarted. He wanted to lash the woman with the accumulated horrors and tragedies of his life, but he could already tell she would bear it all with sorrowful nods and caring gazes. She would not refute his accusing proclamations or battle with him. He could try to craft a barb to scourge her faith, but the thought of it sickened him with its hateful pettiness.

"Many have hurt me, so many," the magus said, his voice flat. "But those people are not why I hate him, not now, at least."

She frowned curiously.

"If it isn't the suffering, it is the squirming?"

A loud, long snarl of laughter tore from Milo's throat.

"Fair enough," he said and gave an approving nod before leaning forward. "It is the squirming. Bad enough He put us here, but then He puts us in a world where even our best intentions, our best efforts even, can make nothing but death and filth and suffering and failure. How dare He put us in such a world?"

The old woman's gaze lowered in thought, and she seemed to notice Milo's uniform for the first time.

"Did you ever think there might be something to learn from that?" she asked, somehow managing to keep the question from seeming coy or condescending. Perhaps it was how earnest her expression was.

"If He wanted to teach us something, He could have told us." Milo shrugged. "This shadow play disguised as life seems a rather poor form of pedagogy."

"Oh, I think He did tell us," she said. "But if you are like me, and I find most people are in this respect, there is a lifetime's distance between my ears and my heart.

"I can hear something and know it up here," she continued, tapping her temple with one yellowed fingernail before tapping her chest. "But it takes a long time to get it here."

Milo shook his head as the light coming through the windows purpled and the light from the votive candles seemed to swell.

"So, what's the lesson then?" He sneered. "I hope you know because if it hasn't reached your heart, what hope is there for us non-fossils?"

The toxic barb flew off his tongue before he could snap it back down his throat, but once again, his words found no purchase. This fragile creature was proving to be harder to pierce than anyone he'd ever met. That only made his faltering attempts all the more pathetic and reproachable, but his guilt was pebbles compared to the Sisyphean stone resting between his shoulders.

"The lesson may be that we never can, never will succeed," she said, her voice tender. "We weren't meant to."

Milo sniffed, his face curdling as though he smelled something rancid.

"Don't you call him Father?" Milo asked. "What sort of man would you call a father who intentionally makes his children cripples? Who keeps them dependent?"

To his utter frustration, she again paused to consider the

question. With flawless, despicable humility, she'd thwarted him from considering her response as some trite quip she'd memorized.

"We'd call such a man a monster because we'd say he was keeping so many good things from his children," she acknowledged, but he saw her green eyes flash in the deepening shadows of her face. "But now imagine that all those good things, the best things, can only be had by being with the Father. Then we would call it compassion, not cruelty, wouldn't we?"

Milo's lips curled back from his teeth, and he twisted his head to the side to hide his snarl. A deep well of resentment threatened to gush forth, and in the wake of that torrent, he wasn't certain what he might say or do.

"If He is so good, then why all this suffering?" he hissed between gritted teeth. "If He is such a good father, why put his *children* through so much?"

The old woman's eyes narrowed, and she spent some time searching Milo's face before answering.

"I suppose I could give you answers to that old question," she said slowly, her gaze seeming to explore every contour of his face. "But I think the real question is why *you* have been allowed to suffer, and given what you said earlier, I imagine it has to do with something you did. Something that did not end as you'd hoped."

She nodded meaningfully at his black coat.

"I…" Milo began hotly, but what almost came out would have been a confession, not a rebuttal. He forced back the outburst with a hard swallow and stared at the old woman. How had she managed to bring him here? Why was he now almost pouring his sorrow out rather than destroying her infantile beliefs?

He tried to speak, but again the words caught in his throat with a click. His mouth, his lips, and his tongue all seemed determined to betray him.

"War can be a heavy burden," she said, her hand straying to

her locket once more. "Intentions are cold comfort when lives are lost and the dead are counted."

Milo felt the tightness in his throat harden into a lump. In his mind, he wanted to resume the fight, to find his rhetorical footing and engage her arguments, but something deeper refused. Batting aside his counter-arguments and protests, the thing he feared was his soul forced his body to nod slowly as something wet prickled in the corner of his eyes.

Thankful for the shadows of the twilit hall, Milo hung his head and fought to keep his breathing even. So intent was he on not sobbing that he didn't hear the creak of venerable wood and older bones.

For the second time that day, he nearly fell out of his chair at the nearness of the old woman when one knotted hand rested lightly on his shoulder. He looked up and saw the elder standing over him, her eyes deep and glimmering wells of green.

"He knows our hearts," she whispered. "And in His frightening mercy, He judges those before our actions or their consequences."

Something hard and clotted in Milo's heart cried for him to lash out and cast off the old woman, but a far stronger part of him savored the gentle touch. He bowed his head lest she see his tears, but he didn't pull away.

The other hand rested softly upon his head, and he heard the woman's voice as she bowed her head over him.

"Heavenly Father, show mercy to this young man," she prayed, the words agony and light in the wizard's mind. "In seeking healing for his pain, let him find you. In Christ Jesus, may he find that peace that passes all understanding."

Milo's soul was torn between wanting to curse her for a fool and collapse before her. As a compromise, he stayed where he was, his head still hanging.

"May he find that peace in You, for he has so much more to do."

The fingers, twisted and stiff with age, squeezed with surprising yet sure strength.

"In the name of the Father, the Son, and the Holy Ghost. Amen."

Her hands rose from him, but he still felt her presence. Tears rolled freely down his cheeks, landing upon the stone floor with the faintest patter. He still kept from sobbing, forcing his breath in and out in measured intervals, but by then, it was to anchor his reeling mind rather than any attempt at dignity.

Breathe in, breathe out, breathe in, breathe out...

Slowly, but growing with each inhalation and exhalation, Milo came back together. There was still a wound in his soul, and he would most certainly lose sleep over it in the days to come, but the overwhelming, crippling horror was gone. The trauma joined a host of others scarring his psyche, though it cut a bit deeper than most.

Your momma was a witch, Volkohne.

Your momma danced naked with the Devil, and out you came.

As his mind and body steadied, his tear-blurred eyes opened to a world lit by scarlet light.

Milo blinked and dragged a hand across his eyes as he looked around in utter confusion. Hadn't the sun gone down already?

As he cast his gaze to the windows, he found Ambrose ambling toward him, a sheepish look stamped on his features.

"Sorry about that," he mumbled softly, jerking a thumb over his shoulder. "Took a bit longer than I expected. A lot to pray for with the world we live in, eh?"

Milo lowered his gaze from the befuddling windows and suddenly realized the old woman was gone. He swept the sanctuary and even squinted into the foyer they had first entered through, but there was no sign of her.

"Everything all right, Magus?" Ambrose asked, his muscles rippling with tension as he began to probe the area with his peripheral vision.

"I…" Milo began as he continued to stare around him, but he stopped suddenly. He'd seen how the old woman had moved when she sat next to him and knew she didn't possess the nimbleness to vanish as suddenly as she seemed to have.

He swung his gaze back to his bodyguard, still frowning.

"Did you see me talk to anyone?" Milo asked and instantly regretted it as he saw the concern sharpen on Ambrose's face.

"What happened?"

Milo ran a hand over his mouth, unsure of what to say. He'd been so sure he hadn't felt magic, but how could all this have happened without it?

"I'm not sure?" he confessed, staring up at Ambrose.

The bodyguard's gaze swept the church, then he cocked his head to one side. A few heartbeats later, he shrugged his massive shoulders and cracked a smile beneath his auburn mustache.

"Entertaining angels without me, eh?"

THESE SIGNS

"It was a joke," Ambrose grumbled as they made their way back to the general staff office under a bruise-colored sky.

The sense of déjà vu Milo felt at walking under his second dusk of the day was disorienting, to say the least. Despite this, though, he hadn't let up on interrogating and theorizing at Ambrose since they'd left the church.

"I'm asking you to consider if maybe it was," Milo pressed, his gaze darting between watching where he was walking and staring intently at Ambrose. "I mean, it's not like we are uncertain angels exist."

Ambrose shook his head as his mustache twitched.

"Fine," he muttered as he bristled. "It is a possibility, I suppose, but I don't think it was."

Milo was frowning so hard he nearly walked off a curb and into the path of a rumbling trolley. Ambrose's meaty hand snatched him back from certain mangling, but the magus only managed a nod as his mind raced behind his squinting gaze.

"What makes you think that?"

"You almost died, Magus," Ambrose snapped. "You're welcome, by the way."

The wizard flapped his hand dismissively at the trolley as though shooing away a retreating insect.

"Yes, yes, thank you," Milo muttered before leaning toward Ambrose's face. "Why don't you think she was an angel? Really?"

Ambrose frowned and gnawed his lip before heaving a sigh. His breath formed an anemic plume in the chill air.

"Two words: 'fear not.'"

Milo scowled, sure he was supposed to make a connection, but if it was a matter of religious esoterica, he was lost. The silence stretched between them as the sounds of the city began their shuffle between the daytime bustle and the nightly susurration.

"Whenever you're ready, *maestro*," Milo grumbled as he came to a dead stop at a street corner. The lamp overhead was broken, leaving the spot in deep gloom, which somehow seemed appropriate.

Ambrose shrugged and looked around. Milo found the little display comical since, given the number of supernatural subjects they could have been discussing, the matter of the angelic was one of the few that wouldn't raise eyebrows.

Satisfied that no one was close enough to overhear them, Ambrose leaned forward and began in an almost conspiratorial whisper.

"In almost every story about angels, they have to tell people not to be afraid," Ambrose began. "Almost every time the angelic gets involved, people are scared, and I think we know why. Remember that moment I was unveiled in the tunnel?"

Milo did.

In the past year of violence, horror, and wonder, that moment in the tunnel still was one of the most terrifying. With a shiver, he remembered the words of living flame, the crimson light of alien stars, and a voice that shook his very soul with a few words. That moment, those few linear seconds of time, had nearly broken him when he saw Simon Ambrose the Nephilim, son of Oro'zion'Nrzim, He of the Flaming Sword.

"I see your point," Milo said, a little deflated and more than a little shaken by the recollection. "Yeah, there was nothing like that going on."

Ambrose nodded, shifting his weight as he noticed the pronounced effect of the memory on Milo. He was silent, allowing the moment to pass as pedestrians skirted around where they stood in the little patch of murk.

"There are some bits in the Scriptures where they didn't scare the pants off everyone," Ambrose said slowly, choosing his words with obvious care. "But I think in each of those, they end up revealing themselves anyway at some point, and it is usually in the scary, smite-y sort of way."

Milo cocked an eyebrow, one side of his mouth hitching up in a grin.

"Smite-y, eh?"

Ambrose chuckled and shook his head.

"Technical term for the biblically literate," he announced archly before cutting a little bow. "We can start reading together if you'd like, and I can teach you all the necessary jargon."

Milo laughed, shaking his head with one hand raised in warning.

"It took the threat of war crimes to get me into a church." He snorted. "I don't want to know what it would take to get me to pick up that book."

Ambrose's smile vanished, and he took the wizard by the arm.

"War crimes?" he growled, a primal noise of alarm. "What war crimes?"

Milo opened his mouth to answer but paused, his tongue still as his throat threatened to betray him with a little quiver of tension. He swallowed and cleared his throat before trying again.

"My little misdirection for Stalin's army at Shatili sort of misfired," Milo said, forcing a smile that was as false as it was uncomfortable. "I'm not absolutely sure, but I think I know what happened."

He hated the lie even as it passed his teeth. Though he couldn't provide more evidence than what he'd said to the general staff, he knew what had happened without a single doubt. Magic, which inherently defied science and other such shackles, was based on intuition and instinct. Those were as solid and real in such matters as any smoking gun or spoken confession.

The wizard knew what had happened in Shatili, and that was what made it so awful.

Ambrose waited, concern and dreadful anticipation etched into the scarred seams of his face.

"The Soviets were left psychically and spiritually vulnerable by Zlydzen's magic," Milo said, forcing his voice to remain level as his vision blurred at the edges. "The shades I'd prepared didn't disrupt and frighten the soldiers, they possessed them and turned them against each other. It seems they killed each other to a man."

Ambrose's eyes widened, his whole body straightening as he drew in a sharp breath.

"How many?" he asked. His voice was gentle, but the look in his eyes burned into Milo like a condemning brand.

"Not exactly sure," Milo admitted, unable to bear the look. He turned away. "Thousands, though the precise number is hard to tell because of the state of the bodies. It would take time to sort out which pieces belonged to who."

"*Mon Dieu,*" Ambrose swore, then bowed his head.

Neither could find the heart to say anything for some time. Young, raucous voices sounded down the street. Milo couldn't make out what they were being so rambunctious about, but he envied the abandon they possessed. He should still have such freeness of spirit, being hardly out of his teens as he was, but life and its horrors, both mundane and eldritch, had ground it out of him.

Instead, he stood in the dark with blood on his hands.

His morose reflections were interrupted by a heavy hand on his shoulder. He turned at the familiar grip and stared into Ambrose's face.

"Listen to me," the bodyguard said in a thick voice, his other hand clasping Milo's other shoulder as they stood square with each other.

Milo struggled to meet the big man's gaze, but he nodded to acknowledge he was listening.

"It isn't your fault," Ambrose said, the slightest tremor in his voice. "Do you hear me?"

He did hear, but he shook his head angrily. He made a half-hearted attempt to pull away from the huge hands holding him, but Ambrose held him fast.

"Milo, I mean it," Ambrose hissed between grinding teeth as he gave him a small shake. "It. Isn't. Your. Fault."

Milo met the man's gaze, his pale blue and Ambrose's sparkling green eyes shining like gems beneath a sheen of tears.

"I set the trap," the magus gasped, trying to straighten and pull away but once again failing. "Those shades were bound to the soul wells by my magic, using my blood. *My* blood, Simon. It doesn't get much more responsible than that."

Ambrose shook his head fiercely, sending glittering tears into his mustache.

"You didn't know," Ambrose insisted, eyes boring into Milo's. "You couldn't have known tha—"

"HEY! What are you two doing?"

The intrusion of a harsh young voice was like an electrical discharge, snapping between the two men with violent suddenness. Milo and Ambrose whirled to face the sound, the wizard's hands adjusting to grip his cane as Ambrose sank into a fighting stance, fists raised, knees bent.

Approaching their little patch of darkness was a band of rangy and snarling youths dressed in some sort of uniform. Their hair was plastered with a greasy product and swept to one side, and though the style of their shirts varied, all bore a distinct shade of brown that was clearly intentional. They loped down the street like young wolves, eyes hungry and bright as their mouths cruelly sneered in obvious anticipation.

"I said," called a tall teen at the head of the group as they came to stand under a lamppost, "what are you two doing?"

Milo and Ambrose exchanged looks and instantly relaxed. Milo lowered his fetish cane's point to the pavement, and Ambrose straightened and crossed his arms over his chest. If these children were planning to intimidate vulnerable civilians, they were sorely mistaken.

"Can't see how that is any of your business," Ambrose said, only the slightest of rumbles in his cavernous chest.

"If you weren't doing anything unsavory, you wouldn't mind telling us, now would you?" the lanky youth snarled, and his pack gave growls and barks of agreement. They arrayed themselves across the pavement as they closed the distance, instinctively moving in lockstep.

"Unsavory?" Milo asked, and he and Ambrose exchanged looks again before bursting into laughter.

Between guffaws, Milo could tell the little posse didn't take kindly to the levity, faces hardening as hands clenched.

"Berlin is for true Germans," the leader roared. "It's bad enough we have Poles and Jews slinking about. We don't need perverts and deviants fouling our streets too."

"I think you're doing enough fouling on your own." Ambrose chuckled, a dangerous edge coming into his voice. "I mean, what gutter did you boys muck out for that sludge in your hair? Your mothers aren't going to be happy about that come bath time."

Several of the young men slung their heads forward as they

hissed curses between clenched teeth and shook fists Ambrose's way.

"Oh, you might get a spanking for using such naughty words, but that might be the point, I suppose," Milo crowed between snorts of laughter before trying to force a conciliatory face. "Sorry, sorry. We're teasing. Settle down."

The wizard leaned on his cane to catch his breath and fought to keep a straight face before the red-faced gallery.

"Now, what is this about? Were you afraid you were being left out?"

Curses, sharp and snarled, drowned out Milo's ensuing laughter. Along with obscenities came several rude gestures and a fair amount of launched spittle. A small voice in the wizard's head told him that this was hardly de-escalating the situation, but for the most part, he didn't care. It was fun taunting the little hellions, and the longing for a fight hadn't left him.

"Oh, don't be like that now, boys," Ambrose called, patting his hands at them in exaggerated placation. "Nothing says you strapping fellows can't take care of each other. After all, what are friends for?"

Ambrose barely made it through the last words before he descended into a fit of laughter. Milo had settled enough to wipe his eyes, and he noticed the clenched fists of several of the young men now glinted with metal or shone with lengths of polished wood. It was a motley collection of coshes, knives, and pipes, but the hateful creatures outnumbered them five to one.

Milo straightened slightly at the same moment Ambrose noticed the escalation, and the laughter died on his lips.

"You boys best think twice," he warned even as he wrestled with deploying a little magic to scare the urban brigands. "You went looking for trouble, and your hot heads are going to get you into hotter water."

The warning had the opposite effect of what Milo had hoped for as predatory grins slid across flushed faces and they edged forward. They'd taken the words as evidence of fear rather than concern for not killing them. The magus suddenly realized he was stupid to envy the immoderation of the common youth.

It was about to get someone killed.

"Does bigotry lead to blindness?" Ambrose asked with a sideways look at the wizard. "Or have these boys' eyes not adjusted from the nursery nightlights?"

Milo seamlessly clueing in on Ambrose's strategy, they both took a step forward and closer to the lamplight. Upon seeing the men's uniforms, a ripple went through the pack. As one, they tilted sideways glances at their alpha. The young firebrand's jaw tightened for a second, but before another heartbeat could pass, he leveled an accusing finger at them, voice raised in a theatrical cry.

"You're not worthy of those uniforms!" he screamed, his voice shaking with fury. "You dishonor the Fatherland and its people with your public depravity."

His fellows all snapped back on pointe, teeth bared as they inched forward, weapons in hand. Things were quickly approaching the point of no return. Milo realized he would soon have to decide if he'd reveal himself or if he was willing to risk being beaten to death to keep his secret safe.

He raised his voice over the growing babble of angry curses and slurs, trying to sound reasonable. As his voice rang out, he had a revelation that the secret of his magic wasn't his but the general staff's as well.

Things had gotten damned complicated quickly.

"Not that it is any of your business," Milo said, squaring his shoulders and trying to exude officerial authority. "We are two soldiers who were sharing old stories. If you're going to go around defending the Fatherland's honor, try enlisting or at least picking a fight over something that actually happened."

The pack advanced two steps, the lamplight shifting behind their hunched backs. One look at the shadowed faces and the feverish glares burning in those sockets told Milo it was too late. Things were in motion and wouldn't be stopped.

"No fireworks," Ambrose whispered out the corner of his mouth, coming to the same conclusion as Milo.

A stocky young boy with a crooked nose broke away from the group, brandishing a short length of pipe atop which sat a large blocky bolt.

"If we can avoid killing them and exposing me," he breathed, sliding the cane into both hands, "that would be preferable."

"I'm going to smash your lying face in," growled the mace-wielding youth as he leveled a finger at Milo. "Then I'll bring that coat back for my commission."

Ambrose cracked a smile as the boy charged at Milo.

"Don't think it works that way, kid."

The rush was wild and sloppy, but the wizard wasn't taking any chances. He wouldn't throw fire and ice or conjure terrifying shades—certainly not for some time—but that wasn't the only magic at his disposal.

Just some speed if you please, Milo thought.

As you wish, master, Imrah answered a touch sullenly.

Milo's body sped up as the pipe came hurtling toward his head, and he tilted away from the blow with consummate ease. The youth was unprepared for a complete miss and therefore was precariously unbalanced. Milo kicked out and the boy went down hard, his head bouncing off the pavement with a hollow thunk.

The wizard was pretty sure he saw the young man breathing as he turned back to the others, but that was the only sign of life.

"Now, I think that's enough of that."

The rest of the pack was already surging in, weapons raised. Milo was glad to find Imrah hadn't been stingy with the magical enhancements as he darted out of the way of several swings at once. Ambrose roared a battlefield challenge as he rushed to

Milo's defense, then everything became the mad kaleidoscope of violence that was close combat.

The young men weren't trained fighters, but they had rage and numbers on their side, attacking with a recklessness that was difficult to take advantage of because there was always another attack by their fellows. Multiple times Milo almost delivered a leveling blow, only to check the swing to deflect or sidestep another attacker. At this rate, they'd eventually get him because he had no chance to fight back and they'd wear him down.

Out of the corner of his eye, he saw Ambrose flatten one teen with a passing elbow as he turned to throw a charging thug over his shoulder. Not for the first time, Milo found himself envying not just the big man's power but the brutal economy of his movements. Magic could provide much, but those reflexes and ingrained movements came with experience alone.

Milo looked away for a second, and as he backpedaled, his foot slipped. A knife was arcing toward his chest, and with wild desperation, he drew deeply on the fetish in his hands and swung out. The magically-powered movement drove the length of the cane across the forearm holding the knife, and there was an audible snap like rain-dampened twigs breaking. The knife tumbled from a hanging hand, and Milo's foot in the screaming young man's chest sent the wretch flying back into his compatriot.

The space this maneuver created was what Milo needed, and he adjusted his grip on the cane and leaped to the attack.

Snarling a curse, he scythed the back of the eagle skull into the hip of the uninjured attacker entangled with the disarmed knife wielder. There wasn't the satisfying crack of bones this time, but the youth's leg gave out underneath him. Already enmeshed with a wailing casualty pawing at him one-handed, the unfortunate young man twisted and then toppled onto his injured hip, and his screams mirrored his compatriot's.

Milo spun to the next two assailants like a grim farmer ready to reap a vicious harvest. The fetish cane's hooked beak imitated a stubby scythe.

The two young men hesitated, and that cost them dearly. A sharp chop to a knee felled each, and rap on the skulls left them sprawled on the pavement.

When Milo's gaze swept around, he saw only two figures left standing. Ambrose was advancing on the tall leader. He had not rushed in with his pack, who now lay in various states of unconsciousness and disarray.

Ambrose's thick fingers were curled, and a terrible grin had spread beneath his bristling mustache. His expression suggested the big man would love nothing better than to devour the whelp after tearing him apart with those hooked fingers.

The young firebrand didn't seem keen on the idea.

"This isn't over," he hissed as he began to shuffle backward, hate and fear shining in bulging eyes.

"Why are you leaving?" Ambrose growled from deep in his chest. "Come a little closer, and we can finish it properly."

The packless alpha skittered back several steps, pausing on the edge of flight.

"The new Reich—the forever Reich—is coming," he screeched at them defiantly. "Soon you and all the traitors like you will be hanging in the streets. Very soon!"

Ambrose sprang forward and the young man bolted, boots thumping on the street.

"Forever Reich?" Ambrose spat, kicking a moaning youth pawing feebly at his foot as he turned and picked his way toward Milo. "What an ass."

A tremor went through Milo as the adrenaline and magical fortification leached from his body and he looked at their handiwork. All of them would live, but several of them would walk with a limp or have to chew on one side for a while.

He'd had the fight he'd longed for, but its source was little comfort.

"Street gangs preaching the coming Reich." He sighed heavily. "That can't be a good sign."

Ambrose nodded, then patted Milo's shoulder.

"Fear not." He started to pull the wizard away from the scene.

"Come along, sweetheart." He chuckled. "We had our fun, but we'd best get you back to the general staff before you're missed."

4

THESE QUESTIONS

Their arrival at the general staff offices was not nearly as casual as their departure.

They'd no more than set foot into the lobby of the building when a grim cohort advanced on them as though they had been lying in wait.

"Milo Volkohne, come with us," instructed a stern-looking young officer with the insignia of the military police emblazoned on his lapel. At his side were two enlisted men with pistols and truncheons on their belts, and something in the set of their shoulders made it clear they were handily proficient with either.

"Am I under arrest?" Milo asked, the skin on his arms prickling as a stone settled into his stomach.

"The general staff has reconvened," the officer said, dismissing the question with a curt blink. "You were not in the lobby when an aide was sent to find you, so we've been asked to make sure you arrive with all speed."

The idea of sitting there stewing in the lobby while the general staff whispered and grumbled among themselves had never occurred to him. It seemed they were not accustomed to having people take the initiative. Good thing he hadn't returned to the hotel room Jorge had rented for him. The general staff would have been left waiting a good long while if that were the case.

"I'm sorry you had to spend time looking for us," Milo said sincerely. "We went to visit a church."

The officer, a first lieutenant Milo noted, gave them a wry look and nodded at Ambrose.

"Bloody knuckles are an odd thing to collect at a church service," he remarked dryly. Ambrose sheepishly ground his fists against the hem of his trousers. "But I was spared the tedium of hunting you down. Colonel Jorge instructed me to wait here and said that you would be along eventually."

Milo blinked rapidly, and his fingers tightened on the cane.

"Jorge is here?"

The officer nodded evenly, but there was a subtle shift in his stance, a slight forward lean like he was preparing to spring after a skittish creature or a naughty child with a truant streak

"He arrived shortly after the recess," he said softly as though afraid his tone might spook Milo into flight.

Milo was sure he looked as nervous as he felt at the announcement of Jorge's arrival, but he couldn't think of anything to say to break the tension. Thankfully, Ambrose cleared his throat and drew the eyes of the looming trio.

"So, instead of the tedium of stretching your legs in Berlin, you endured the tedium of the lobby for the past few hours?" Ambrose asked, arms tucked behind his back now that he had given up on cleaning his knuckles. "There's decent coffee, and the scenery isn't half bad," he added with the ghost of a smile haunting his lips. At the desk behind him, a buxom administrative assistant was closing up shop at her workspace.

"You came just in time." He nodded and swept an arm toward the conference room. "Shall we?"

Milo followed, Ambrose at his shoulder.

They made it to the double doors of the conference room,

behind which could be heard a general hubbub. The lieutenant stepped forward and spoke to Milo.

"I'm afraid your aide will have to wait here," he said in the formalized conciliatory tone that made most unpleasant things palatable. "He can stand out here with us if you'd like since we aren't allowed to enter either."

Milo met the officer's gaze levelly.

"He's not my aide but my bodyguard," Milo said, his chin rising in challenge.

"I can't imagine there is anything in that chamber that dangerous," the lieutenant said with a faint chuckle that ceased as his gaze hardened. "And if there is, it's not something one body-guard can save you from."

Ambrose gave an audible grunt, but the wizard knew there was no point. He'd faced the old hawks alone before, and having a dustup with those Reich louts didn't mean the hierarchy was about to shift.

"I'm sure you'll find something to amuse yourself and stay out of trouble," Milo said with a warning look at the big man.

"If you say so, *sir*," Ambrose said as he threw himself into an exaggerated salute that looked more like a bout of epilepsy than military decorum.

The lieutenant's eyes darted between the two of them, but he decided sorting out such things was not his problem. With a nod to Milo, he stepped aside and let the wizard stride into the belly of the beast.

"How good of you to join us, Volkohne," Jorge remarked over his shoulder with a warmth that made his welcome sound sincere.

The head of Nicht-KAT and the man who'd plunged Milo into a world of darkness, magic, and violence was seated in the same spot the wizard had been in earlier that afternoon. Unlike

Milo, the venerable officer seemed perfectly at ease under the gaze of Ludendorff and his cronies, even as the bristle-lipped crowd scowled and murmured as much or more to the colonel as they had to Milo.

"You can have a seat right here," Jorge said, bobbing his head slowly at a seat at his left. "I don't imagine this will take much longer."

There were further signs of irritation from the bearish gathering of military officials, but Jorge acted like a duck in a summer rain. Milo quickly moved to the proffered seat, unsure if Jorge's ease was a good thing or merely the velvet sheath around a descending blade.

"We are about finished, I think," Jorge said as he turned to the general staff with an expression that was far more steel than sunshine. "I believe it is a matter of a promise made and some documents signed."

"The general staff has not decided to accept your perspective on the situation," Ludendorff pronounced archly, leaning toward Jorge with a deepening scowl. "Even if we do, this business with Russia is—"

"Something I think you'd much rather I handle," Jorge cut in without raising his voice even a little. "And the general staff knows it would be ridiculous to expect me to do the work it needs while snatching the tools I have out from under my command."

It took Milo an instant to recognize that he was silently nodding in agreement with the colonel, even as he was being described as a tool. Blithely ignoring the wizard's mute support, Jorge continued in a mild conversational tone.

"The reality is that I've been working on your behalf for years now, and you were very happy to give a crippled soldier something to occupy his time until you realized the value of what I've brought to you."

Jorge placed a hand on Milo's shoulder. He couldn't help

straightening and trying to look noble. Painfully aware of where his tattoos showed and the scars on his face, Milo held himself tall and proud, even as the staff murmured and growled around them.

Perhaps it was from being in the church, but at that moment, Milo remembered a stylized stained glass panel where an angel hovered, one hand out, over a man at whose feet lions prowled.

"You haven't dragged this young man in to judge the rightness of his actions, or even for an explanation of how it was achieved. You've brought him in here to remind him who is in charge and to ensure that he knew that he was yours. You discovered you have a weapon to win the war, and you wanted to make sure it couldn't turn on you before you could strike the killing blow. Do not waste any more time pretending it is otherwise."

Jorge's voice wasn't raised above a conversational volume, but the severity of his tone, the hardness of each syllable struck the snarling general staff. By the time Jorge had finished speaking, he'd beaten them into submission with the steady hammer strokes of his unyielding words. Silence reigned in the conference room, and Milo failed to keep a smile from creeping across his face as he looked at the glowering officers.

The stillness stretched until Milo lost his confidence and looked at Jorge to see if things had gone too far. The colonel was a veritable bastion of serenity, settled easily into the chair while he looked without fear or challenge at every face before him. Everything about him exuded "Don't worry, I can wait," and Milo envied him fiercely for it.

When Ludendorff finally spoke, it sounded harsh and braying, yet there was not the anger Milo might have expected. The most powerful man in the German Empire simply sounded tired.

"Is he trustworthy, Colonel? Is this someone upon whom we can stake the fate of our Empire?"

Jorge met Ludendorff's eyes and opened his mouth, but before he could speak, another man did.

"He's not even German," said a tall officer with a curling dark mustache a few seats to the right of Ludendorff. His voice did not echo the guttural noises of his fellow staffers, but there was a sharpness to the simmering baritone that couldn't be missed. He tapped out a cigarette and nodded at the colonel as he continued.

"I'm sure Jorge had something very eloquent and witty to tell us about this sorcerer's character, but one simple fact remains," the man continued, turning now to look at Milo with a burning intensity at odds with his otherwise calm features. "He is a Slav, a motherless Russian savage plucked from the streets of Petrograd. Try as he might, he will never be a true German, and as such, he can't be trusted."

The back of Milo's neck prickled as he glared at the officer, a sensation familiar to anyone spotting an enemy for the first time. He'd heard of the Reich, felt their influence, and fought men inspired by them, but now, here, so close to the seat of ultimate power in the German Empire, he met one of their number.

The wizard, having a long experience with bullies and bigots in his relatively short life, narrowed his eyes but bided his time. Now was not the moment when he could strike a meaningful blow.

That didn't seem to apply to Colonel Jorge, though.

"I don't believe his parentage was asked about, Mayr," Jorge remarked dryly. "But I appreciate how you so keenly illustrate that even a very smart man is capable of saying something very stupid if he's determined to make an ass of himself."

Mayr's gaze swung back to Jorge to reply, but the colonel continued in that same even and unstoppable tone of voice. It was like a rhetorical engine driving a verbal spike with an unhurried but undeniable relentlessness.

"General Ludendorff, to answer your question simply, I say yes on both counts," he said, his eyes meeting those of the addressee with resolution in their depths. "Milo Volkohne has proven himself to have greater honor and virtue than even he realizes, and we both know that is a rare quality in any man worthy of the name. He can be trusted to do what is right, and considering the power he wields, that is the best any of us can hope for."

Milo knew he would look like a fool, but he couldn't keep from glancing at Jorge. Something caught in his throat, but his emotional expenditure for the day had drained him for the next decade, so he only regarded his commanding officer with softly dewed eyes.

"But he's not German," Mayr pressed, his eloquence beginning to fray as his voice showed the anger in his eyes.

"If you are going to keep repeating yourself, you might want to find something worthwhile to say, Mayr," Jorge retorted, eyes flashing in the first sign of temper he'd displayed.

Mayr slammed his fist down and prepared to launch into a scathing tirade, but a thick, hoary voice croaked loudly enough across the conference room that nearly everyone jumped at the violence of the exclamation.

"Enough, Mayr!" Ludendorff cried, his eyes boiling in the porridge that was his sweaty face.

Mayr glared at the old man, but after a surreptitious scan of the room, he sank back without another word.

"Very well, Jorge," the general said after reluctantly turning his gaze back to the colonel. "You will have your way yet again, but remember that the terms are the same as before. Do you understand?

"Perfectly." Jorge nodded, folding his hands on the table in front of him. "Are we free to get back to saving the Empire and ending the war now?"

Ludendorff gave Jorge one more long look and shook his head, a smile working its way across his flabby face.

"Volkohne, report to Colonel Jorge immediately," the general instructed without bothering to look at Milo. "This special conference of the general staff is hereby dismissed."

Jorge's hand once more descended to Milo's shoulder, and the man drew him into a whispered conference.

"I've had an office cleared. We need to talk."

Milo and Ambrose followed him down the corridors. As unhurried and unflappable as ever, he led them to a room with an ornate brass "7" over the door.

"You've got to be joking," Milo groaned as he looked at the number emblazoned on the door.

"What?" Ambrose asked, following Milo's eyes to the digit.

What is going on? Imrah whispered.

Milo looked at Jorge, who beamed at him, his weathered face beatific.

"A little inside joke between the magus and me," the colonel said softly as he led them into the room.

It was a small space with rudimentary furnishings, the desk being a metal table with wire filing baskets stacked on either end. There was a bookshelf on one wall beyond the table, where a few dusty files sat unmolested by time or attention. The glow of the city played across the bookshelf from the slightly open window, which also circulated a cool current that kept the room from becoming miserably stuffy. One chair sat opposite the door on one side of the table, and two more sat with their backs to the door. Jorge shuffled to take the seat opposite the door, and Milo and Ambrose sank into the two remaining seats.

Jorge eased down into the chair, and Milo was once again struck by how at the turn of a moment, the colonel could transition between being in absolute control to seeming helplessly fragile. He remembered Jorge's wry remark about being a "crippled soldier," and once again, he wondered at the tale of Colonel Jorge before he was head of Nicht-KAT.

"It seems I did not arrive early enough to spare you," Jorge said, giving Milo an even look. "But not so late that I couldn't save you some of the worst bits."

Milo and Ambrose exchanged surprised glances.

"What might the worst bits have been?" Ambrose asked. Milo realized he didn't want to know.

"Oh, I imagine you would have been thrown in a cell and threatened with all sorts of horrible torments," Jorge replied with about as much concern as a man might use to describe an errand he ran the other day. "You probably would have been slapped around a bit by Mayr's bully boys, most certainly called all sorts of very rude names, and then forced to swear some ridiculous pledge or oath to the Fatherland while men were threatening to shoot you."

Yes, Milo was quite certain he could have done without all that. He gave Ambrose a sour look, which prompted a defensive reply from the big man.

"Well, at least they weren't going to kill you," he spluttered, crossing his arms. "It was all a show to try and make sure you toe the line."

"Quite," Jorge responded. "Needless to say, they can't very well kill you now that they know what you are capable of. You're far too valuable for that."

Milo's stomach lurched as he thought about what he was capable of, and it took considerable effort to keep the anxiety and frustration out of his voice.

"The thing is, Colonel," he began, the words almost painful in his suddenly dry mouth, "I'm *not* capable of it. It was all an accident, a fluke. I didn't know the Soviets would be vulnerable to possession by the shades I'd left, and to be honest, sir, knowing what happened last time, I'm not going to do it again."

"I wouldn't say that too loud," Jorge cautioned as he nodded sagely. "But the fact that you believe that is one of the reasons I stuck my neck out for you in there."

Human squeamishness is so quaint. Imrah's thought slithered through his mind icily. *It is a wonder your kind has survived this long.*

Shut up, Milo warned. *Or I'll start using you to scrape muck off my boots.*

The ghul promptly decided her council was not necessary, and he felt her consciousness sink into the essence of the cane, the closest thing she had to sleep.

Milo looked away from the momentary distraction to see Jorge watching him over steepled fingers.

"Oh, uh, thank you, sir," Milo muttered weakly as he fought to recall the threads of the conversation. "For, uh, sticking your neck out, that is, sir."

"Quite welcome." Jorge nodded, but his increasingly pointed stare didn't waver from Milo.

"Sir?" Milo asked. He had the feeling that Jorge was waiting for him to say something, but for the life of him, he didn't know what. Milo held up his hands in surrender and stole a glance at Ambrose, who seemed to be choosing between pretending he was asleep and diving under the desk for cover.

Jorge took a deep breath and very slowly leaned forward onto his elbows, his eyes boring into Milo's as he spoke

"Milo, I understand that you and Mr. Ambrose have a rather loose perspective on military discipline and hierarchy, and I've allowed you as much leeway as could be afforded and then some."

The magus struggled to keep from wincing as he realized what was going on. He knew the collar was sliding around his neck and the slack being taken up in his leash even if he couldn't see or feel them dangling from his neck.

"But," Jorge continued with that fatal conjunction, and Milo felt his shoulders sag, "that ends now because you are officially under scrutiny by the general staff. It might seem silly to explain this to you, but I need to make sure you understand. The military thrives on hierarchy, one man in higher authority knowing without fail that the men beneath him will follow his orders, also without fail. If you can't be trusted under that system, not even your incredible power will spare you from their wrath. A soldier who doesn't take orders is a weapon that can turn on its owner, and you know what they do to a weapon like that."

Milo didn't like being compared to a weapon but forced a smile onto his face in defiance of the grim thought.

"Send it back home to let it live in peace?" the wizard asked with an exaggerated cheer as he grinned hopefully at the colonel. Jorge didn't bat an eye at his attempt at levity.

"They dismantle or destroy weapons like that," the colonel said gravely. "So unless you want someone to change their mind about you, you need to be on your best behavior after Georgia."

"You mean Georgia, where we single-handedly ended a communist coup on the southern border of the empire?" Milo replied tartly. "Or do you mean Georgia, where we again single-handedly captured one of the most powerful Red warlords and his right-hand man to deliver to military intelligence?"

"I mean Georgia, where you risked the operation multiple times while acting in direct and belligerent defiance of a senior officer," Jorge stated coolly. "An officer I happen to hold in some regard, mind you."

Milo wasn't sure which he disliked more: Jorge reminding him of the constant near-failures or stating plainly that he had regard for Captain Lokkemand. Ambrose stirred from his seat and cleared his throat, sparing Milo the burden of his thoughts on that score for the moment.

"Or maybe the Georgia where you won over the support of a powerful fey to our allies, the Shepherds, while mastering a new form of magic," Ambrose added as though Jorge hadn't spoken, frowning thoughtfully beneath knit brows. "Or the Georgia where we repeatedly fended off American agents and their mercenaries to save a member of that same group of allies I mentioned."

Jorge stared at the pair, his face a practiced mask of disinterest and his eyes flat.

"My, we do sound heroic when you put it that way," Milo said, looking at Ambrose, who smiled, white teeth flashing beneath his mustache. "Do you think they give medals out for such things?"

"If they don't, they should." Ambrose chuckled.

"I'm gone for a little while, and you boys start developing delusions of grandeur." A silky voice behind Milo and Ambrose made both jump.

Before either of them could turn around fully in their chairs, Rihyani had reached between them to lay a folder on the table in front of Jorge.

"As you requested, Magpie," she said softly as her traveling cloak brushed Milo, and her dark lips smiled teasingly in his direction.

"Thank you, Contessa," the colonel replied as he took up the folder and began reading.

"Rihyani," Milo blurted and made to rise, but she settled her hand on his shoulder, and he sank back into his seat.

"In a moment, darling," the fey said softly and bowed her head to press her wine-dark lips against his mouth.

Milo's shock turned to delight, and he suddenly felt that perhaps the travails of the day were not quite so bad after all. He took the fey's long fingers and their hands intertwined as she stood at his shoulder.

"Nothing for your favorite cook, then?" Ambrose called, looking forlorn with a great puckered frown.

Rihyani rolled her eyes and leaned over and planted a peck on his proffered cheek.

"I'm glad to see you too, Simon," she said, squeezing his hand. "Thank you for keeping my young rascal alive in my absence."

"*J'aurais fait n'importe quoi pour toi,*" Ambrose replied before pressing a kiss on her outstretched hand. "It is good to see you again, my dear."

"I'm glad to be back," she said softly, then retrieved her hand and clasped it over her and Milo's interlocked fingers. "I've missed you both."

Ambrose smiled as he settled back into his chair. Milo looked up at Rihyani, who was smiling down at him. She nodded at Jorge, and Milo turned and saw that the colonel had put down the folder, and despite his best efforts, a small smile had formed on his lips.

He realized he was smiling too, and for one moment, a moment that seemed etched in stone, Milo understood that everyone he cared about, everyone he loved, was here in this small room in Berlin. The world was at war, there were nefarious schemes afoot, and danger lurked around every corner, but right then, this mad bunch was bound together in the shared joys and smiles of reunion.

For a moment, Milo wondered if all the magic he'd learned would equal what flowed between and through each of them at that moment.

But precious moments are fragile, and it soon ended. Jorge sniffed, Ambrose shifted in his seat, and the fey's hands let go of Milo's, though one hand settled on his shoulder.

"Yes, well." The nearly unflappable Jorge floundered for a moment as he looked down at the folder he'd been perusing. "To business."

"Something is going on in Russia," Rihyani said solemnly as the colonel gathered himself. "The forests around Moscow have been dangerous for some time, but something much bigger than bandits is happening."

Ambrose leaned forward keenly, and Milo felt his stomach tighten.

Thinking of Russia reminded him of the man he'd dragged as a penitent to the general staff. Milo remembered the Georgian who had once come so close to ruling all of Russia and remembered the name he'd hissed into Milo's face on the night of his capture.

He recalled the name that burned in his mind and made the card in his pocket chafe like an iron shackle.

Milo fought to remove the swirling thoughts and emotions from his head as Jorge cleared his throat.

"Our garrison at the village of Sergio-Ivanoskye has sent some rather troubling reports, the most recent being that the nearby town of Gzhatsk was secretly emptied overnight. Given your report from Imrah about Zlydzen and his allies camping near that area, combined with Rihyani's network of sources, I'm inclined to believe that this is something that will require your attention."

Milo recalled the dwarrow's declarations of his plans and damning proclamations before he'd fled in Georgia. Given the power his magical creation had in enthralling the minds of men, it was within the realm of possibility that he could enslave an entire community in a night. But to what aim? Nothing good, that he was certain of.

"We have all sorts of questions about what is going on out there but no answers," Jorge summarized, both hands opening in front of him as though waiting for solutions to land in them. "I need you three to go there and find me some answers."

"Have you extracted any more information from the prisoner we brought in?" Ambrose asked, not hiding his sidelong glance at Milo. The wizard didn't begrudge him the look, though he had to batter down a surge of annoyance. They both knew it was a sore subject.

"Stalin's interrogation results have been strictly mundane thus far," Jorge said, looking at Milo and Ambrose in turn as though trying to keep them both in his sights like creatures that might attack.

Milo supposed if the colonel was going to make the effort, he might as well oblige.

"Which is exactly why we should be handling the interrogation," he said flatly, staring into Jorge's weathered face. "He has reason to fear us, and we know what sort of questions need to be asked. The general staff hiding him so they can keep up this game is ridiculous."

Jorge slowly took off his glasses and massaged the bridge of his nose.

"The responsibility for Stalin's interrogation was transferred to Nicht-KAT two weeks ago," he declared quietly, a man sighing under a heavy burden. "The Ludendorff was concerned about members of the general staff sympathetic to the Reich interfering to protect Röhm from the part he played in allowing Stalin's forces to move freely through German territories."

Milo and Ambrose sat silently for a moment, chewing the news like gristle.

"Two weeks ago? *Two?*" Ambrose said slowly, clearly on his way to the same revelation Milo was chasing. "The magus put in a request with the general staff to debrief Stalin four days ago."

"A request they immediately rejected," Milo said through clenched teeth. "Without one word about him being transferred to the custody of the very division we serve in."

"The general staff does have ultimate authority," Jorge reminded him with a shrug. "Even over Nicht-KAT operations."

Milo spat a short string of curses to make it clear how little he thought of the answer.

He got a gentle warning squeeze on his shoulder from Rihyani.

Careful, Milo, her thoughts whispered to him via the Art. *There may be much here that we don't understand.*

Then how about someone starts explaining? he shot back as Jorge leaned forward, looking at Milo and Ambrose from under his eyebrows.

"The decision to restrict access to Stalin was mine," the colonel said, not flinching from the angry stares both men gave him. "And it was made for a variety of reasons I am not inclined or able to share with either of you at the moment."

Milo tried to remember the closeness he'd felt with Jorge only moments before. He tried to recall the relief and pride he'd felt as Jorge had swept in and stood against the most powerful men in the German Empire on his behalf. He wanted to focus on that, but all he could think of was the name Stalin had whispered.

"Stalin will give us everything in time," Jorge said, a sharp note of finality in his voice as he snapped the folder in front of him closed and slid it toward Milo. "In the meantime, your business is with an abandoned town, not a humbled warlord. It's as simple as that."

Ambrose opened his mouth to argue, but another quick look at Milo changed his mind.

Visibly seething, the wizard leaned forward and took the folder off the desk with trembling fingers.

"You're making a mistake," Milo murmured as he rose and made for the door, thinking he should leave before things escalated irreparably.

"You are dismissed," the colonel called after him.

5

THESE MEMORIES

The train rolled on through the rainy night, the churning throb of the engine giving a voice to the undercurrent of tension in the compartment where Milo, Rihyani, and Ambrose now sat.

After the meeting with Jorge, Milo and Ambrose had retired to their room at the hotel, with Rihyani joining them a little later. She'd arrived via the window and informed them that Jorge had arranged for a train to take them east. Both men acknowledged her news, but neither felt much like talking. Ambrose had gone to bed rather quickly and was soon snoring. Milo had sunk onto the bed with his thoughts and stared at the ceiling. The fey had laid next to him, one hand resting upon his chest while she ran long fingers through his hair.

Milo couldn't remember when he'd fallen asleep, but at some point, eyes burning and shoulders knotted, he'd slid into a sleep where there was nothing but doors arrayed along a dark corridor. He felt with certainty that one of these doors was an escape from something, something chasing him, and so he'd raced over and tried the first knob. The knob wouldn't turn, and the door didn't so much as rattle when he threw himself against it. He saw that the name "Volkohne" was carved into the door. Something, not a sound but a feeling, told Milo his time was running out, and he rushed to another door.

Again, no movement, and he looked up to see "Volkohne" engraved into the pitiless portal.

His fear growing as *something* neared, he'd rushed to the next door, checking for what letters were carved into the wood. Volkohne...Volkohne...Volkohne over and over, until near-blind with panic, he came to a door into which Petrovich had been scored with a smoldering chisel. Knowing that whatever was coming was at his heels, he twisted and pulled. The door opened, and black fire sprang forth to embrace him.

Milo had awakened in the same position, Rihyani still lying beside him. He'd looked into her dark eyes and saw the question, but he brushed it away as he stood and went to the bathroom.

The aching silence had followed them from the car Jorge had sent to take them to the station to the compartment where they now sat watching rain streak across the window as the engines churned. The pressure of the silence weighed down the air, muffling everything and making time a slippery thing. Sitting there, Milo was unsure of how long they'd been traveling and had no idea how far they had gotten in their travels. He couldn't even have said he knew for certain when the storm had started. Each moment seemed a cramped eternity, yet he knew things were passing him by without his notice.

Would he look up from contemplating the worn compart-ment floor to discover they were disembarking into the Russian forest? And what was keeping them all silent? Anger? Distrust? Fear?

Wasn't morale something an officer was supposed to address? To make certain his men were ready for whatever lay ahead?

Milo didn't think he was a good speaker, certainly not the type to rouse the troops. He supposed he ought to do something, but what? What words could he offer either of them or even himself that weren't hollow platitudes and lies? Some people might appreciate such sentiments, but not these two. How do you encourage a Nephilim nearly two hundred years old and a fey older than most civilizations?

Milo looked down at his black coat and felt the card in his breast pocket. He shouldn't have felt it, the card not being big enough or his clothes thin enough to explain it, but he was aware of it all the same.

Quietly, Milo reached inside his coat and drew out the folded card. His fingers played over the ragged edges he knew better than he did his own body, and he felt a terrible certainty steal over him. Like a crank gaining momentum, his thoughts worked around and around, coming back to the same point faster and faster.

If he couldn't say something encouraging, at least he could say something true.

"I've got something," he began, his voice a horrible bleat in his ears. "Something to show both of you."

Ambrose and Rihyani both stirred, looking first at Milo's downcast face and then at what was in his hand. Ambrose recognized the tarot card, and a mixture of interest and bemusement played across his face. Rihyani, to whom he had never shown the card, narrowed her eyes at the object in Milo's hand but said nothing.

"I know we are heading into what could very well be the belly of the beast," Milo said, the words clumsy things tumbling from his tongue. "And if that is the case, my head shouldn't be back in Berlin, stewing over the choices Jorge is making about Stalin."

"It wasn't right for him not to talk to us about it," Ambrose offered helpfully, offering Milo a supportive nod.

Milo's head shook slowly, and Ambrose's face contorted into a frown.

"Jorge is the superior officer, and he sees things differently than we do," the magus said, catching Rihyani's eye. "And it's nobody's fault that he makes the decisions he does. We need to respect and trust him."

She bowed her head slightly in appreciation, then her head rose, and he felt her appreciative will brush aetherically past him as her head tilted to one side. She'd felt something in that brief contact, and it gave her pause.

"But?" she asked slowly.

"But Jorge has his concerns and perspectives and I have mine," Milo continued. "I want access to Stalin, not just because I think I can get him to talk about Zlydzen, but because when we captured him back in Georgia, he said a name in reference to me. A name that proved he knows something about...about where I come from."

Milo took a deep breath, feeling more uncertain than ever about this confession.

"He called me Petrovich," the wizard said as he unfolded the tarot card and held it out for them to examine.

The card was a woodcut, its dark lines leaving distinct marks pressed into the stock. The entire card was framed in domino diamonds that encased whorled spirals which gave the impression of a storm or possibly a fire. At the center of the card, a figure sat upon a throne whose legs were tree roots and whose armrests were human bones. Over the back of the throne a banner hung, with the words Petrovich Burned in Russian script. The banner was held by a fine, delicate hand on the right and a bestial black claw on the left. On the throne sat a man in dark princely furs, a broken sword across his lap and wounds on his hands.

The features of the figure, wrought in the woodcut's strict lines, were Milo's.

Ambrose and Rihyani squinted at the face on the card, then back up at him, then down again.

"When Roland and I were picked up by German soldiers, this card was my only possession." Milo quietly told them what he'd told only one other human being. "Only the person on the throne was me at five."

He took a shaky breath.

"Like me, the picture didn't stay a child."

His companions exchanged concerned looks, then Ambrose slid back in his seat while Rihyani held out her hand, long fingers scant centimeters from the ragged, curling edge of the card.

"May I?" she asked, looking into Milo's face.

Milo wanted to say yes and hand the card over, but he found that his mouth wouldn't form the words and his arm was locked. A thrill of fear rushed through him at his sudden paralysis, his eyes widening in horror that his body would not obey him. For an instant, he wondered what new and insidious magic he was facing, but a hurried examination of himself using what he knew of both the Art and necromistry revealed nothing. Yet he hung there immobile, even as Rihyani continued to look at him with beseeching eyes, fingers extended.

"Milo?" she said softly, leaning forward as she studied his face, fingers drawing closer to the card. A surge of panic that was almost painful gripped his chest, and an instant later, he felt a corresponding flood of low, burning anger and resentment.

Didn't she know what she was doing? Didn't she understand how this made him feel? To think she could snatch something he'd hidden in fear all his life! How dare she!

"Magus, what's wrong?" Ambrose asked, sitting up in his seat. Both of them were staring at him with looks of concern.

Milo realized his chest was heaving with rapid breaths.

What was happening to him? Why did he feel this way?

Rihyani's hand withdrew even as she leaned closer. Milo felt rigid lines of tension he hadn't noticed before melting along his shoulders and neck.

"Milo, it is okay. I am not going to take it from you," she said softly. "I just wanted to look at it. I'm sorry."

His breathing began to slow and his arm, almost vibrating

with tension, throbbed as he reflexively drew the card to his chest. He cradled it there like a child, the urge to fold and squirrel it away sweeping him again. It brushed aside his thoughts and desires in a tide of mental programming rooted in fear.

"I..." he began, but his throat caught as shame and years of fear bore down.

Ambrose and Rihyani exchanged looks of open concern before gazing at him with sad, knowing eyes. They realized what Milo did: that this wasn't a magical malady or eldritch possession.

Milo had been hiding this secret, this burden since he was a child. The psychic architecture he had constructed to protect himself and ensure the concealment of it was not easily breached. Years of habit, years of terror about others learning the truth, years of quietly but ferociously dismissing something that could not be had brought their full weight to lock his body down. Confessing it was one thing, but handing it over was another. Having another person take hold of the wicked thing had been a fear similar to death for as long as he could remember.

"This card, this thing..." Milo said, glaring down at what he was still cradling. "I've been trying to hide it from others for so long, I... "

He took a steadying breath, hating how Ambrose and the fey stared at him with such concern and pity.

"I'm sorry, I didn't think it would be this hard," Milo explained, forcing himself to straighten and pull the card away from his chest, though only so it hovered over his lap. "This card has been the only hint about where I came from and who or even what I am. I knew if anyone ever figured out its magic, fear, pain, and death would follow."

Ambrose's mouth tightened beneath his mustache for a moment before he spoke.

"How would anyone know it's magical?" Ambrose asked. "I mean, I understand you figuring it out, but anybody who didn't know your story about the card aging with you wouldn't know it was anything but an old tarot that looks like you, right?"

Milo nodded. He understood the confusion, but the effort of formulating an answer was monumental. Instead, he reached inside his coat to the carefully shaped edge he kept in the lining and nicked his scarred thumb. He then held the card in one hand over the bloodied thumb.

"Because of this," Milo said and snapped to ignite the blood-catalyzed magic. The green-tinged flame danced across the edge of the card, kindling it almost instantly. The card began to roll in on itself like a dying spider as the emerald light lapped across every surface, leaving nothing but black crust and a tracery of sullen orange fire. Milo let it fall to the bare floor of the train compartment, where it quickly crumbled into a few black curls that gave up a few pitiful wisps of smoke and then nothing at all.

Milo met Ambrose's and the fey's bemused faces with weary boredom, face slack and lids drooping as he pressed a foot down on the floor, turning the remainders of the card into a dark smudge. Still looking at his companions, he bent down and ran a finger through the stain, and then held his darkened fingers up for inspection.

Satisfied that they'd seen absolute proof of the card's destruction, he reached into his breast pocket and with clean fingers, he drew out the folded card. He unfolded it as he had done upon his initial confession, holding it out for them to see. He then pointed at the floor, which showed no sign of the dark smear from a moment earlier.

Ambrose gave a long whistle.

"On my first day in Dresden, one of the orderlies took it out of my pocket and ripped it to shreds before tossing it into the trash bin."

Milo looked down at the card, a swirling amalgam of anger and nostalgia simmering in his eyes.

"I found the card in my pocket, completely whole before I'd been shown to my room. It was inescapable."

Milo stared into his own face on the card, the woodcut's expression, as it always had been, one of royal stoicism, vaguely dismissive and utterly remote. He remembered practicing making the face in a mirror sometimes when no one was looking, but every time he came close to achieving it, he'd shivered and run away from the mirror.

"My attempts at getting rid of it have always been unsuccessful," the wizard said, looking up at them, forcing himself to meet their eyes. "It's been a curse I couldn't escape and also the one hope I had of knowing my past. In a strange way, I love and hate it at the same time. Does that make sense?"

"Yes," Rihyani said, and to Milo's immense relief, he saw something other than pity reflected in her dark eyes. The fey's expressions were not as transparent as humans', but Milo had learned enough to know that he was looking at understanding. She was no longer looking at him with pity or concern or even curiosity. She was knowing him.

Somewhere within him, Milo felt something long broken heal.

He looked down at the card, shook his head once, and held it out to her.

"Go ahead," he said, unable to believe what he was saying. "You can look at it. It's okay."

As Rihyani's hand stretched out to take the card, the compartment lurched around them, and all three of them were thrown to the floor.

Ambrose bounced back to his feet and tore open the compartment door as Milo and Rihyani were still struggling to disentangle themselves. From where they were on the floor, Milo realized the sudden jolt had brought on a rapid decrease in speed, but the humming vibration of the rails under them could still be felt. The engineer must have spotted something that caused them to slow.

Milo could only think of one reason for that.

"I'll see what's going on," Ambrose called over his shoulder. "You two ought to make sure your contingencies are in order, Magus, sharpish!"

"Contingencies?" Rihyani asked, staring into Milo's face from where she'd landed on the floor.

Milo was up on hands and knees, with one arm reaching over Rihyani's shoulder and one leg between her thighs.

"Uh, yes," Milo said, acutely aware that he was having a hard time forming precise thoughts. "I, uh, I'll need your help."

"Sort of hard to do anything like this," she said with a glance down the length of his body. "Or at least anything practical."

He flushed and started to rise, a half-formed, half-meant apology on his lips, but Rihyani hooked her arm around his neck. For a second, he thought she was trying to use his body as leverage to pull herself up, then he felt her cheek against his and her lips at his ear.

"I love you," she murmured. "Don't forget that."

Milo froze, Rihyani hanging from his neck as her supple legs entwined his thigh.

"The timing is awkward," he said, his voice sounding breathless and peevish to his ears.

"You brute!" she hissed and nipped playfully at his earlobe. "That's not how a lover responds to his beloved!"

Milo blinked, suddenly aware of how close she was, how much of her body he could feel pressed against him, and what she most certainly could feel pressed against her. It was absurd given the circumstances but had death and danger not been so near at hand, he wasn't certain what he might have done.

Or rather, he knew exactly what he would do, but he was determined not to think about it.

"I love you, too," he said, dizzy from the emotional rollercoaster he'd been on for the last few minutes. "But I *will* need your help to pull this off."

Rihyani lowered herself back onto the floor and gave an immense roll of her eyes.

"What can I do for you, my love?" she asked with a sigh.

"Camouflage," Milo said as he climbed to his feet with a grunt.

He bent and offered his hand, which the fey took kindly enough despite her efforts at pouting.

"To hide the train?" Rihyani asked, brows arching in doubt.

"Not for the outside," Milo said as he pulled her to her feet. "For the inside."

Standing eye to eye with him, the fey continued to look at him doubtfully. Then her eyes widened, and a sly look crept over her features.

"Especially the third and fourth car?"

Milo nodded, giving her a devious grin.

6

THESE MESSAGES

Milo was standing at the end of the fourth car when Ambrose shuffled down the passage at gunpoint. The rain-lashed German soldier behind him couldn't see the expression stamped across the big man's face as he frog-marched the bodyguard down the aisle, gun pressed to his head.

"This better work," encapsulated his feelings well enough.

The other patrons in the car sat very still, most not daring to look up from where they huddled in their seats. They were a motley collection of travelers, ranging from men in drab business suits to a pair of old women in the vibrant apron dresses common in the most rural parts of Belarus. They were bystanders, non-combatants suddenly and frightfully aware that they were caught up in a conflict not their own.

One or two whispered prayers with bowed heads while others leaned over children, offering what fervent if feeble protection their bodies could afford.

Despite this absolute inoffensiveness, or perhaps because of it, Milo watched the sodden soldiers shuffle behind Ambrose's warden's jeer, threatening the passengers. They hissed and snarled and carelessly swept their rifles this way and that, laughing as people cringed and lurched away. One even reached out with the barrel of his rifle and began to knock the hats off of those he passed. As the tormented stole frustrated and fearful glances at the bully, he snarled in German, "Look down, pig!" before moving on to another target.

Milo gritted his teeth, willing himself to maintain his composure.

Not yet, he thought. *Just a little longer.*

This plan may not be feasible, Imrah offered, and the wizard ground his teeth all the harder as Ambrose came to stand in front of him, the rifle barrel still pressed to his head.

"Look who came for dinner," Ambrose said and bit back a curse as the rifle barrel was jabbed hard against the back of his head.

"Shut up," the big man's escort spat, glaring past his captive at Milo.

Milo's temper flared, and the plan nearly failed then and there.

"Be careful," Milo said, distilling his anger into a tone as cold and sharp as a flensing knife. "If you're here for me, you know I could kill every last one of you with a single word."

The eyes of every soldier in the column in the aisle swung to Milo, and for a moment, no one dared to move.

"You're not going to do anything as rash as that," said a familiar voice in crisp German.

Milo looked at the front of the car, where the officer with the curly dark mustache from the general staff meeting stood watching him with glittering eyes. In the uneven light of the general staff conference hall, Milo hadn't noticed that the man's eyes seemed greedily amphibian. He might have been a handsome man of middle age if not for those bulging, glassy orbs watching the world as if everything might be his food. A twisted imitation of a smile wormed its way across the officer's face as he continued to leer hungrily at Milo.

"You won't do that because I have soldiers in the next car ready to kill every civilian present if things get out of hand. Do you understand?"

To illustrate the point, the soldiers in the compartment turned and leveled their rifles at the rows of seated civilians. The innocent gasped and shivered but stayed where they were, trembling and crouching.

Milo tightened his grip on his cane as his thoughts whispered to Imrah within.

Both compartments. Are we sure this will work and not get us killed in the process?

It is not a question of power but focus. Make certain you excite but don't ignite.

Milo looked at Mayr's goons, their expressions slack, almost bored, and terror gripped him.

What if they've been hollowed out like the Soviets?

Then focus will be even more important. Now, attend to the situation before you are shot.

Milo hadn't realized he'd been ignoring Mayr, who had not only been talking to him but now had a pistol in his hand and was walking toward Milo as his soldiers shuffled to one side of the aisle or the other. The passengers forced into proximity with the menacing Germans cowered back in their seats.

"Don't tell me you're losing your nerve," Mayr growled as he came to stand in front of Ambrose, pistol held out at waist level. "I promised the Reich that you would be a valuable asset, but I'm afraid no one will believe me if you go all moonstruck anytime guns are involved."

Ambrose gave a low growl and shifted to shield Milo from the pistol. Mayr looked at him as though just seeing him.

"Please move," he said in a brittle, polite tone, twitching the barrel of the pistol to one side. "My business is with the warlock, not his imp."

"You're not worth the effort some devil took to wipe you

from his ass," Ambrose snarled back, one hand curling into a fist while the other settled into a claw.

Mayr met Ambrose's stare, and as was the case with any mere mortal, he quickly looked away, but the man would not be so easily cowed. Shaking his head with a sigh, he ceased pointing his pistol at Ambrose and Milo and instead turned and held the pistol in the face of a small girl sitting next to her mother. Both were dressed in traditional Belarusian attire, and when the pistol was leveled, the mother hid her daughter's face against her patterned apron. The child made small snuffling sounds as she shook against her mother, while the woman glared up at Mayr in tearful defiance.

"I feel that things are getting out of hand," Mayr said flatly. "Perhaps you should convince me otherwise."

Milo rested a hand on Ambrose's shoulder and drew him back so they could trade places.

The big man resisted but finally looked at Milo and then beyond him. His eyes narrowed with predatory focus.

"Batch moving up five," he reported in a clipped whisper as Milo shuffled past him. "They're mine."

Milo wanted to tell the bodyguard to not do anything so risky, but then he was standing in front of Mayr, who was pointing a pistol at the back of a girl's head.

"Well, I'm not dead," Milo said with a practiced swagger as he gave Mayr a dismissive once-over. "So you must not want to kill me."

The smile that spread under Mayr's mustache was cold enough that Milo was amazed his voice didn't fog in front of him.

"I do very much want to kill you," Mayr said icily before turning his head to gaze at the cowering passengers. "As I'd like to purge the world of every one of these subhuman sheep and the parasites that cling to them. Even their would-be defenders, the simpering English and the limp-spined French, deserve only the shallowest graves history can afford."

He glared at the mother who defied him with her stare, and Milo could practically see the hateful calculations playing out behind the man's cold-blooded eyes. The wizard harnessed his will in preparation for what would come next and wished he could offer up a prayer, but nothing came to mind.

"But all things in good time." Mayr shrugged, and in one fluid movement, holstered the pistol at his hip. "I'm not here for that sort of thing today."

"Then what are you here for?" Milo asked and nodded to the man's damp coat. "Besides enjoying the weather."

Mayr eyed his dripping sleeves and gave Milo a small, self-assured smile.

"Well, obviously I'm here to recruit you, my little warlock," Mayr said as though the wizard were a very silly schoolboy. "The Reich doesn't necessarily need a creature like you, but you could certainly make certain aspects of our operations far more productive."

Milo blinked, for an instant certain that he misunderstood.

"Well, your pitch could use some work," Milo said, crossing his arms as he stared into the toadlike eyes that watched him. "But more than that, you seem to have forgotten yesterday evening where you called me a Slavic savage and a motherless Russian or something along those lines."

Mayr flapped his hand at the words and shook his head before resuming his condescending tone.

"If you're going to let that bother you, it won't be easy working together," Mayr said with a roll of his eyes. "I know you're not like the rest of the parasites, that you're a different sort altogether, but appearances must be kept up. If I hadn't spoken up at that meeting, some might have gotten the wrong idea."

"Wouldn't want them to think you weren't a raging xeno-phobe, would we?" Milo said with mock understanding. "That would be awful."

Mayr again shook his head and waved his hand even more aggressively as though trying to dismiss an unwelcome smell.

"I don't blame you for your ignorance of our organization and its purpose," Mayr said, reaching up to flick rainwater from his mustache. "The nature of our operation has required secrecy, but now that we are preparing to take a great leap into the future, I feel we can start to lift the veil, as it were, and reach out."

Milo looked pointedly down the aisle at soldiers still training their rifles on the seated civilians, then gave Mayr a long look.

"This is your idea of reaching out?" Milo chuckled, gesturing with his cane at the pistol on the officer's belt. "Again, your pitch needs work."

Mayr shrugged and took a step back toward his soldiers.

"I want you to understand what we are offering, whatever your choice may be. Join us, and you buy yourself time to carve a place in the new world order as we build a better, purer world through ruthlessness and strength. Stand against us, and discover that nothing and no one is safe from our wrath. Think of all you have to lose, all that we could take from you if we become your enemies."

Mayr gave the woman and child he'd threatened a pitying look.

"Better to run with the wolves than cower with the sheep, no?"

Mayr's face lit up with an idea, and a tight, cruel smile opened under the amphibian's hungry stare.

"Don't," Milo warned, but that only made Mayr's smile wider.

"Oh, come now." Mayr chuckled darkly. "I think it will serve as a perfect lesson about who we are and what we are capable of."

"Do—" Milo began, but Mayr drew his pistol with startling speed and snapped off two shots, punching gory holes in the child's back and her mother's face.

Fear and outrage should have erupted across the car in the wake of the pistol's crack. Children should have wailed as men and women screamed and shouted in terror and anger, yet no voice was raised. There was a deathly stillness across the entire car.

Milo felt Rihyani's will ripple through the Art she'd stretched across the car, and a grim smile spread across his face. It was time; no turning back now. Mayr and his soldiers stood looking around the car for a moment, suddenly unsure as every cowering face turned to them with a dead-eyed stare, the woman and her daughter among them.

"It's your turn for an education," Milo said, his razor focus raking across his slumbering horrors. "Now you will see who I am and what I can do!"

The soldiers opened fire as Rihyani released her illusion in a befuddling eruption of broken images.

The car was revealed to be empty of passengers or seats or anything but a drift of black grit. The soldiers began shooting despite this, rifles going off in a crazed series of blasts that chased the fractured visual stimuli Rihyani had spread around them. Glass shattered and shots gouged and ricocheted about the interior as the rain and wind began to pour in. Mayr was shouting something, but it was lost as an incredible shivering buzz filled the car.

At Milo's command, a storm of si'lat emerged like an abominable locust swarm from a mad sea and broke through Rihyani's now-dissipating illusion, engulfing the soldiers. Not bothering to take concrete shape, the necromist creation swept over the terrified bullies, making a mockery of their attempts to fight back as it drove them toward the front of the car.

Like men trying to grapple with an attacking swarm of bees, the Germans screamed and swatted and reeled, but their antics only allowed the flurry of black grit to gouge and rasp exposed flesh with greater speed. Every way they turned and every movement they made opened new avenues of attack as the shade-driven particles slid under clothing and dug into orifices.

They began to huddle and press against the door to the next car, but if they hadn't been tearing at their own eyes, they might have realized that there was no safety beyond it as the soldiers left there faced another colossal si'lat.

Milo stood, sweat beading his brow as he sought to keep his creations in check. He heard movement behind him and Ambrose's bellicose roar, but he couldn't be bothered to turn around. The si'lat required all his attention lest they fly free and kill every enemy at hand. A typical si'lat was more than capable of killing a man and ripping him to shreds in short order, much less these huge expansions, but Milo didn't want to kill everyone on the train.

He wanted to send a message, which he supposed would be easier if there were any to carry it.

Behind him, Milo heard the bark of a gun firing an instant before the viewport at his back exploded in a crash of broken glass. Then a man screamed, but the sound seemed to move quickly away from the train before ending abruptly. With the viewport gone, rain and wind sent shivers over Milo's back, and his mind was nearly knocked off point by the sudden chilling stimulation.

Focus, Imrah growled, and the wizard could feel the cane trembling in his hand.

Milo had herded animated corpses before, but this was something else entirely. The shades within practically exploded to inflict themselves on the world around them. Inside each, he could feel the bound soul wells like throbbing dark stars. Without the intimate connection his blood gave the magic and the assistance from Imrah, Milo knew he wouldn't be able to control the living, slashing storms of sable sand.

There were further sounds of smashing glass, and Milo

looked up to see the soldiers hurling themselves out the windows. The si'lat chased them, tearing off strips of cloth and flesh as they fell screaming. As the sand left to chase the fleeing Germans, he could see more of the car.

One of the soldiers lay on the floor with a trench knife buried in his chest. Another looked like he might have fallen asleep, but Milo knew better since he saw the man's face and arms scoured until pink-stained bone gleamed in the lights of the car. Milo felt a twinge of sympathy for the men and then noticed the one with the knife in his chest was the sadist who had walked along knocking hats off. He turned away.

True, the hats and their wearers had all been part of Rihyani's masterful illusion, but the soldier hadn't known that, had he?

As he considered and more of the si'lat swarm slid from the car into the night, Milo saw that there was one more figure left in the car with him. Legs out before him, Mayr leaned against the battered train car portal. His face looked like he'd tried to shave with broken glass, and blood dribbled freely from a freshly broken nose whose shattered bridge pressed jaggedly against the skin.

The toady's eyes were so swollen and moist that Milo wondered if the slimy things would pop free and roll away. Instead, they looked up at Milo and widened, then Mayr fumbled for his pistol with si'lat-gnawed hands.

With a flex of his focus, he gathered what remained of the black storm into a tendril that snared Mayr's fumbling hand. The treacherous officer screamed as the fractured edges of the condensed grit sawed into his flesh.

More of the si'lat reluctantly returned, called inexorably by his will back into the car. They poured in through the shattered windows, freshly christened with the rain outside. Milo bore down on the shades, willing them to congeal into tendrils of jagged, coagulated darkness that coiled around Mayr's remaining limbs and then dragged him upright. The shade-animated tentacles stretched Mayr against the front wall of the car, arms and legs straining out in a tortured X shape.

The muscles in Mayr's neck stood out like cords as the web of black sand extended his limbs millimeter by agonizing millimeter.

"Stop!" Mayr gasped. "For the love of God!! Please stop!"

Milo began to stalk toward Mayr, reminding himself that he was sending a message but wondering exactly what that message was.

"Do you think that's what the subhumans will say when your Reich goons will come for them?" Milo asked, stepping over the soldier with the dagger in his chest. "When your bands of zealots attack them in the streets and drag them from their homes, will they call out for mercy?"

Mayr's right wrist began to slide a little more and soft clicks could be heard, and then a sound like bone rasping against bone. Mayr started to scream, then that wrist gave a wet pop and pain robbed him of his voice.

"When you shoot the children in front of their mothers, will they say prayers to Heaven for you to laugh at?" Milo asked, hardly noticing when Mayr's arm gave a sharp click and the officer whimpered.

"Please!" Mayr wheezed as he hung there panting and watching himself be pulled apart bit by bit. "Please, what do you want?"

Milo paused to consider the question, even reaching out a hand to still the si'lat from pulling the man into pieces.

"What do I want?" Milo mused as though the novel question intrigued him. "That is an excellent question."

Mayr stared at him between huge heaving sighs, unable to relax since the tendrils held him fast. As Milo wiped sweat from his brow and tapped his lower lip thoughtfully with an upraised finger, Mayr strained against his broken ribs to get enough air to speak again.

"Maybe I was wrong," he moaned, and his eyes bulged in fear when Milo looked up and leveled an icy glare at him. "I was wrong. Am wrong."

Milo lowered his hand to rest his palm on the cane as he planted it in front of him. Sweat running in rivulets down his face, he looked expectantly at the magically racked officer.

"Yes?" he prompted in a forcedly unhurried tone.

Mayr struggled for air, the movements eliciting whimpers of pain as his ruined joints popped and ground with a sound to put teeth on edge.

"I could explain this to the others," he hissed through clenched teeth. "We didn't understand, didn't appreciate your power."

"No, you didn't," Milo said distractedly as his focus thrummed against the other si'lat swarm, which had gone to chase its share of soldiers into the night. The shades pressed against his control, hungry for blood, but he drove them back mercilessly. Milo felt the si'lat swarm sluggishly turn back to the train like children sulkily returning home for dinner.

In the distraction, the si'lat swarm binding Mayr had begun to gently pull again, greedily lapping up the fear and pain dripping freely from the man.

The trapped officer couldn't manage words this time, only a whining keen as one of his knees gave a slurping pop that made the hair on the back of Milo's neck stand up. The si'lat stopped once it felt Milo's mind bristling at its subversive initiative, slackening the coils a little. Mayr's head slumped forward, though his body remained stretched in four directions.

For a moment Milo thought the man had passed out, but a sob escaped his lips, and though he didn't look up, he raised his voice in a low groaning plea.

"What are you going to do to me?"

Milo looked at the broken man hanging before him and decided he was done. He knew what message he wanted to send. He felt a twinge of guilt that it had taken him so long to make up

his mind and that unnecessary pain had come because of it, but now that it was settled, things seem to take on a momentum of their own.

With a flick of one finger, another coil of black sand, smoother than the others, stretched out to Mayr. It wrapped gently around his neck and lifted his head to look at Milo. There were tears in the officer's eyes as he looked at the wizard, fear and hate twisting together like two vipers behind his gaze.

"I am going to use you to send a message," Milo said slowly.

A flash of hope enlivened Mayr's gaze, all the more nauseous to witness for the man's desperate nod.

"I can do that," he said eagerly, his voice nearly breaking.

"I know you can," Milo said, and at his nod, the immense si'lat pulled sharply in five different directions. There was a soggy thump as something damp and heavy hit the floor amidst the patter of additional fluid falling as freely as rain came in through the windows.

Milo turned away from the grisly scene as Ambrose and Rihyani stepped into the car from the rear. Both advanced a few steps before stopping and staring at the mess. Their eyes took in the scattered remains before settling heavily on the magus.

"What happened to sending a message?" Ambrose asked.

"More than one way to do that," Milo remarked dryly as he walked past them to their compartment in the fifth car, the red-stained si'lat sliding along the floor in his wake.

When they rolled into Gzhatsk, none of them felt prepared for what waited for them—which turned out to be nothing.

The rail lines didn't run directly to Sergio-Ivanoskye and the camp there, so they were supposed to arrive at Gzhatsk and be promptly picked up by transport from the camp. As they moved into the train station, it became clear that their escort was as absent as the occupants of the town.

No sight, no sound, no trace of anyone having ever dwelled in the place other than the buildings. As Milo climbed off the train with Ambrose and Rihyani, he could have believed that Gzhatsk hadn't just been abandoned but forgotten. It felt as though humans had fled the place years ago, maybe longer, and as he looked out and saw fresh vegetation creeping in and around the buildings, he wondered if this wasn't the case.

"When is the escort from Sergio-Ivanoskye to arrive?" Milo asked over his shoulder as he looked up and down the street outside the station platform, which was barren except for tufts of grass and ground cover.

"They were supposed to be here to meet us," Ambrose said, his Gewehr in his hands as he swept the area. "At least, that was what I was led to believe."

The low hiss of the train engine was the only sound any of them heard as they slowly stepped out onto the street. The dark windows of the hollow buildings arrayed before them were like vacant eyes staring down at them indifferently.

"How far is it to the village from here?" Rihyani asked, her dark eyes looking first at the ground and then squinting at the sky.

"Twenty or so miles due west," Ambrose muttered distract-edly, then nodded at what looked like an inn or hotel across the street. "We should get our effects and head over there. Not wise to stay out in the open."

As though summoned by the mention of their luggage, one of the junior engineers cursed and dragged a trolley laden with their luggage onto the platform.

"So quick to see us off, eh?" Milo called, then cringed at Ambrose's wince. Perhaps, standing in the street and shouting wasn't the best plan.

Sweating and still swearing, the junior engineer shuffled to the stairs leading off the platform, where he managed to keep the trolley from descending catastrophically down the steps.

"Chief says to off-load and quick," the young man said breathlessly as they started to climb the stairs. "Says he wants clear as soon as possible."

He looked anxiously from the three companions to the train as though fearing they might leave him if he didn't discharge his duties fast enough. Milo thought the fellow's fears weren't entirely unfounded.

It had taken no small amount of cajoling and threats to get the train moving again after the encounter with Mayr. None of the train's crew had been injured when the Reich had stopped the train and boarded, but that experience had been frightening enough before Milo had released the two immense si'lat. The chief engineer had ranted about how his rig was not a military train and that he and his crew were not soldiers and could not be expected to operate under such conditions. Ambrose had seen fit to remind the man that according to dictates from the current German government, all trains were military trains if it was deemed so, but to no one's surprise, that did not satisfy the man.

"I don't want any part of this strangeness," he spluttered, giving Milo and Rihyani furious glares. The chief then proceeded to say he was going to turn the train around at the nearest wye track.

Even with Milo promising that the crew would be compensated and repairs to the train paid for, it took the wizard threatening to show the man more strangeness to get them moving again with no plans for any detours until they arrived at Gzhatsk.

"Then let's not keep him waiting," Milo said as he reached the trolley.

The wizard nodded appreciatively at the youth and scooped up his pack and a satchel holding the alchemical reagents he'd collected while waiting for the general staff in Berlin. Usually, he kept such things in the enchanted pockets sewn into his coat, but some of them were too sensitive or too dangerous to keep on his person, which tended to get jostled around quite a bit. Among the ingredients were the si'lat swarms, condensed beyond physical reality into two fist-sized orbs.

"Tell your chief we appreciate his cooperation," Milo said. "And please remind him that any and all requests for compensation need to go to Colonel Jorge at the office of the general staff."

The others snatched up their things as Milo spoke, leaving a single crate on the trolley.

"That," Milo said, pointing at the crate. "That goes back to Berlin to the general staff office. I'm sure they'll compensate you for the trouble of transporting it, and if not, leave a note for Colonel Jorge."

The young man stared doubtfully at the crate, frowning as he tried to find some way to refuse the instruction.

"I'm not sure that the chief planned for this," he said, looking at Milo beseechingly.

"Stow it in back and handle it yourself then," Milo said with a wink. "I imagine you could charge the general staff just about anything for personal delivery. Make sure you don't open it."

The junior engineer might have argued the point, but the train whistle sounded. After looking torn for a second more, he swore one last time and scampered back to the train, trolley and crate in tow.

Milo stood watching the train roll out, bearing his message.

"I'm still not sure that was the best idea," Ambrose said at his shoulder as he kept watch on the abandoned town.

"It's too late for second thoughts now," the wizard murmured. "Let the chips fall where they may."

7

THESE SURPRISES

Their ride still hadn't arrived to take them out of Gzhatsk nearly four hours after the train had left the station.

They'd entered the hotel and found its dark halls as eerily vacant as everything else they'd seen in the town. They'd quickly found the dining hall was the most comfortable spot, not only because of the ample seating but also because the large decorative window over the bar offered ample light from outside. Ambrose had done some pilfering of the choicest liquors and nonperishables from the bar and that parlor behind it, but that was consumed all too soon.

This left the three companions to sit in an empty hotel dining room and hypothesize what could have emptied the town.

"Maybe it was something like Kimaris," Ambrose had suggested as he got up from where he'd sat on the hotel bar across from the passage to the front entrance. "Some sort of demon that swept through and swallowed up everyone."

Milo shook his head as he twirled the cane to bore a hole through the thick dust on the dining hall floor.

That feels oddly pleasant, Imrah informed him, which was

Milo's cue to stop immediately. A decidedly disappointed impression radiated from the fetish.

"Something like that would have left some sign of its passing. Damage or something like it," Milo said, looking at the caked dust on the wooden floor and wondering when feet had last scuffed these boards. According to the reports, it was only a few weeks, but it looked like ages.

"What do you think, Rihyani?" Milo asked, rocking back in his chair, which gave a slight squeak of protest.

Rihyani had been silent for most of the brainstorming, quietly moving around the tavern. She seemed to be looking for something to catch her interest as he and Ambrose chatted. She was currently standing next to a window, sliding her fingers down the drapes. Beyond the window was a veranda, where other tables looked out toward the forest that hemmed Gzhatsk in with a wall of evergreens. Staring past the fey for a moment, Milo couldn't help but wonder if it was his imagination or the trees really were leaning in.

"Rihyani?" Milo called as he shook his head to dismiss thoughts of maliciously inclined trees. He had enough to worry about without making enemies of the vegetation.

"Yes?" the fey said without turning around.

Milo climbed to his feet, a frown tugging at the corners of his mouth. It wasn't like Rihyani to be so quiet.

"Ambrose and I were discussing whether it could have been Kimaris or not."

"What about Kimaris?" she asked, her voice rising with a subtle note of irritation. With more force than was probably necessary, she yanked the curtains to one side and began a minute inspection of the window frame.

Before Milo could press the question, Ambrose, who had wandered to a window on the opposite wall from Rihyani, thumped the wall with a fist.

"About damn time," he swore and turned back to his companions with a grin. "Lokkemand finally decided to show up."

The wizard shook his head at the announcement but stopped as he noticed Rihyani had pressed herself to the windowsill and seemed to be sniffing its length.

"I'll go out and wave them over," Ambrose said as he ambled his way across the hall, leaving Milo and Rihyani alone.

"What are you doing?" Milo said, trying and failing to keep the irritation and concern out of his voice.

"Something seems wrong about this town," the fey said as she raised her head.

"You mean, besides the fact that it was abandoned?" Milo asked as he looked around the vacant room.

"Yes," Rihyani growled, then raised a hand as her fingers grew wicked claws.

"Rihyani, what's going on?" Milo demanded, feeling the need to look every direction at once. She didn't reshape like this except when danger was about. He spun around to face the empty room, every shadow seeming to hold a dangerous secret.

"I'm not sure," Rihyani said in a wet, leonine voice as fangs replaced her teeth.

"Then give me your best guess," Milo hissed, looking over his shoulder in time to see the fey's talons rake across the windowsill.

Milo had expected the sound of wood being gouged or scraped and thought he would see flecks of paint and splinters go flying. When there was a ripping sound like canvas parting under a knife instead, he balked. When blood ran freely from the rent windowsill, rolling down the wall darkly, he nearly cried out in surprise.

"Hiisi," Rihyani snarled, the word sounding like a wildcat's yowl.

When gunfire erupted outside the hotel and the window they stood next to exploded into a hundred glass fragments, Milo was almost relieved.

Being shot at was something he was intimately familiar with.

"Hiisi are Folk, right?" Milo shouted as he and Rihyani crept along the wall to the hotel entrance, thankful the exterior was brick. The crack of rifles could be heard as bullets came whining through the broken window.

"Yes," she said. "They marked the building with their runes."

"Are they shooting at us because you spotted it?" Milo asked as they neared the door to the front of the hotel. "Or just on principle?"

"I am almost certain this isn't them," Rihyani yelled with a look over her shoulder at the window and the forest beyond.

"We're under fire," Ambrose shouted as he burst back into the dining hall, chased by half a score of near-misses.

"Thank God you're here," Milo bellowed. "I might not have noticed all the bullets flying around."

Ambrose swore and kicked one of the double doors shut as a trio of shots punched through the wood. Blood ran down one side of his face, and his eyes blazed like emerald stars in his face.

"We're pinned down," he rumbled, working the action on the rifle to chamber another round. "I popped two of the rats running around out there, but there's plenty more."

"What about Lokkemand's men?" Milo asked as more shots from outside gnawed the dining hall doors into mere formalities.

"Likewise," Ambrose spat as he spotted the window, where the occasional bullet still whizzed through. "They had half a dozen rounds rattle off the lead vehicle and they circled the wagons, as it were."

"They brought wagons?" Rihyani asked, a wild incredulous laugh bubbling out between her fearsome teeth.

"Figure of speech," Ambrose said as he began to slink to the broken window, careful to stay out of the line of fire. "Point is, if they've got troops enough to pin us all down, they might have enough to storm this spot to get a better line on Lokkemand's men."

"We need to get out of here, or we'll be overrun," Milo said, wincing as a stray shot ricocheted about the room.

"Thank God he's here," Ambrose remarked dryly as he sank to one knee next to the broken window, the Gewehr coming to his shoulder.

Rihyani gripped Milo's shoulder and pointed at the large window over the bar.

"Break that and we can wind-ride out," she shouted.

"We'll be exposed out there," Milo protested and pointed at Ambrose. "And if we take him, we'll be easy targets for sure."

Ambrose pivoted on his knee to fire a shot with the Gewehr before swiveling away from a torrent of return fire.

"Don't worry about me," Ambrose growled as he ejected a spent shell and chambered a fresh one. "I can give them something to worry about while you two get clear of the place."

"What about the si'lat?" Rihyani offered.

Milo shook his head.

"I don't know if I can keep them from going after Lokkemand's men," he said, his gaze wandering over to the window opposite them, where he could see the road between the curtains. "The si'lat won't differentiate between one group of men with guns and another, and unless I can see everyone to direct them, they're likely to waste time tearing up the town."

"That and you can't wind ride while controlling those monsters," Ambrose added before swiveling around for another shot. This time he was greeted by so much return fire, Milo felt certain the window frame and the wall around it were both about to collapse into rubble.

Thinking quickly, Milo snatched out his pistol and snapped off a trio of shots to send the window above the bar tumbling to the floor in a shower of dazzling daggers.

"We'll get out and clear that patch of woods," Milo shouted, pointing over Ambrose's shoulder at a patch of woods to the right of where he'd been shooting. "When you see witchfire, get moving."

Ambrose nodded despite the scowl on his face. Milo turned to Rihyani as he returned his pistol to his belt and gave her his most dashing smile.

"Come on, dear, let's fly."

Milo hadn't taken any opportunities to practice wind riding since Georgia, and it showed as he clung to Rihyani's hand and lurched through the air.

They cleared the broken window easily enough, but the wizard was sluggish in both turning and acceleration. Rihyani, who had millennia of experience, dragged him along, but she could only compensate so much. Instead of darting out the broken window, they lurched out, with Milo nearly gashing his dangling legs on the way.

Thankfully, Ambrose took the opportunity to pump shot after shot into the tree line, which was probably the only thing that saved the wind riders from coming under fire immediately.

As it was, they were diving for the trees when the first enemy shots hissed past them, a scattering of panic fire as they came down on what turned out to be exactly where the enemy had congregated. They were ragged figures in the baggy khakis of the Russian forces—a dozen men all told, huddling amongst a tight stand of young pines.

As Rihyani and Milo sailed over their heads, Milo saw their eyes widen with terror even as their mouths snarled feral curses. They swung around to bring their rifles to bear.

Before another shot could be fired, Milo focused, and at the speed of thought, sensed their minds. With an outward shove of his will, he scattered images of him and Rihyani in every direction, some breaking into more images until the canopy was darkened by the illusory targets.

The squad of men was still firing and spitting curses into the trees when Milo and Rihyani touched down. One of the soldiers stepped out of his cover, screaming and shooting into the tree branches before his head snapped to one side, half of it missing. The Gewehr's report sounded as the corpse crumpled to the ground.

A few of the soldiers returned to firing at the hotel window, but the rest remained intent on firing up at the images of Milo and Rihyani above them.

"Come, darling." Rihyani laughed in a liquid roar as she bared her fangs. "Let us be terrible together!"

I am learning to like her, Imrah chimed in Milo's head, and a ferocious smile spread across his face.

"Who am I to argue with a lady?" He chuckled, the onrush of adrenaline and excitement turning the laugh into a wild roar.

As one, they rushed between the tree trunks and sprang like wolves to the kill.

Rihyani shed her traveling cloak in one rolling shrug, then she bounded forward, sometimes on her feet, sometimes on all fours. Milo drew on the cane's empowering essence and threw himself after her in great rushing leaps. The eagle's eye sockets burned with witchfire, and he brought it back as if to smash them with great crushing strokes.

Screaming their joined fury, Milo and Rihyani fell on the ambushers like a hammer on rotten fruit.

Rihyani pounced on the nearest man. He spotted her charge, but he was too slow to get something between her claws and his chest. He went down gasping and wheezing as she ripped her talons from his chest and whirled to look for her next victim.

Milo swung the cane, and a lash of green witchfire tore across four men with rifles pointing toward him. The sorcerous flames ripped into them, biting deep into flesh and finding it to their liking. All four collapsed as emerald fire gnawed up and over their bodies with a ravenous light.

"More demons!" shouted one of the remaining men, and without another word, they all turned and made a dead run back into the forest.

Milo and Rihyani were left standing in the crackling glow of the dying soldiers, more than a little confused as Ambrose came jogging up.

"Spotted the fire," he said as he took cover against a sheltering tree trunk, Gewehr held across his broad body. "That was quick."

Milo and Rihyani looked at each other and then in the direction the men had run.

"Took us by surprise as well," Milo admitted, straining his ears to hear the men crashing through the trees over the crackling gunfire along the roadway.

"Do you think they are trying to reposition for a counterattack?" Rihyani asked, the ferocity leaving her voice as she squinted curiously between the trees.

Ambrose cocked his head to one side, frowning deeply.

"Doesn't sound like it," he snarled, his eyelids sinking to half-mast as he strained his preternatural hearing. "Those men are running for their lives."

Ambrose's eyes flew open a heartbeat before Milo and Rihyani heard the first screams. Wild and piercing, a babble of pleas, curses, and shrieks cut through the air and chilled the blood. Milo had heard men cry out in pain and fear many times, but this was one of the worst.

"They're dying ugly," Ambrose growled, his head wagging slowly as some voices fell silent and others rose to new shivering heights.

"Hiisi," Rihyani said breathily and turned to Milo. "We need to get to Lokkemand's men. Now!"

With a ripple of will, the traveling cloak poured over the fey's body, then she was heading for the sound of gunshots.

Milo and Ambrose knew better than to argue, but they shared concerned looks as they began to trot along the tree line toward the road. All three kept a sharp eye out for the ambushers still firing on the German forces as they bounded along. It went without saying that it wouldn't do to race into the kill zone.

"Are they in more danger from the Hiisi than the Russians?" Milo asked as he jogged up alongside Rihyani. "What are we protecting them from, exactly?"

Rihyani threw a worried look over her shoulder, and Milo realized the screaming had stopped.

"The protection isn't for them," Rihyani explained, quickening her pace. "It's for us."

By the time they'd made it to the road, the Russian ambushers had begun to die.

The trio didn't see what was killing them, but given the sounds the dying made, it seemed clear that whatever had killed their fellows near the hotel was preying on them now along the road.

The German caravan had ceased firing when the Russian salvos had given way to desperate screams. They couldn't see what was happening, but the horror on the soldier's faces grew with each rustle amongst the branches that preceded more auditory torment. They sat listening to men beg and pray and cry before their voices became incoherent yowls and wails that seemed too tortured for human throats.

The soldiers were so captivated by the morbid symphony around them that they didn't spot Milo, Ambrose, and Rihyani on the ditch-hemmed side of the road. The trio, seeing that they didn't need to worry about being caught in the crossfire, made for the vehicular triangle formed by two open-topped kubelwagens and a canvas-backed truck. The wizard had to pound on the side of the truck to draw the men's attention away from the horror in the forest.

"You can sightsee on your own time, gentlemen," he shouted in German. "As it stands, you are hours late, and the service so far has not been up to standard."

Blinking like owls awakened before dusk, the German soldiers swung around and stared at Milo and company. The magus thought about jumping aboard, but there was a tension in the men's shoulders and faces that gave him pause. Time was of the essence, but rushing a crowd of emotionally fragile men with guns seemed unwise.

"Permission to come aboard?" Milo asked, throwing a jaunty salute as his eyes searched for a black coat or at least the NCO of rank.

"What the hell is going on in there?" someone asked, and the question was repeated by several soldiers.

"Bad things," Milo said quickly, taking half a step toward the open backseat of a kubelwagen. "Now, can we please be on our way before bad things start happening to us?"

"Did you do this?" one man asked, his face hardening as another called behind him, "Or did she do it?"

"Neither," Milo said, fighting to keep his temper in check. There were now only one or two wretched voices begging for their lives, which meant the Hiisi, whatever they were, were most likely headed their way.

"What did you summon, warlock?" a voice demanded, and Milo heard hissing whispers that sounded a lot like *"De Zauber-Schwartz"* moving amongst the ranks with less than friendly connotations.

"Look," Ambrose said, his mustache bristling furiously. "Take us prisoner if you like, but you don't want to meet whatever is out there. Get your heads out of your bungholes and get this caravan moving. NOW!"

To Milo's relief and no small amount of envy, the big man's thunderous voice and battlefield demeanor won out. Like shame-faced children scolded by a gruff uncle, the soldiers hopped to and began to break up their impromptu fortification. The trio was crammed into the back of the lead kubelwagen since both the truck and the other kubelwagen were being used to transport men wounded in the initial ambush.

Within a minute of Ambrose's bellowed orders, the caravan moved out.

Milo felt comfortable enough to lean forward and call to the driver. "Good thing Captain Lokkemand sent out a full guard for a priority pickup, eh?"

The driver looked uncomfortable as he wiped his forehead, and he kept swiveling his gaze to the dirt road and along the forest edge. He gnawed his lip for a moment, then replied without looking back.

"Begging your pardon, sir," the man replied, shouting over the sound of three engines working in close proximity, "but we travel like this always. We can't do it any other way. The bandits are thick as moss on Pfeiffer's backside."

The man seated next to him, who must have been Pfeiffer, spat out the window, clutching his rifle in both hands. Despite that, the man's eyes were calm, almost apathetic with all that was going on around him.

"If I got moss, it came from Schultz's mother," he growled, looking left and right before giving them all a sidelong grimace over his shoulder. "Woman's a mangy old goat, but 'needs must when devils drive' is how the saying goes, right?"

"Did you just call my mother a goat?" the driver Schultz growled, one hand curling into a fist.

Rihyani shot Milo a concerned frown over Ambrose's bent back, and her thoughts rushed into his mind.

Do those two intend to start fighting at a time like this?

Milo shook his head even as the driver's fist struck Pfeiffer's shoulder with a dull smack and the man rocked against the door of kubelwagen.

They're blowing off steam. You know, banter, Milo explained. *None of these look like Lokkemand's old escorts, so they're new to all this, though I'm sure they were briefed.*

Rihyani gave Milo an incredulous stare as blistering streams of invective and profanity flowed freely between the two, but true to Milo's word, it quickly settled into chuckles as they rolled further down the road and out of Gzhatsk.

"Glad we're clear of that mess," Pfeiffer offered as he leaned against the window, eyeing the trees suspiciously.

Milo and Rihyani felt Ambrose tense next to them, and Milo saw the look of concern on his face turn to wrath in an instant.

"Not clear yet," the bodyguard rumbled and began to wriggle his way to his feet as he swung his Gewehr toward the forest.

"What is it?" Milo asked, rushing to join Ambrose. One hand held his fetish cane while the other probed for one of the si'lat swarms. He didn't imagine the soldiers would feel very comfortable with the vicious black cyclone, but he figured dying like the Russians had was even less appealing.

As though summoned by the thought, three bloodied and harried figures in khaki uniforms lurched out of the forest and into the middle of the track. Their heads were twisted back to watch for whatever horror had pursued them here, but their hands were raised in surrender.

"Help! Save!" they cried in stilted German. "Save! Please!"

Pfeiffer leveled his rifle their way, but a sharp word from Milo stayed his trigger finger.

"Damn it, man, they're unarmed."

The defeated men staggered forward, still trying to watch the woods they'd left as the caravan rolled to a stop.

"I thought we needed to get out of here?" shouted the driver of the truck. "Put on the gas and they'll move."

"Load them into the truck bed," Milo shouted back,

motioning to the Russians to head for the truck.

"Letting those rats in with the wounded? Are you mad?" the driver bellowed, revving his vehicle's chugging engine and menacingly halting the Russians in between kubelwagen and the truck. "Get out of the way, or I'll roll over you and the cowards!"

The Gewehr roared, and the side-view mirror of the truck sprang free of its mount in a shower of sparks and broken glass.

"A superior officer gave you an order. A DIRECT order!" Ambrose roared, his rifle's aim now adjusted to the cab of the truck. "Think very hard before you open your mouth again, soldier."

The tension crackled in the air like barbed lightning, and Milo felt Rihyani's will brushing against him.

This does not seem like banter, Rihyani thought. *If Simon fires again, I think the one called Pfeiffer will attempt to shoot him.*

Milo didn't dare turn around as the standoff ached on second after second. He considered stretching out his will and trying to soothe or at least befuddle Pfeiffer but thought better of it.

If he does, try to stop him without hurting him, Milo instructed via resonations of his own will. *We still need these men to cooperate with us while we work out here.*

Rihyani's will throbbed with affirmation, then she left his thoughts.

Milo looked askance at the Russians standing between kubelwagen and the truck before clearing his throat, drawing all eyes to him.

"This is ridiculous," he said in his best no-nonsense commander's impression. "We've got an unknown hostile, and we are exposed. Get the prisoners in your vehicle, and let's get the He—"

The air was suddenly filled with a cacophonous clamor of raucous cawing. All eyes turned toward the woods, searching the branches and jagged tops of the evergreens for the source of the terrible sound. The limbs rustled and creaked as the canopy suddenly erupted in a storm of croaking ravens. With a precision and cohesion uncommon to carrion birds, the immense flock swept down and encircled the caravan in a wheel of beating black wings.

The Russians screamed and crouched with hands raised over their heads.

"Get those prisoners loaded NOW!" Milo bellowed, his finger stabbing at the truck.

Not needing any further prompting, the would-be prisoners scuttled to the back of the truck and got on board with terror-fueled speed.

"*De Zauber Schwartz*," Schultz cried, and for the first time that day, it didn't sound like a curse to Milo. "What do we do? I can't drive through this."

Milo wasn't sure the man's grasp of physics was very reliable if he thought his blocky battering ram of a vehicle couldn't punch through a wall of birds, but he didn't think it was time to correct the man. Instead, he reached into the case and drew out the heavy orbs that held the si'lat swarm.

Milo held a sphere out in front of him and began harnessing the focus necessary to not only rouse but master the shades. He knew he'd need as much control, if not more, than he had used aboard the train. It would be even harder now since he'd had plenty of time to prepare his mind and body for the rigors of magic then. He liked the si'lat better than dousing the birds with witchfire or eldritch ice, but he understood that if he lost control, it would very likely cost the soldiers their lives.

"When I give you the word, floor it," Milo called as his eyes centered on the undulating black spheres in his hand. Milo could feel the vibrating essence of the trapped shades, their secondhand hate and hunger twisting over and around each other like so many tangled vipers. The harder the knotted shades pulled away, the tighter they were bound, which was part of the magic that Milo was secretly proud of. To unleash them, all he had to do was untie one little knot at the center of the writhing mass.

"Come out and play," Milo whispered as he opened the end of his scarred thumb and ran the welling blood across the top of the sphere in his outstretched hand.

"Magus! It's coming!" Ambrose shouted as something far bigger than a raven broke through the wheeling barrier of black birds.

The knot unbound, and the ebony orb stretched out exploratory tendrils as Milo drove his command home with a burning stake of intent.

KILL

Black grit erupted as a ravening dervish fit for the banks of the Styx.

"GO!" Milo screamed as the si'lat swarm spun up and over them to crash drunkenly into the rotating ravens. The terrible crowing was interspersed with death rattles and screeches as birds died in droves. The sound was so deafening that Milo could barely hear the revving of the kubelwagen engine, but he felt it buck under him as Schultz slammed down on the accelerator.

His feet came off the floorboard, and to his surprise, they never returned. The same instant this happened, Milo felt a crushing pressure in his shoulders as though a vise had clamped over them.

He saw the massive corvid digits clamped on his shoulders. Those taloned feet rose into a twisted, sharp-angled body that seemed as though man and raven had been mashed and folded into each other.

As Milo rose into the air, before he was plunged into the gouging, ripping tide, the creature carrying him jerked its head around to glare at him with a raptor's hungry stare.

The magus screamed when he beheld the jagged, misaligned beak and mangled plumage, and the creature's talons drove down deeper, crushing the breath from his lungs as they pierced his coat to burrow into his flesh.

8

THESE NAMES

Milo emerged from the congress of ravens more or less the same way he had entered it, which could be summarized simply as not well. His shoulders ached from where the monstrous bird-thing's claws gripped him, and he had a few other scrapes and nicks across his face and hands from birds and branches as he was dragged out of the trees and into the sky.

Done assessing his state of being, Milo decided he was also done with his sudden flight.

Focusing his mind to bring his magic with the talons digging into him proved difficult, but thankfully the grip on him did not prevent him from reaching his belt. Milo drew out his pistol and aimed straight up. The creature, the Hiisi, must have felt his movement since it had enough time to look down and see the barrel leveled at it before Milo pulled the trigger.

One, two, three, the pistol barked, but before the second muzzle flare could singe feathers, the corvid horror had exploded into icy wind, the smell of rotting meat, and dozens of black-winged shapes. Where once had been a creature large enough to carry Milo off like a rabbit in a raptor's claws, there was now only stink, chill, and the flutter of wings.

And then Milo was falling.

A raw scream tore from his throat as the treetops seemed to lunge up from the ground, eager to impale his plummeting, pinwheeling body.

Wind ride, Imrah called, sounding almost bored.

Milo tried to orient his brain, but fear was like a weighted pendulum knocking his thoughts askew with each pass.

Quickly would be best. The fetish-bound ghul sighed with irritation.

Milo felt a wave of familiar anger at her criticism, and that more than anything else allowed him to lay hold of his will and change the world around him to make reality accept him as being buoyant even as he plunged to his death.

His falling slowed until he halted only a few feet from the top of a lightning-scarred pine. As he hung there trying to right himself, he had time to study the tree. It was old and whorled with ancient wounds, and Milo thought it almost looked disappointed that he would not be adorning its branches.

"Not today," Milo muttered, feeling as though his internal organs had just caught up with the rest of him.

Grunting and being careful to take long, slow breaths, Milo let himself sink toward the tree. Hands outstretched, he descended until he grabbed a branch that looked like it wasn't about to break. Steady and levitating, Milo swept his eyes across the horizon and saw the breach in the forest that was Gzhatsk to his right. It took a minute longer to find the thin gap in the trees indicative of the road, the process made slower by the nagging certainty that his pistol had only bought him a reprieve, not victory.

Despite the thought, he saw no trace of the black-feathered fiend, but he wasn't quite ready to hope that it had been scared off. He thought he would have felt some freedom under the open sky, some safety from ambush, but Milo knew that any flying creature, much less a magical one, would be far more comfortable than he was fighting in the sky.

After another moment spent considering making his sluggish way due west, Milo shook his head and began the slow, careful process of climbing down. The relative weightlessness was a great boon, and he was on the forest floor quicker than he expected.

Standing there getting his bearings, Milo felt a tug upon his mind, and he remembered the si'lat swarm he'd unleashed before his abduction. His ability to control his creation over a distance was not unlimited, and he felt his grasp on the swirling shades slowly slipping.

Had Lokkemand's men cleared the flock of ravens? Had Ambrose and Rihyani gone with them, or were they even now braving the tempest of black wings and darker spirits?

Who was he fooling? He knew Ambrose and Rihyani were looking for him.

His mind narrowed to a needle-pointed hook, and with a sweeping grab, he snatched the thin strands of essence that bound the si'lat to him and gave them a savage twist.

RETURN

The shades resisted, straining until Milo feared they would break free, but then he felt his blood and soul humming through the connection. As long as he lived, the construct could not— would not—escape his control. In some perverse way, it was part of him.

Milo's mind returned to the world around him, and he tried to decide where he was going. Conscripts were for fighting and dying, more the latter than the former, and as such, his training in fieldcraft amongst the penal forces was lacking. That was compounded by the fact that his youth had been spent in strictly urban environments. Milo looked at the venerable trees standing as though in silent judgment around him, and he felt the unease of being in an alien world. He was unfamiliar, unwelcome, and unprepared.

He was considering either wind riding up to the canopy again or trying some creative necromistry when he jumped at the sound of wings fluttering overhead. He whirled, cane and pistol both raised.

On a low branch of a nearby tree, the monstrous bird squatted, except it was lessened.

The huge, twisted avian was now human-sized and had it stood on the ground, Milo doubted the top of its feathered head would reach his chin. More than being humanoid in size, the creature now seemed closer to human in shape as well. Its wings resembled elongated arms tipped with fingers, no less, and the legs had changed direction so that it now sat on the branch with feet dangling over the forest floor.

The head cocked to one side, round black eyes staring and inscrutable before the malformed beak opened.

"Funny!" it cried in a harsh and braying attempt at Russian. "Funny little man!"

Milo glared at the creature, eager to launch lead and eldritch energies at it but hesitating as it continued to watch him. If it wanted to kill him, it didn't seem to be in much of a hurry, and since he felt the si'lat swarm seething toward him, he decided he would take advantage of this.

"So, you don't seem in a rush to kill me anymore," Milo called without relaxing. "Does that mean you'd rather talk than fight?"

The corvid creature twitched its head to the other side and back again before its feathered shoulders bunched into a sort of shrug.

"Maybe," it squawked and continued to stare.

Slowly, Milo lowered his pistol, half-expecting to be rushed by an unseen attacker. When no attack came, he lowered the cane, planting it in front of him as he slid his Luger into its holster.

Do you have eyes on it? Milo asked, one hand resting lightly on the eagle skull.

Yes, Imrah replied, though he felt something like a crack in her stoic presence. *But Hiisi are not to be trusted.*

"Depends on what I have to say, huh?" Milo replied, chuckling a little, but he froze when the bird suddenly stiffened. Milo thought he'd caused offense and was scrambling to think of an apology when the crow's beak gaped wide and it let out a grating screech of laughter.

"Yes, yes," it squawked, taloned feet dancing in mid-air as it chortled like a hideous child. "Depends on the answers. Answers for Borji."

The wizard frowned, struggling to keep his edge as he watched the buffoonish antics of the creature sitting in the tree. Could this be the same monster that had snatched him up and borne him away?

"Borji?" Milo said, determined to keep talking. He sensed that the si'lat swarm was a minute out, maybe two. "Is that your name?"

The raven-thing did a quicker and less raucous version of the ugly laughing routine. Milo was fairly sure it was answering in the negative, but nothing much about the creature made sense, and Imrah's warning was still fresh in Milo's mind.

He couldn't afford to take anything for granted.

Do you want me to cook the cretin? Imrah offered. Milo felt the fiery energies build in the raptor's skull until his fingers felt sweaty where they rested on the cane.

Not yet, Milo thought, watching as the little bird-man hopped up to stand on the branch and then sprang into the air.

"Black sand nice trick," it croaked as it beat its wings in an ungainly flutter. "Lempo will peck this from your brain. Some day!"

Milo flinched as the creature—Lempo?—darted between the tree branches and out of sight.

"Well, that was one of the strangest conversations I've ever had," Milo muttered as he rolled his bruised shoulders and heard a series of clicks. "But at least I can get back to the others."

Don't move, Imrah warned, the words rolling up to Milo's mind like an icy waterfall in reverse.

"What is it now?" he groaned, looking through the trees for whatever new madness awaited him.

Straight ahead, Imrah whispered to his mind. *Don't panic and run.*

Milo stared between the tree trunks and was about to demand the ghul be less vague when he noticed the deepening darkness moving toward him. It took Milo a moment to realize how large it was, not because of the darkness which accompanied it, but also because his mind was rebelling at the silence of its advance. Whatever was coming had to be at least as massive as a draft horse, long-bodied and hulking, but there wasn't even the rustle of evergreen needles as it came. Nothing that big should be so quiet, and Milo felt a prickle of fear on the back of his neck as the primal corners of his brain sounded the ancient alarm: PREDATOR!

Milo gripped the cane in both hands, squeezing the unyielding stone in his clammy palms, an anchor to counter his hammering heart. Where was the si'lat? Would it even matter?

"Borji, I assume?" Milo called, proud that there was only the barest tremble in his voice.

A low growl echoed through the forest, as wet as a torn throat and echoing from a depth somewhere under the Styx. Every instinct in Milo urged him to run, but his fingers tightened around the cane until his knuckles popped and his palms throbbed.

"YOU ARE BRAVER THAN MOST," howled a voice that belonged in a nightmare. "AND THAT IS THE ONLY REASON I WILL EXCUSE THE INSOLENCE OF THAT NAME THIS ONCE."

Between the trees, Milo saw huge red eyes advancing. The huge creature paused, and he received the impression of something vaguely lupine standing in the unnatural shadows. A snout beneath the glowing eyes parted to speak, and Milo saw the glint of fangs as long as his hand.

"I have many names, whispered with fear through ages by heroes and gods. I am the one your kind feared as they huddled around stolen fire and he who you still worship with your walls and torches."

Milo swallowed heavily but then heard a faint rustle at his feet.

He stole a glance downward, hoping it just looked like he was losing his nerve, and he smiled to see the tiny filaments of black grit coiling at his heels. The si'lat had found him. His shoulders squared and his heart steadied.

"I'm going to need to know what to call you," Milo said as he prepared his mental focus to unleash his summoned weapon. "Do you have a shorter name or title?"

The monster within the dark pressed forward until its huge head breached the shadows. Jaws that could have snapped him in half hung open so he could count each tooth that could have ended his life. Milo wasn't sure that this thing looked like a wolf so much as a terrifying impression of what a wolf might look like in Hell.

"Borjikhan shall do, little monkey," it rumbled. "I had Lempo bring you here that you may bear my will to your kind."

"I'm squarely on the tall side for my kind," Milo shot back as he felt the bulk of the si'lat swarm settle across the ground around him. "But if you've got something to say, I'm listening."

Borjikhan sniffed the air and narrowed its red eyes at Milo, clearly sensing the change in him. Its lips curled back from the fangs in a smile that beamed with a sadist's joy.

"If any of your kind comes to these hovels or to the woods beyond," it began, the words resounding less from its throat than its vast chest, "the lives of every human in a hundred miles will be forfeit. These lands now belong to the Hiisi of the first wood, and we will brook no challenge."

Milo felt Imrah seethe within the fetish in his hands and remembered her words about Zlydzen's connection with the Hiisi of the First Wood. Given that the monstrous creature was issuing a warning rather than killing him, it seemed likely it hadn't been briefed on him by the dwarrow. Milo had a hard time believing that there wouldn't be a standing order to mangle his person on sight.

"What happened to the people of Gzhatsk?" Milo asked.

A thick chuckle bubbled from the monster.

"Set foot in that mausoleum, and you'll soon find out."

From somewhere behind Milo, a distant but familiar voice bellowed between the trees.

"MAGUS!" Ambrose shouted. "MAGUS!"

Borjikhan snarled, and even with the si'lat secretly arrayed around him, Milo felt like his knees gave out.

"Perhaps an object lesson will impress upon you the severity of this command."

One huge paw reached out from the shadows, revealing black fur that smoked with shadows as claws like sickles sank into the loamy earth.

"MAGUS!" Ambrose hollered again, his voice closer and ragged with desperation. "MILO!"

Wrath, righteous and blazing, blossomed in Milo's chest and rushed through his veins like liquid fire. The air brushing his skin felt cold, but only because of the heat of his anger. This beast bragged about its mass murder and then decided to maim and kill Milo's friend to make its point. His anger increased to a deep and terrible rage.

"How dare you?" Milo snarled as the si'lat rose around him in curling tendrils.

The wizard's mind commanded the si'lat at his feet, not with the precise instructions, but with a raw instinct that set the bound shades to quivering. The black coils wrapped around Milo and drew him upward even as more of it rose around him. The coils lengthened and stretched until they were vast black wings whose wicked points could have gripped a tank end to end with ease.

Borjikhan snapped his jaws with a force that sounded like a thunderclap, and spittle flew from its fangs as it hissed, "My patience wears thin, little man."

Milo's voice, amplified to shake the heavens by the Art, drowned out the coming threat.

"You've had your say, now I'll have mine!" Milo thundered. "You may be an ancient horror with names and stories stretching back into forever, but let me tell you who *I* am."

The pinions became black lances, plunging in front of Borjikhan and driving it back between the trees as the magus advanced, glaring furiously.

"I am Milo Petrovich, Magus, Slayer of Demons, Crusher of Tyrants!" he declared, his chest swelling as though ready to split with the power of the words. "Orphan and Prince, I was oppressed so I would crush oppressors, and if you ever think to threaten me or mine again, all your names and all your stories will be forgotten. Your tale will become that of one more monster I defeated!"

The si'lat, driven by the fire in his blood, ripped across the tree trunks, sending the lupine terror bounding back in a hail of smoldering splinters.

"You've made your threats, and I've made my promises," Milo growled, looking down his nose at the red eyes glaring up at him. "Now retreat to your den, lick your wounded pride, and hope we never meet again."

For a moment, Milo thought it would attack, but Borjikhan gave an unconvincing snort of derision and snapped its jaws one more time.

"I will remember this," it growled.

"I'm counting on it," Milo spat, his black pinions rising in menacing promise. "Now go!"

Borjikhan gave one final snarl, then like a patch of smoke on the wind, it was gone.

It took a few moments for the heady mixture of righteous wrath and power to leach from him, but it did, and with a long sigh, Milo bid the si'lat swarm lower him to the ground. Feeling drained and parched, he struggled to draw the si'lat back into its bound form. He finally managed it, though his shoulders had begun to bow.

He was sliding it back into its case when he felt eyes behind him and saw Ambrose and Rihyani staring at him.

Milo looked back to the savaged trees behind him and back at the shocked expressions of his friends.

"Sorry." He shrugged as he trudged over to them. "A little dramatic, but I guess I'm getting a little sick of bullies."

Ambrose and Rihyani kept staring for another heartbeat, and Milo felt a swelling pang of loneliness. Had he gone too far?

Rihyani's arms went around him and her mouth, hungry and tender, met his. The loneliness melted, and for a moment, Milo couldn't think but just was, and was with her. When they came up for air, Rihyani gave that achingly beautiful laugh that made him believe he would love her forever.

"You were amazing," she said before crushing him in another embrace.

Milo looked over her shoulder at Ambrose and saw the big man smiling at him.

"Well, I'm not going to kiss you for it." Ambrose chuckled. "How about I raid Lokkemand's stores for a hero's feast, eh? I know you're hungry."

"Always." Milo laughed and allowed himself to be drawn into another kiss.

9

THESE EXPECTATIONS

"It would've been great if Lokkemand had seen your little display," Ambrose muttered as they rolled into the camp outside Sergio-Ivanoskye. "It probably would make this next part easier."

"I doubt it." Milo yawned, knowing he should be more concerned than he felt. "Lokkemand's never lacked appreciation for my power."

Ambrose snorted as the kubelwagen pitched and yawed over the mounded earth that broke up the approach to the central palisade ring.

"Just lacks a healthy fear of it," Ambrose said, his mustache doing an anxious little dance.

Milo shrugged, recognizing that fatigue was contributing to his nonchalance rather than any sort of maturation where the captain was concerned. He didn't have the energy to hate him.

"I think he's terrified of your power," Rihyani shared as Schultz slung the kubelwagen around to park in front of the wooden wall. "He understands better than most what you are capable of, and it scares him to no end."

It was Ambrose's turn to shrug.

"It makes a sort of sense," he muttered as he stood and stretched. "What do you think, Magus?"

Milo shook his head as he rose and managed to pour himself out of the kubelwagen onto the muddy ground. Right then, he felt that Lokkemand could have hated him for his eye color, and he couldn't have cared less. He was hungry and tired and wanted nothing more than to fill his belly and then collapse.

"Hey, Schultz, Pfeiffer," he called, his voice raw and peevish even in his own ears. "Where can I get some food?"

The garrulous pair had been silent since Ambrose and Rihyani had led Milo back to where the caravan waited on the road. Their banter had been absent on the drive to the camp, but the wizard had been too weary and distracted by hunger to notice. Now Milo could practically smell the aura of fear emanating from the two soldiers.

Fear of Milo, of *De Zauber-Schwartz*.

"Look alive, soldiers!" Ambrose barked with the bristling authority of a training sergeant. "An officer asked you a question."

Both men continued to stare at Milo with a mixture of terror and loathing worked into the lines of their faces. A rumble that would have done the monstrous Borjikhan proud resounded in Ambrose's chest, and both soldiers straightened and squared to attention, their gazes locking forward.

"The mess is located in the eastern corner by the village," Pfeiffer announced in a professional tone so sharp it nearly cut Milo's ears. "But we were supposed to make sure that you met with the captain first."

Ambrose looked at Milo, who gave a heavy nod as Rihyani slid up next to him, a silent yet strong support.

"Might as well get it over with."

Ambrose turned to the two soldiers, standing rigid as poles in front of him.

"Well, you heard him," he barked. "Take us to your leader."

"Captain Lokkemand," Milo said as he took in the familiar sight of Lokkemand standing over an expansive map while aides punched typewriters. "I appreciate you sending an escort to pick us up."

Lokkemand rose from his maps to look down at Milo, herculean and stoic. The captain's gray eyes bored into the magus, a scrutiny that left him feeling even more tired and exposed.

In the months since they'd last parted ways, Milo had forgotten how tall and powerful the captain was, and he remembered the single punch that one massive fist had delivered, which set his chest to aching. Milo tried to remind himself that he'd intimidated an ancient monster like the Borjikhan into flight. Right then, looking at the towering captain took all the fight out of him.

Let Lokkemand jab him with verbal barbs or rail against him. Milo wasn't going to fight back.

"I understand that not only was the escort late in arriving," Lokkemand said gravely, "but that when they did arrive, they stumbled into an ambush."

It was not the opening salvo Milo had expected, which left his fatigue-burdened brain struggling to catch up.

"Yes, uh, well, they weren't the only ones who came under fire," Milo managed with a shrug. "And I'm not sure it was an ambush so much as the Reds were fleeing from one thing and seemed to think we might object if they kept running."

"Yes, I see," Lokkemand said, rubbing his jaw as he sucked his teeth. "Well, regardless, I wanted to first apologize for their tardiness and ineptitude before thanking you for getting them out of there alive."

Milo stood dumbstruck. This was not going how he had expected at all. Too tired to be surreptitious, he looked over at

Ambrose, who seemed just as gobsmacked. Rihyani caught his eye, and she nodded meaningfully at the waiting captain.

"Oh, er, you're welcome, Captain," Milo stammered, forcing himself to smile and nod appreciatively. "And there is nothing to forgive. Such things are part of the fortunes of war, right?"

Something pained, almost desperate, flitted behind Lokkemand's eyes, but it disappeared in an instant as a smile broke across his face.

"Well said. Fortunes of war indeed." He beamed. "Now, I'm sure that you are all tired and hungry and in need of some time to get yourselves settled. We can review possible operations tomorrow when you are ready, but I insist you spend some time recovering."

At that moment, Milo could have kissed the man, but he settled for a loose-jointed salute.

"Yes, sir," the wizard mumbled. "You don't even have to insist."

Lokkemand's smile held and he even threw a wink, something Milo would have previously thought the man's granite features were incapable of.

"I'm glad to hear it," the captain said as he returned the salute. "Dismissed."

Milo turned to leave, giving the wide-eyed Ambrose a wondering shake of his head as he did so.

"Volkohne," Lokkemand called, and Milo turned on the spot.

This was it.

"Yes, Captain?"

This was where the other shoe dropped.

Lokkemand struggled to meet Milo's eye, his gaze wandering down to the table or off to the side of the tent as he spoke.

"I know that in the past we had our problems," he began, his lips peeling back as he sucked his teeth again, "but I can't deny that you've accomplished great things for the Empire."

Milo wasn't sure what he could say in response to that, so instead, he just watched as Lokkemand struggled through.

"I am a soldier in a long line of soldiers, and perhaps that's why your unique perspective on authority is very difficult for me," he continued, arms rigid at his sides and back painfully straight. "But regardless, you get results, and as a military man, I can appreciate that, and I do appreciate it. How you came out of Georgia was nothing short of commendable."

"Thank you, sir," Milo said, certain this was an appropriate time to say something. "I couldn't have done it without these two, but we all appreciate the recognition."

Despite himself, Milo had begun to feel sorry for the captain. This couldn't have been easy, but he was making a go of it in front of Ambrose, Rihyani, and his staff. That wasn't a small thing.

Milo stole a quick look at his companions to confirm their appreciative expressions. Rihyani nodded with the sort of elegant nobility he'd come to expect from her. Ambrose seemed not as ready to bury the hatchet, bushy brows lowered in plain suspicion as his mouth twisted into a lopsided frown. He caught Milo's eye, and for a single instant, the two were locked in a battle of wills.

The wizard leaned his head slightly toward Lokkemand, and Ambrose's eyes narrowed. Milo kept his head at that angle as he held Ambrose's gaze, but it was a near thing when Ambrose finally relented. Milo heaved a heavy sigh as his bodyguard bobbed his head in a curt display of affirmation. It wasn't much, but Lokkemand took it well enough, returning the nod eagerly.

"I hope that from here on out, we can work together in light of this new mutual understanding and respect," he said, his face folding into a warmly expectant smile.

The olive branch was now fully extended.

"Absolutely, sir," Milo said, returning the smile with one that was far weaker but no less genuine for that. If this reconciliation took much longer, Milo was certain Ambrose would have to carry him out.

"I'm glad to hear it," the captain said, looking away quickly, but not before Milo caught that same pained look in the man's eyes. He doubted then whether he could ever fully appreciate what the moment had cost Lokkemand, but he valued it all the same. This was the first time that he could remember someone in authority acknowledging their mistakes and seeking to move forward in light of that.

Milo wished he wasn't so faint so he could savor it.

"Go get something to eat, Volkohne. That's an order," Lokkemand said with a brief but sincere smile.

"Yes, sir," Milo muttered, meaning it for perhaps the first time.

"I don't like it," Ambrose rumbled as he plopped another bowl of stew in front of Milo. "There's something off about the man."

Milo's mouth watered and his teeth itched eagerly as he dragged the bowl to himself. This was his third helping of the hearty and pungent solyanka stew, but he knew he'd give this one as much ravenous attention as the last two.

"Come here, darling," Milo cooed as he dug out a thick spoonful.

"Magus, are you listening?" Ambrose growled as he thumped down on the bench opposite him.

Milo looked up from his spoon with a scowl before shoving it between his lips emphatically. The potent yet pleasing combination of sweet and sour hit his tongue as his jaws began to chew through the multiple glorious meats in the composite stew. He found it impossible to keep his scowl as he chewed, but he spared Ambrose a long sideways look as he savored the bite.

"I'm not saying it wasn't a surprise," Milo said around a mouthful before a few more chews, and a swallow cleared things up. "But Jorge himself said he respected Lokkemand, and this is probably part of why. He's not quick about it, but he can admit he's wrong."

Ambrose shook his head and ground his teeth, raking his spoon back and forth across his bowl.

"Saying he's sorry, which he didn't directly do, I might add, would be about a tactical error or something like that," Ambrose explained, his eyes darting around as he leaned forward to impart in a conspiratorial whisper, "If he'd told you to go left and he should have sent you right, I could see that Lokkemand might have the decency to apologize, but this isn't that sort of situation."

Milo had put away a few more bites and was raising his spoon for another when he paused and looked at Ambrose over the steaming lump before him.

"What sort of situation is this?" he asked before taking in the bite.

Ambrose battered the contents of his bowl a little more before pushing it to the side to tap the table with one thick finger.

"He excused your disrespect and your flouting of the hierarchy," he hissed, leaning so far forward his thick, muscle-banded stomach pressed the table edge. "Officers born and bred with blue blood in their veins and iron in their souls don't do that. Hierarchy defines them."

Milo swallowed his bite and looked at Rihyani for support.

The fey had eaten only half a bowl of the stew before handing it to Milo, and since then had been puffing lightly on her cigarillo, not saying much but listening intently.

Seeing Milo's look, she let out a long ribbon of smoke, then glanced at the bodyguard.

"I'm with Milo on this one, Ambrose," she said with a helpless shrug. "I think Jorge is the sort to see the value of an officer who is strong and resolute, yet humble and mentally flexible enough to see where he's wrong."

Milo, munching happily, turned to Ambrose with a smug

smile, but he stopped smiling when he saw the veins grow thick and ropy at Ambrose's temples as his face reddened.

"But he's not wrong, and that's the point!" Ambrose growled, his teeth working the words between his clenched jaws. "Fact is, from a military standpoint, we were repeatedly insubordinate, and if anyone apologizes, it should be us, which is why this doesn't make any sense!"

Milo resignedly put down his spoon and raised his hands to squeeze his temples. He had begun to rally around the food in his belly, but now it only made him feel sluggish and uncomfortably dense as he sat staring at Ambrose.

"I'm not sure what you are getting at," he said slowly, spreading his hands out before Ambrose as though waiting for a gift. "What doesn't make any sense?"

Ambrose opened his mouth, teeth bared, but promptly shut it and took a steadying breath. When he began again, his voice was noticeably lower and slower.

"Lokkemand could apologize for giving you a bad order or bad command," Ambrose said, each word measured carefully. "Any good officer could and would do that."

"Okay," Milo said, rotating his open hands to signal Ambrose to continue.

"What Lokkemand would never do is excuse or be apologetic about you not following orders," Ambrose said, the words coming out even heavier and slower than before. "Soldiers follow orders, even bad ones, and Lokkemand would never, ever accept or apologize for not understanding our insubordination. There is no way he believes that hog spit about 'unique perspectives on authority.'"

"Why say it, then?" Rihyani asked, tapping ash into her empty bowl. "He didn't have to say any of it, so why did he?"

Ambrose rocked back and shrugged his shoulders.

"I haven't a clue." He sighed and dragged his bowl back in front of him. "That's part of what's eating at me."

Milo took up his bowl but found himself twirling the spoon between his fingers as he digested more than several helpings of meat.

"He didn't have to say it, but he did," he began, eyes focusing on the middle distance. "And he didn't mean what he said, but he said it trying to sound genuine. That all adds up to one thing, doesn't it?"

Ambrose and Rihyani looked at each other and then at Milo, bemusement stamped on their oddly juxtaposed features.

"What?" they asked in unison.

"He's trying to manipulate us to get us to trust him, maybe even let our guard down?"

Ambrose's mouth became a grim line barely visible beneath his mustache, while Rihyani's eyes narrowed, golden pupils flashing.

"Why would he do that?" she asked with the barest hint of a feline snarl in her throat.

Milo shrugged as he dug up another hearty spoonful and held it before him.

"I don't know," he admitted slowly as he considered. "But regardless, we can't let our guard down."

He suddenly didn't feel quite so enamored with the meal, though intellectually he knew it was a fine culinary creation. He'd lost his enthusiasm, but he eyed the bite and the rest of the bowl with determination. He took the bite with gusto, ripping flesh between his teeth.

"We can't afford to trust," Milo stated as he swallowed and looked doggedly at his bowl. "With the Shepherds and the Reich, there's too much at stake."

He was going to finish the whole thing. He had a feeling he was going to need it.

THESE FRAGMENTS

The Russians who had surrendered to them on the road were probably wishing they'd reconsidered their options.

At least Milo would have felt that way if he were them, naked and bound to chairs hand and foot, shivering in a tent stinking of fear and urine.

After a night's rest, Rihyani had stated she would take stock of the area using her fey wiles, which left Milo and Ambrose to see to the prisoners.

Both men felt their eyes watering as they stepped into the cloud of stink, but that was nothing compared to the hard knot that formed in their chests at the pathetic sight. Milo was unfamiliar with the vagaries of war, but the scene turned his stomach, and he was certain that something was wrong.

Ambrose wasn't nearly so ambivalent.

"These are prisoners of war," Ambrose snarled to the soldiers standing guard. "Soldiers of enemy armies are to be treated according to the Hague Conventions."

The guard frowned and looked past Ambrose at the prisoners, his lip curling.

"What does the Hague say about bandits?" the guard shot back. "Or murderers and rapists?"

Ambrose looked at the men sniffling and quaking on the chairs.

"What do you mean?"

The soldier's eyes were chips of ice in a mask of leathery skin, his features blank but with subtle trembles of tension in his neck and arms. Milo knew the look of a man who'd seen enough that he had armored himself within, but the hardening hadn't come soon enough. He was drowning inside that mental armor as unhealed traumas filled it from within.

Yes, Milo was intimately familiar with that look.

"These are Reds, belonging to one Soviet commander or another." The guard spat at the center of the tent. "For years, their kind has been ripping through these parts before wandering east to fight the Whites. If we handed them over to the villagers, they wouldn't be nearly so hospitable."

Ambrose frowned and glanced at Milo, his consternation unspoken but written on his face.

"How do you know these men did those things?" Milo asked, staring at the men, his mind caught between imagining himself in their position and seeing Commissar Beria's face on each man.

"They were wearing the same uniform." The soldier shrugged. "There is little difference between one Slavic rat or another."

A rumble in Ambrose's chest rose to challenge the statement, but Milo stilled the oncoming tirade with a raised hand. The guard started to smirk but stopped as he came under the wizard's piercing stare.

"I doubt you want me to punish you for everything the German Army's ever done," Milo remarked icily. "But regardless, I'm going to interrogate these prisoners, and I want them comfortable enough to share information."

"Captain said we were to keep them like this until he was

ready to deal with 'em," the soldier growled, unable to hide his clenched jaw as he thrust his chin at the prisoners.

"Are you refusing to comply with my direct order?" Milo asked.

The soldier didn't respond, only stared at him.

Milo took a second to exhale slowly and keep any heat from his voice. His pale eyes flashed for an instant, but otherwise, there was no sign of his temper.

"The first thing then will be for you to unbind them," he said evenly, nodding at the prisoners without breaking eye contact. "And do so gently, please. I wouldn't want to report that information was lost because you damaged them."

Milo saw the man's eyes blaze in defiance and something came to his tongue to argue, but he checked himself at the very last second. His mouth clamped shut, and with his teeth grinding furiously, he moved to the first soldier and began to loosen the cords binding his hands.

"Weird, isn't it?" Ambrose muttered at Milo's shoulder, his voice pitched for only the two of them. "Lokkemand being friendlier than he's ever been, and the common soldiers are nastier than they've ever been."

Milo gave his bodyguard a sidelong glance as he watched the second prisoner be unbound. The naked man rubbed his wrists as he cringed on his chair.

"It does seem that things are shifting," Milo answered softly out the side of his mouth. "And certainly not for the better."

Ambrose nodded and leaned closer as the last prisoner was being untied.

"I've got a feeling that we need to conduct our investigations outside the chain of command."

Milo listened to the suggestion without making a response. He could see the validity of it, but to accept it put certain things in doubt. After Lokkemand at least made the appearance of burying the hatchet, Milo felt it would seem rather uncooperative to go back to his old habits of sneaking around and working outside the command structure. Also, if things fell apart, as they were wont to do, wouldn't that point the finger at him again?

And there was still the nagging matter of Jorge's confidence in Lokkemand. At dinner, it had seemed a simple, reasonable thing to be suspicious of Lokkemand, but now when it came to actions, it was not so simple. Would this be what finally changed Jorge's mind about his usefulness?

"Anything else, *sir?*" The German soldier sneered as he shuffled back from the prisoners. His expression was puckered and angry, made all the worse by the strong smell of ammonia now clinging to his boots.

"Where are their clothes?" Milo asked.

An ugly grin came to the man's face.

"Burned them, sir. Didn't want anything catching to get around the camp."

Milo fought the urge to shove his fist a few centimeters through the man's nose.

"Then I suppose you will have to make yourself busy finding them something to wear," Milo said, looking at the man imperiously. "And make sure it is warm enough since these men seem a bit chilled."

The guard's body clenched as though he was bending his whole frame to keep from saying something. He settled for one snorting breath that might have been "Yes, sir" before he turned on his heel and left the tent. There was a long moment of quiet, the only sound the shivering breaths of the naked prisoners. Though autumn was upon them, it wasn't that cold in the tent. Milo imagined a good deal of their unsteady respiration was due to fear.

"Don't be afraid," Milo began, switching over to Russian. "I'm probably your closest thing to a friend here, and all I want to do is talk. Are you hungry?"

He knew they were after one look at ribs pressing against

their skin and the deflated sag of their sunken stomachs. They were starving, but he wanted, no, *needed* them to engage.

The men blinked and looked at each other before all nodding at once.

Milo nodded at Ambrose, who produced a round loaf of dark bread. With two quick twists, he tore the bread into pieces and stepped forward to hold them out to the three men. As he did so, Milo saw the Gewehr swaying on its strap over Ambrose's shoulder, and the thought of one of the men lunging for the weapon in desperation became inescapable. Milo doubted any of them possessed the strength, even working together, to pry it from the Nephilim, but in the scuffle, the rifle could go off.

Not liking the possible outcome of a rifle firing blindly in a crowded camp, Milo decided to ply the Art upon the men's wills. It was a subtle, ticklish sort of magic, especially what he was trying, which amounted to all three prisoners suddenly finding everything about Ambrose incredibly boring and thus beneath their attention. It worked so well that the last prisoner almost didn't notice the big man until he shoved the bread into his dirty hands.

Milo gave them a moment to lavish ravenous attention on their food before he spoke again.

"There is no reason there can't be more than bread," Milo said, meeting each man's eyes over their last few bites. "Last night I ate some solyanka that was quite good, and if the mutters mean anything this morning, we'll be eating something just as delicious for dinner. I don't see why you three couldn't have some."

It was an obvious ploy but seeded with just the right pressure from the Art to inflame their hunger, the words were silver in the ears of the prisoners. Their eyes became feverishly bright as they looked at each other. Milo noticed this time that two of them were looking intently at the smallest and oldest of the trio, a man whose stubble was gray and black, peppered with stark white. The man watched the world with the sort of pinched eyes that suggested lifelong spectacle use over a prominent nose and thick lips.

The senior Soviet turned to Milo and spoke slowly in a rough voice barely above a whisper.

"We would like that very much," he said, then pointed to his throat. "But in the meantime, could we please get some water? We are all very thirsty."

Milo smiled and waved Ambrose forward. Having prepared this morning, the bodyguard had three full canteens waiting. He handed all three to the spokesman of the trio, who quickly gave two to the others. As soon as the canteens were distributed, the prisoners slurped down mouthful after mouthful, hardly pausing even as they choked and coughed on the greedily guzzled water.

Milo gave them time to savor before he spoke again in a calm and reasonable voice.

"I'm glad to see you are all reasonable sorts," he said with a small smile. "Some soldiers aren't nearly so reasonable, and that's why I wanted to apologize for the rough handling you endured when you came. I didn't save you on the road to Gzhatsk just to do this to you."

Again, he kneaded their wills with the Art. He was someone who saved them, decent and respectful. He felt all three of their wills give, though the senior Soviet was the least elastic. Still, Milo could tell that all three were becoming more tractable from Milo's efforts juxtaposed with their earlier treatment.

"We accept your apology," the senior Soviet said after pawing off some water that had wet his fleshy lips. "And we understand that the generosity you've shown comes with certain expectations."

After the bread and water, the man seemed remarkably revived, affecting an air of authority at odds with his stature and current condition.

Milo had to admit he was impressed. He wouldn't have

thought it possible for any man to look that resolute sitting naked on a chair he'd just been untied from.

"I'm glad you've grasped the situation so quickly," Milo said, the gentility slipping from the sharp edges of his tone. "The fact is, I don't want to see you men put through more than you've already endured, but I can only make sure that doesn't happen if you cooperate."

The senior Soviet looked at the other two, who watched him with large, pleading eyes. In an instant, despite his manipulation, Milo knew those two would die at a word from the elder. They didn't want to, but seeing the way they watched him, Milo knew if called to attack, even in their current state, they wouldn't hesitate.

The aged soldier nodded, then tilted his head back to suck the last few drops from his canteen. Milo noticed the bulge in the man's stomach where the bread and water sat.

"My name is Lev, and this is Fedor and Izac," the senior Soviet said. "We were soldiers in the Red Army under the command of General-Commissar Trotsky."

"Were?" Milo asked with a single raised eyebrow before nodding at Ambrose to produce the next portion of their interrogation gambit. A bottle of schnapps and three pewter cups appeared from the Nephilim's pack.

Lev smiled, warmth touching his eyes as he took the first cup and threw back a healthy swallow.

"Oh, that's not bad." He chuckled as color began to climb into his wan cheeks. "But yes, I said we *were* part of that army. It doesn't exist anymore."

Fedor and Izac ducked their heads at the confession, barely raising their chins as they imbibed the liquor. From the droop of their shoulders and the way Izac kept blinking, Milo imagined these men weren't forced conscripts, or if they were, they'd adopted the cause and were as good as volunteers now.

The revelation wasn't vital intelligence, but it at least it relieved him of the burden on his conscience that these might have been unwilling combatants.

"Does that sort of thing happen often?" Milo asked as he nodded for Ambrose to dole out another round.

"To the smaller bands, maybe." Lev shrugged as he took a sip and then sniffed diffidently. "But not Trotsky. His army, like Stalin's and Voroshilov's, was originally formed after the Revolution began, and we've been fighting the Whites and their Cossack allies across Russia for nearly two decades."

Lev's chest swelled as he made the declaration. Milo heard pride and anger in the man's voice.

"But not anymore?" Milo said and nodded at the men's state of undress. "The army was disbanded?"

Lev took a mouthful of schnapps and coughed, then shook his head hard enough to sling droplets of alcohol off his face.

"No, no, not disbanded," Lev corrected, his voice forceful and clear. "It was dismantled and absorbed by another force. You'd be closer to the truth to say it was devoured. The Red Army of Trotsky, our army, was decapitated and then gutted."

Milo stole a glance at Ambrose at the mention of decapitation.

"Decapitated?" Milo wondered aloud. "What happened?"

Lev had emptied his cup and was holding it out for more, a request acquiesced to with a nod from Milo. As Ambrose began to fill the glass, the wizard pushed a little harder and was pleased to see Lev's stalwart will give a little more. It seemed sad stories and alcohol were the combination that loosened Russian tongues and wills.

Lev took his schnapps and spent a moment staring into the cup before a magical nudge from Milo had him taking another belt.

"After Stalin went and got himself killed or captured or whatever, a meeting was called."

Milo leaned forward eagerly, the Art rippling out in waves of reinforcing will. Lev wanted to tell his story; he needed to get it all off his chest. Izac and Fedor caught the wake of it, and Milo was glad to see them nodding eagerly, willing Lev to share their tale of woe.

"Now, this meeting wasn't among a few of us Reds, or all of the Reds, or all of the Reds and our allies," the elder Soviet said, swaying a little as he leaned toward Milo. "It was supposed to be everyone: Reds, Whites, Cossacks, even some of the bandit chiefs who were big enough to merit attention. Everyone was to meet in Moscow."

Milo nodded, pushing Lev to keep drinking and talking. He imagined if things kept going, they'd need more drink and probably more food, but Milo would cross that bridge when he came to it. For now, he leaned into the performance.

"So, Reds and Whites and a few of those bandits show up," Lev said and paused to take another drink.

"The Cossacks weren't there?" Milo asked, daring a slight interruption for clarification.

Lev shook his head and then leaned forward dangerously far, a finger pressed to his lips.

"Shhh, don't interrupt," he chided and gave Milo a wink. "But I did hear that they were busy fighting amongst themselves. Something about the Bloody Baron or whatever, but it doesn't matter because it wouldn't have changed what happened."

Milo fought the urge to verbalize the obvious question, nudging instead with the Art again. He felt a prickle on the back of his neck that something remarkable was coming, but it would take patience to draw out in its fullness.

"So the meeting was called, and Reds and Whites stood in the same theatre without shooting each other." Lev giggled and practically snorted into his cup. "More of them might have lived if they'd started with that."

"So, you were at the meeting?" Milo asked quickly, to which the elder Soviet nodded.

"Trotsky's second in command," he muttered. "Right there in the damn theater."

Milo turned to check the bottle in Ambrose's fist and saw the man mouth "theater" at him, but Milo could only shrug. As expected, when Milo turned back, he saw Lev holding out his cup for more. Ambrose complied without question, topping off the other two's vessels as well. There wasn't much schnapps left, and Milo was beginning to consider that he might need to send Ambrose off to find something else to drink.

"But anyway," Lev continued, drawing Milo's full attention again, "the meeting was getting started, and despite some bickering, everyone knew something needed to be done because you Germans aren't playing fair."

Milo realized Lev was glaring over his cup now, his pinched eyes watery but simmering with sudden anger.

"Bad enough you scoop up pieces of the Empire like pebbles on a beach," he hissed, spittle flecking his lips. "But then you press into the heart of Russia and not only with your armies, but with your promises and lies. You promise the future and get some gangster to build it for you!"

Milo blinked, befuddled. Weren't they talking about Moscow? What did Petrograd have to do with anything?

"Well, he's got all the help he needs to build that future now," Lev snarled and twisted in his chair after throwing back the last of his schnapps. "Isn't that right, boys? Isn't it! I escape that rat slaughter of a meeting and find that Ephraim is in charge and is already mobilizing our forces to move to Petrograd. I'll bet my left hand and a bit of my right that once they get there, he'll give them all the same treatment! Bastards!"

Milo looked at Izac and Fedor during the rant but only saw them nodding along, hot, angry tears rolling down their cheeks.

"Who is Ephraim?" Milo asked, then took a step back as Lev surged to his feet. Milo felt Ambrose surge to his defense, but he waved him off with one hand when the older man didn't advance.

"Ephraim Sklyansky!" Lev snarled, throwing his cup to the fetid mud at his feet. "He *was* the second in command of the only true Red Army in all of Russia! Now he's another tool of that gangster, that tattooed thug."

Lev stood on unsteady feet. Tears and snot ran freely down his flushed face, yet the wounded indignation that emanated from him was nothing short of majestic. Izac and Fedor clutched their heads but could not tear their eyes away.

"I thought you said you were second in command?" Milo said.

Lev's face twisted. Enraged and drunk, he'd been caught in a lie. He wasn't the second in command of Trotsky's forces, but the obvious loyalty of the two men behind him bore out that he was a leader, and Milo believed him when he talked about the meeting.

Lev's and Milo's eyes locked, and understanding passed between them.

"I'm sorry for your loss, General-Commissar Trotsky," Milo said softly. "Such a betrayal can't be easy to bear."

Leon Trotsky deflated and shrank back in his seat, a tired, naked, hungry old man once more.

"I'm not sure it was a betrayal of me as much as a betrayal of nature," he said, sliding his back against the chair and placing his hands on his knees. "I escaped the gas that filled the room by falling into the basement. I heard the others dying, Ephraim among them, yet when I finally crawled out of there and tried to reach my men, there was Ephraim."

Trotsky shivered then, gooseflesh spreading over his body.

"I looked into his eyes, but he wasn't the man I knew," he muttered, his knuckles going white as he clenched his knees. "It was like something had crawled in and now lived behind those eyes. That thing denounced me as a traitor, and to my horror, I saw everything unraveling."

Trotsky hung his head and coughed and gave something like a sob that turned into a defeated laugh.

"All the petty rivalries and perceived slights, all of it came up like vomit," he cried in a wrenching croak. "And just like that, I was running for my life with only a few loyal soldiers beside me."

Izac and Fedor, their eyes dry now, squared their shoulders and thrust out their chests. They might have once been impressive specimens, but in their dilapidated state, their poses only made them seem more tragic.

"This gangster," Milo asked, feeling an impossible premonition nibbling at the back of his mind. "The tattooed one. Who is he?"

Trotsky shrugged and shook his head, refusing to look up.

"I don't know," he said. "He's Russian, I could tell that from how he spoke, but he had a strange accent."

The ousted general looked out from under his brows at Milo.

"Sounded a bit like yours." He smirked, a sour, humorless expression.

Milo felt tightness in his chest, and a place in his mind and heart hardened with refusal. He was being silly; it simply wasn't possible. It was stupid to keep asking.

Despite this condemnation, his eyes darted to Izac and Fedor, his mouth working in defiance of his rational mind.

"What about you two?" he asked. "Did you hear anything?"

Fedor shook his head, but Izac considered the question for a moment, then sighed and shrugged.

"I heard a name once. Roland," he said uncertainly. "Does that mean anything?"

THESE GHOSTS

"You don't have to talk about it if you don't want to," Rihyani said as she held Milo's hand. He knew it was a lie, though one she believed.

She'd returned from reconnoitering the area, giving the report that indeed there were signs of Hiisi only a few miles from the encampment and the village. She'd begun to describe the nature of those signs, something Milo had asked about, but stopped when she looked into his eyes.

Ambrose had promised to join them after seeing to Trotsky and his men. They would soon need to decide how much to share with Lokkemand.

Now they both sat at a rough-hewn table in a hovel afforded them by the village. Milo hadn't noticed it the night before when he'd crashed on a cot to sleep, but now he was certain the place had served the needs of animals more than humans. The floor was packed earth layered with fresh straw, but the musky smell of beasts was everywhere. It was not oppressive as much as one more indignity among what felt like a pile heaped on him.

He not only had to face demons he thought he'd finally escaped, but now he was going to tell of his relationship with them inside a pile of stones that smelled of dung and donkey hide.

"I might as well be honest with you," Milo said, angry at how weak and watery his voice sounded. "Ambrose has bits and pieces of the story, I think, but I've never told anyone all of it. It never seemed like it would matter to anyone else."

Rihyani's fingers tightened on his hand, and he realized his gaze had wandered to the crumbling seams between some stones in the far wall. In the back of his mind, he imagined Roland tunneling rodent-like through the joints until he burst into the room.

Milo shook off the image and looked at Rihyani, who watched him with concern bending her face into a deep frown.

"Roland was there at the beginning of what I can remember," Milo said, swallowing hard as he tried to keep his voice steady. "I was young, five or six maybe, and alone on a street when men on horseback nearly ran me down. Roland saved me, though he was probably only a few years older. After that, we were together."

Rihyani nodded in gentle, wordless encouragement, but Milo felt himself swallowing a rush of bile. She pitied him, he could feel it, and that galled him to his soul, but he knew he couldn't expect anything different. He couldn't even hold it against her. The reasons he'd not told this tale were many.

Milo gritted his teeth and forced himself to bear the pitying gaze that tore at his heart and needled his pride.

"We survived in the city until one of the German reconnaissance patrols found us, starving and hours from death in the cold," he continued, remembering the rough laughs of the men who'd pinched and prodded them while trying to squeeze some useful intelligence out of them. "I was scared of the soldiers, but Roland was there, arm around my shoulder, telling me to be brave."

"He was like your big brother, then?" Rihyani asked. "Why?"

"I asked him that more than once," Milo said, shrugging as he shook his head. "I hoped that it was because he knew me and thus my past, but he claimed he'd just met me that night. He said he saw me in trouble and didn't want me to get hurt, and that was it."

Rihyani nodded and massaged the top of his hand with one thumb.

"I'm sorry, go ahead," she said softly.

"It's all right." Milo sighed, forcing a smile. "The fact is, there's so much I barely understand."

The door to the hovel creaked open and Ambrose walked inside, eyes downcast and sheepish.

"Sorry to interrupt," he muttered as he shuffled over to the table. "Trotsky and his boys are sorted, and I picked this up."

A green glass bottle appeared on the table, and a second later, Ambrose had tugged a cork out. Milo didn't have to pick up the bottle to feel the smoky tickle of country vodka in his nostrils.

"Managed to snatch this from Command while I was out," Ambrose said as he patted Milo's shoulder with one huge paw. "Thought it might lubricate the process."

"Are you sure that is a good idea?" Rihyani asked, but the bottle was already in Milo's hand.

"No," the wizard answered before raising it to his lips and throwing back a heavy slug.

Milo felt it burn down his throat, tasting of metal and woodsmoke. It reached his belly, where it formed a molten lake. He coughed and gave a growling laugh as he set the bottle on the table.

"It's good," he muttered hoarsely. "Thank you."

Ambrose nodded and ambled over to sit on his cot and listen.

"So, we were sent to Dresden, and Roland made sure we were kept together," Milo said with a sniff as his fingers played with the neck of the bottle. "He lied about his age to make sure we were in the same dormitory, and soon the children and even the adults in that hellhole knew he was my guardian. Neither of us could avoid everything, but I had a much easier time than most because of him."

Milo raised the bottle to his nose and savored the way the smell of the vodka prickled.

"At some point, we started sneaking out to steal things," Milo continued after taking a small sip. "I'm not sure why, but once we learned we could, it was like discovering ourselves. We were no longer rats scampering from shadow to shadow under the boots of the orderlies and the older children. Out there in the dark, we were predators, stealthy and clever."

Milo raised the bottle again and felt the burning pool inside him radiating a soothing warmth across his whole body. He wanted nothing more than to keep filling those depths until they swallowed him. Only by sheer force of will did he lower the bottle to the table again, dragging his fingers down the smooth sides until glass ended and the wooden table began. With the tips of his fingers, he began to rotate the bottle idly.

"Before long we had a crew, other orphans like us, along with a few strays living rough in Dresden. We moved from simple snatch jobs to schemes more grandiose and violent. I was eleven the first time I held a porter at knifepoint while the crew emptied his wagon. I was twelve when I killed a man we were mugging."

"The little one in the top hat," Ambrose said, nodding slowly. "I remember."

"Me too," Milo muttered and took another drink.

He didn't bother to look at Rihyani's and Ambrose's faces as he took a swallow he could be forgiven for. He stifled another cough when the swallow turned out to be larger than he'd expected, though not as rough as the first.

"I cried hard that night, but Roland was there, arms around my shoulders, telling me to be brave. We learned from that night, and I only had to kill two more times before things all fell apart. One of those times was a handsy orderly from the orphanage who'd followed us out one night when I was sixteen. No great loss there."

Milo rolled the bottle on its bottom in a slow oscillating pattern, his hand on the neck. He waited for a few heartbeats and then gave a quiet sigh of relief. No one had asked about the other murder.

"So there I was, about to turn seventeen and looking at the reality that we were going to be sent to the war or a factory. Roland had this plan for us to steal a shipment of arms off a train and use it to start up as gun runners along the eastern edge of the Empire. It was daring, it was inventive, and it was either a victory or a firing squad once we started, so we were all in. By then we were old hands at sneaking, stealing, intimidation, and general miscreant behavior, so despite the risks, we were confident we'd succeed. Then the worst happened."

"You were discovered?" Rihyani asked, leaning forward, still holding Milo's hand. "The plan fell apart? You were betrayed?"

"No, no, and yes, in that order," Milo said with an ugly snicker before drawing on the bottle once more. He was surprised at the ease of his confession but also by how light the bottle was feeling. He couldn't have drunk that much, could he?

Milo looked up from considering the bottle and saw Rihyani and Ambrose staring at him, faces taut with a pained combination of interest and frustration. He'd been telling them something, he knew it...

"Ah," he said with a lurching start, thumping the bottle down once more. "So, we pulled off the job, managing to snatch no less than a dozen machine guns with, uh, well, a lot of ammunition, along with several crates full of rifles and even some grenades, I think. We left Dresden and hadn't made it to Poland before we made a deal with some Red sympathizers in Berlin to sell off most of what we stole. We went from being hand-to-mouth orphans to rich men in less than two weeks. That night we rented the best hotel and had so much alcohol brought into the room we could have drowned in it."

Milo's gaze swung back to the bottle, which he began to raise to his lips.

"Much better than this stuff," he muttered, then giggled as he winked at Ambrose. "No offense."

Ambrose's face was hard and fixed to the point it nearly looked waxen and mask-like. When the grim line of a mouth spoke to him, Milo started in shock.

"When did the betrayal happen?" he asked.

"Yes, that," Milo said, pointing with a finger even as he swung the bottle about. "So that night, I'm drunk, much drunker than I am now, and he, Roland, that is, he has me come back to his room. On the bed is all the money from the sale, which was odd because he'd handed it out before we started celebrating. That was why we were celebrating after all, right?"

Milo tried to laugh, but it caught in his throat. To dislodge the trapped laugh, he drained the last of the bottle, but there was hardly anything left, and it only frustrated him. Memories, long kept under lock and key, were bubbling up, and he'd been fool enough to not only let them see daylight but now the warden was drunk at his post.

The bottle came down with an angry thunk as his words started to flow out hot and slurred.

"He'd stolen all the money, he had, swiping it while we drank and bragged about how we were going to spend our money. He calls me in and says, 'Milo,' and I says, 'Roland, why's all the money here?' and he smiles and tells me, 'we're running away, Milo, running away like we always wanted.' 'What about Rush-sh-shia and the gun selling' I says, and he says, 'no trust me, trust me, Milo, we's, uh we're better than that, we're going west not east.' I shakes my head and says 'why?' and he says 'we can be together' and I just looks, just stares at 'im, an' you know what he does?"

Milo swung an exaggerated stare across the room in an inebriated attempt at a dramatic pause.

"He puts his arms around my sh-shoulders and tells me to be brave, like always."

Ambrose and Rihyani frowned, vague disappointment in their expression, which spread a twisted, hard smile across Milo's face.

"Then he kisses me," Milo said as he slouched back into his chair. "Not like always."

Rihyani shook her head slowly, and Ambrose muttered a curse under his breath. Milo nodded, a heavy, aggressive slamming of his head up and down.

"That's right, and I yell, and he's telling me to be quiet, but I'm drunk and confused, and he's grabbing me and I'm scared, and then the others come in and see him grabbing me and all the money on the bed."

Milo shivered as ice crept up from the bottom of the molten lake in his belly as he remembered all those red-rimmed eyes shifting from confusion to anger. Suddenly the vodka was like a cold, jellied weight in his stomach, the liberating buzz gone with a splash of frigid water on the inside.

"I was too drunk, too scared, and too stupid to explain and then Roland tells them I stole the money and came to him with the plan to run away. I can see they believe him, so I try to pull away, and he holds tight since he's always been bigger and stronger, and desperately I grab a bottle and hit Roland. He lets go, and I start rushing out of the room. The others are drunk as I am, maybe more, so I somehow rush through them and start running."

Milo raised a hand to his mouth and began to curl in on himself, the sudden weight of the hastily drunk vodka dragging him to the edge of his seat. He'd let go of Rihyani's hand and was now wrapping his arm around his stomach.

"Dear God," he gasped and swore as the smell of the room mixed with the vodka vapors in his nostrils. "Uh, so I was suddenly on the run, not even eighteen, no papers, no money, and with my best friend—hell, my big brother—having turned my only other friends against me. It was only a matter of time before I was cau—oh, God, before I—"

Milo lurched to his feet and stumbled to the rickety door of the hovel, knocking his chair over as he did. He clapped one hand over his mouth as his gorge rose to the back of his throat, yanked the door open, and managed a couple of strides before pitching forward on hands and knees. His body bowed, and his stomach emptied its contents in spattering heaves.

He managed a groan and sometimes a curse between each body-arching expulsion until he had nothing left, either in words or further fluids to evacuate. Mouth dripping, he hung there, crouched over his vomit, wanting to recoil from the rank smell but lacking the strength. Every muscle ached, and his bones felt as though they were grinding against each other as his body temperature plummeted. He shivered and then managed to sink back onto his haunches, arms limp at his sides.

It was in that broken and vulnerable state that he looked up and saw Trotsky, Fedor, and Izac standing against the palisade wall.

"Who let you out?" Milo wheezed as he sank onto his backside, clutching his knees as he continued to shiver.

As he watched, he saw all three men were shaking but not from cold since each wore the clothes that the guard had managed to find. They seemed agitated, talking to each other and maybe to others, trying to speak emphatically and gesture even though their hands were behind their backs. Milo stared, trying to understand their strange behavior.

Then he heard a voice—Lokkemand's voice.

"FIRE!" he bellowed, loud enough that it could still be heard as a chorus of rifles answered the call.

Trotsky, Fedor, and Izac twisted, jerked, and crumpled.

"What's going on?" Milo heard Ambrose roar as he emerged from the hovel.

Milo's vision had cleared enough that he could see Lokkemand at the head of a column of soldiers, all with their rifles out. They were turning toward the hovel now, faces set, eyes hard.

"That didn't take long," Milo grumbled as he sat beside his effluvium, watching the soldiers level their guns his way.

"Get him out of here," Ambrose bellowed as he drew a trench knife from his belt. Without a backward glance, he began stalking toward the oncoming soldiers.

Rihyani had her hand on Milo's shoulder, but she shouted after the big man as she tried to pull him to his feet.

"Ambrose, don't!" she cried, as Milo forced himself to clumsily stand up.

Some of the soldiers were already leveling their rifles at Ambrose, who kept walking forward, knife in hand. Milo knew that even with his preternatural strength and speed, it could only end one way, and that was not with a surprise victory on Ambrose's behalf. There were too many, they were coordinated, and all he had was a knife.

"Ambrose!" he shouted, which sounded more like a donkey braying than anything else. Despite this, Milo called out two more times as he lurched forward. Ambrose stopped a few strides away, blade still in hand.

"Get out of here, Milo!" he growled without turning around. The soldiers were a dozen strides away and had formed a line. Their rifles were at their shoulders, Lokkemand looming behind them.

Milo staggered next to Ambrose and rested his hand on the big man's shoulder.

"If they wanted us dead, they would have blown us up," Milo

rasped before hawking a mouthful of sour phlegm at the hovel. "I'm not sure what game Lokkemand is playing, but it seems to involve keeping us alive."

"He's gone over to the Reich," Ambrose hissed. "That's what this is."

Lokkemand cleared his throat, and the soldier in front of him slid aside to allow him to stand facing Ambrose squarely, hand held behind his back.

"Nothing so dramatic," the captain said, straightening to stare down his nose at Milo and Ambrose. "I'd rather eat a bullet than join those zealots, but the realities of the situation in this godforsaken country require me to make certain compromises. One of them was the assurance that the operation in Petrograd remained secret. You can see how things have been complicated."

Milo spat again, this time toward Lokkemand.

"How does doing their dirty work not count as joining their side?" he snarled, wishing the world would stop lurching in and out of focus.

To Milo's surprise, the captain laughed as he continued to glare down the field at Milo.

"You are very brave and sometimes even clever, Volkohne, but you never seemed to grasp that we are a branch of military intelligence."

Milo chose to blame his inebriation for his failure to put the pieces together and kept glaring at Lokkemand.

"I've brokered an arrangement with the warlord in Petrograd, and soon I'll have enough to bury the Reich," Lokkemand replied archly. "It's not as dashing as midnight raids and quests to discover magic secrets, but it gets the job done."

"Except it caused the murder of three men and has you pointing guns at allies," Ambrose growled, ready to explode across the intervening space. "Maybe you should try our way."

"I do what I can with what I have." Lokkemand sniffed. "And these guns will only be used if you choose to misbehave. If I was as depraved as you thought, I'd have put you down while you slept."

Lokkemand gave a sharp wave of his hand and the rifles trained on them were lowered, though still kept in ready hands.

"I can't have you blowing this operation, but I meant what I said yesterday," Lokkemand told them. "I want to work together. I don't want us to be at odds."

Milo laughed, but the burst of sound made his head hurt.

"You've certainly had a funny way of showing it," he said, wincing.

"If you send a report back to Berlin about Petrograd, the Reich will know, and that means the warlord will know," Lokkemand said, his voice holding the flat certainty of a man stating facts.

"His name is Roland, that warlord," Milo told him as he held his head.

Lokkemand's eyes narrowed, and Milo could almost hear the wheels humming and the gears clacking.

"Well, once this Roland is informed, I will lose my access to information about the Reich, and that can't happen," Lokkemand said, then he took a step forward, hands knotting into fists. "That can't happen! You can't understand the cancer those monsters in the Reich represent. If I miss this chance, there may be no stopping them from turning my country into something hideous."

Milo remembered the raw hate in the faces of the youths under Berlin's streetlights.

"I think I've got an idea," Milo said. "But what you don't understand is how dangerous Roland can be, especially if he's sided with Zlydzen."

The fierce light in Lokkemand's eyes still burned as he looked suspiciously at Milo

"We're not just talking Germany, Lokkemand," Milo continued grimly. "We're talking all of Europe."

Milo and the captain stared at each other, wills grappling over the muddy expanse between them.

"My oath is to the Empire," Lokkemand replied, looking away. "Not the continent. I'm not saying you are wrong; I'm saying I can't sacrifice the soul of my country even in the face of Armageddon. If we act now, too much of the Reich survives, and chances are we won't be able to stop them next time."

Milo found himself struggling not to see Lokkemand's side of things. The threat that Roland and Zlydzen presented couldn't be understated, but it was a nebulous doom to the captain, not like the disease he saw infecting the very fabric of his country. They needed some way to tie the two sides together, to provide information, or even better, evidence to damn them both. With such proof, they could catalyze the general staff and thus all of the Empire to attack.

"So, you have contact with Roland?" Milo asked, feeling another mad scheme forming in his alcohol-addled brain.

Lokkemand saw the madness in Milo's eyes, and he gave the magus a wary look.

"Yes, in a fashion," Lokkemand breathed. "What do you have in mind?"

A smile spread across the wizard's face.

THESE DECEPTIONS

"This is a terrible idea," Lokkemand muttered as he frog-marched Milo up the steps to the train platform.

"Steady, Captain," Milo murmured as he tried to keep from tripping over the shackles on his ankles while viewing the world through one bruised socket. Lokkemand had insisted they had to sell Milo's capture and had thus proceeded to shackle and bludgeon the wizard. The fact that Lokkemand had been doing the binding and the hitting made Milo a touch uncertain as to the captain's motive at being so thorough.

Still, they were here now, and Milo was being led to a waiting train, with Ambrose being carried behind him in a pine box. Ambrose had traded his uniform for some tattered remnants smeared with the blood of one of the Soviets. It turned out the Red's clothing hadn't been burned; it was just that the guards were petty. Here they were, one captured black coat and one Russian spy's corpse, all being served up to Roland. They just had to make it past some watchdogs first.

"What is this?" asked the officer standing on the platform as he nodded at Milo with obvious disdain.

He was a gaunt man with a long face with heavy brows over a pair of busy, worried eyes. He stood with arms crossed and foot tapping, trying to affect a stance of irritated boredom, but his eyes betrayed him. Nothing passed beneath his sight that was not scrutinized minutely.

Milo's stomach clenched, and his mouth suddenly felt dry. He hoped the man didn't start questioning him, lest he give himself away with a careless word or gesture.

"A gift for our Russian friend," Lokkemand said in an enviably steady voice. "I thought you might drop him off since you were headed that way."

The officer threw a sour look at Lokkemand.

"We're not a parcel service."

Lokkemand laughed, a strong, genuine chuckle that made the officer wince.

"Oh, Karl, always with the jokes," Lokkemand said as though the two were old friends. "We both know you've got plenty of room, and this particular bit of cargo could prove very useful to our allies' schemes and thus to ours."

As Lokkemand spoke, Milo gently reached out his will and prodded the officer's psyche with the Art. To Milo's eyes, Lokkemand's jocular tone seemed to be putting the black coat on edge, thus putting the magus on alert. Was this all a grand deception, an excuse to put Milo in as compromising a situation as possible?

"Even with that coat, he won't be trusted near the men," Karl replied, looking at Milo with a curled lip.

Milo found the officer's will to be incredibly responsive, and in an instant, he discovered why the black coat became edgier the friendlier Lokkemand was. Karl was insecure. In a flash of tangled emotions and memories, Milo saw that Lokkemand was everything this man wasn't, and Karl knew it. Lokkemand's friendly tone made him certain the captain was mocking him, and he was so fixated on that, he was paying less attention to Milo.

"Oh, of course not," Lokkemand replied. "I imagine a smart fellow like you'd want to stash him with the rest of the shipment, though I might assign a man to watch. He's a clever little rat."

Lokkemand rapped Milo's head with one large knuckle and chuckled.

"Can't be too careful with the beasts," Lokkemand said with a wink to his fellow officer.

"Yes, of course," Karl simpered as he leaned forward to gloat over Milo's humiliation. As he did, his eyes swung past Milo's shoulder and settled on the box containing Ambrose. "What's in the box?"

"Oh, yes!" Lokkemand exclaimed with self-deprecating laughter. "How could I forget?"

Lokkemand pushed Milo at a trio of soldiers standing to Karl's right.

"Mind him, would you?" he said in the off-hand way a man of authority gives a command phrased as a question. Lokkemand motioned for Karl to draw close as he moved to the box and lifted the lid.

"Dear God!" Karl gagged as a wave of stench emerged from the box.

Milo had ensorcelled some bits of meat and giblets from a butcher in Sergio-Ivanoskye to emit the putrid smell as they sat splayed across Ambrose's stomach. It had been eye-wateringly convincing when he'd made it, and Milo was glad that the smelly mess hadn't faded too quickly.

"Yeah, I hate it when all the bits pop like that, but this one was run down as he tried to escape," Lokkemand said before pointing at something within the box. "I think you can still see the wheel tread on that bit right there."

Karl turned from the box, his face pale and sweaty and one hand raised to his mouth.

"What would the Russians want with that thing?" he

demanded, his legs trembling as the other hand sank to brace his stomach.

With his head bowed, Milo hid a devious smile. Being a true German of the Reich didn't spare one from having a weak stomach.

"Didn't you see the uniform?" Lokkemand said, his voice pitched to suggest shock and bewilderment as his gray eyes pinioned his fellow black coat. "Surely, you noticed it was wearing one of the Reds' uniforms, didn't you?"

Milo felt Karl's will twist and squirm with fear as the insecurity bloomed into nerve-rattling terror. The man was terrified of looking incapable or incompetent, especially in front of Lokkemand. Milo subtly stoked the fear toward defiant anger.

"Of course I did," he replied brusquely, a little color returning to his face as his cheeks flushed.

"Then I'm sure you know what this means when matched with your other cargo," Lokkemand said, his voice dropping to a low whisper as he nodded meaningfully at Milo.

Milo, still using the Art to keep a thumb on the pulse of Karl's will, felt unease and fear bloom again. Karl, it seemed, did not have a clue what it meant, but thanks to the anger, his fear of Lokkemand was growing into a vitriolic hatred.

Lokkemand's expectant silence stretched, and Milo became afraid that his manipulation of Karl might get out of hand. If the black coat decided to be spiteful to the captain because of his growing hatred, their whole plan could be thwarted, and things would become much more complicated.

Milo couldn't handle any more complications. He decided then and there to do something he'd never attempted before.

Using the Art, he sent the suggestion of images dappling across the black coat's will, but instead of trying to affect his physical senses, Milo tried to affect his mind. He wasn't convincing Karl that he was seeing or feeling anything, but that he was thinking something. It was akin to what he and Rihyani did when they communicated wordlessly, but far more subversive and thus far more likely to go wrong as he pressed the fabricated thoughts into another's mind, where they could change at the subject's will.

If the Art was a scalpel, it was like attempting to do surgery inside a body belonging to a living and active creature by touch.

"Karl?" Lokkemand said, and Milo's eyes snapped back to the physical world around him, his will retreating. "Captain Karl Franks?"

The officer stood for staring at nothing, his expression slack.

Had he gone too far? Had he damaged the black coat with his efforts?

Milo's hands began to sweat as he reached out to Karl again with the Art, but then Karl's lip curled, and he gave a derisive snort as he turned to glare at Milo.

"So he's a traitor, then," Captain Franks said, narrowing his eyes at Milo. "A filthy rat passing along sensitive information to the Slavs."

"Precisely," Lokkemand said, hiding his unease. "Nothing gets past you, Karl."

Karl turned back to Lokkemand, still glaring.

"How do we know they didn't both work for the Russians in Petrograd?"

Lokkemand leaned in, and Milo didn't need the Art to sense the fearful revulsion. It was written across the insecure little creature's face.

"See, that's the beauty of this," Captain Lokkemand said in that same low, conspiratorial tone. "If he was, then it sends a nice message that we found him out. He kills the traitor to cover his tracks and is down an agent."

Karl nodded, his eyes sliding back to Milo.

"And if he wasn't?"

Lokkemand's smile became positively predatory.

"Well, then we've turned over a spy to the one most likely to find who's holding the strings. The Russian in Petrograd is better able to track down which Red he was talking to, and when he does, we get the glory for unmasking the scheme."

Karl was already nodding, his teeth glistening in a greedy grin.

"Well, that sounds like something I could get behind," he said with a chuckle that was too high and tight to be anything but painful to the throat and ear. "Good work, Captain Lokkemand."

Lokkemand smiled back, and Milo saw the flash of his white teeth beneath twinkling gray eyes.

"I'm proud to be of assistance to the Reich, and of course, to a fellow officer."

Milo developed fresh respect for Captain Lokkemand as Captain Franks' chest swelled with pride. The Nicht-KAT officer had played the Reich cretin's insecurities like a virtuoso plays a violin. If Milo hadn't fiddled with Karl's emotions, it probably would have gone off without a hitch.

This newfound respect for the man's subversive talents struck a chord in Milo as the soldiers began to herd him onto the train, along with Ambrose's box. If Captain Lokkemand really was such a maestro of manipulation, was he playing Milo too?

***

Things were not going according to his plan.

They'd shoved Milo into a small compartment created by metal shelving units bolted and welded to the floor inside a freight car. Along with him was the large box that contained Ambrose. A pair of soldiers, one at each end of the car, stood watch, rifles at their shoulders.

This was an expected complication, but nailing Ambrose's

box shut was not. Milo heard them muttering about the container spilling open and stinking things up, and he wondered if his putrefying magic had perhaps been a bit too effective. For good measure, they'd wrapped chains around the box and bound Milo to the crate with the excess of the chain. Every time he moved, his shackles tugged on the chain, which rattled against the pine box.

More than once, as Milo had tried to surreptitiously reach inside his coat, the chain raised a racket, and he found both his wardens glaring at him. If he'd drawn the unlikely items necessary for the next bit of magic out of his coat, he'd be a sitting duck.

He thought about using the Art to distract or disguise himself, but he was afraid anything that would find purchase in their mind as believable might provoke a response from the rest of those on the train. Illusions while under direct scrutiny were easier to maintain if they shocked the senses, relying on the befuddling effects of fear and anger to gloss over the imperfections of the projection of will.

So Milo had stood there for some time, leaning against the crate, trying to decide what he would do. While wondering what would happen first, Milo heard a rap from within the crate. It was barely audible over the sound of the train, but it was certainly there, so soft Milo could only hear it due to proximity.

Ambrose was up.

They'd been traveling longer than Milo had thought.

He'd fashioned an elixir for Ambrose to render him in a death-like sleep, and by the time it was done, Milo was supposed to have liberated himself and given the all-clear sign for Ambrose to emerge. Travel to Petrograd took seven to eight hours by train, so the plan was to escape inside enemy territory somewhere inside the six-hour mark. They needed to see Roland's operation, but as scouts, not as captives. The Reich was only providing the necessary means to get them close enough without worrying about Hiisi or Russian patrols.

Ambrose began knocking again in a slow rhythm, and Milo winced as one of the soldiers glared at him between the shelves. The man shook his head angrily, his mouth pulling into a tight line as he shook his head and patted his rifle.

Milo bobbed his head apologetically and averted his eyes as his will reached out to Ambrose's.

Stop knocking, Milo thought, and to his relief, the sound ceased.

Ambrose couldn't respond to him, but he could at least hear him.

I'm still bound, stand by, he sent as he felt a wave of frustration and anger ripple from Ambrose. It seemed he was quite ready to be done with his time in the box.

Milo's mind raced as he stole glances at his guards and then at the box. He needed something that would draw them in but not get one of them to go running for help. It had to not only surprise but intrigue them, something they didn't expect.

Start knocking again, Milo instructed as an idea came to him. *Not hard, but make it erratic or frantic sounding.*

Milo felt Ambrose's indecision, but the murky emotions hadn't begun to clear before a soft, irregular thumping began inside the box.

Milo pressed his will outward even as he noted the watchful soldiers glaring at him and the box. They were hearing something they didn't expect, and that made the application of the Art much easier.

"Help! Help me, please!" said a soft feminine voice inside the box. "They put me at the bottom! I can't breathe! Help!"

Milo forced his eyes wide and stared at the box, then looked at the soldiers with his mouth hanging open in stunned shock.

"I think there's someone in there!" Milo called over the hum of the train on the tracks. "Someone's still alive."

The guards locked eyes across the compartment, but Milo interrupted the conference with more illusory pleas.

"Help! I can't breathe! *Help!*"

The cries were followed by pained retching and gasping.

"I think she's dying!" Milo cried, sending out a wave of the Art to stoke fear and concern. As the final spur, he drove in a flashing mental image of a little fair-haired girl with wide, tearful blue eyes trapped in a box of rotting meat. It was not delicate work as with Captain Franks, but given the emotional tumult he hoped to create, it didn't need to be.

For a second, Milo felt a lurch in his stomach as he wondered if the likes of Reich loyalists had enough humanity to be moved by a desperate young girl's cries. His fears were put to rest as both men slung their rifles over their shoulders and scuttled between the shelves to where Milo stood.

"Up against the wall," one snarled at the magus, his eyes fixed on the box, where the knocking sound was growing fainter.

"She's getting weaker," the other guard said, brow knotting as his eyes bulged. "She can't last much longer!"

"Get up against the wall!"

Milo was thrown bodily against the wall of the compartment, but his chained arms played out the slack so they nearly came out of their socket. The tension dragged him hard to one side, and he lost his balance. Milo cried out with dismay a second before his head bounced off one of the metal shelves on his way to the floor.

Thus distracted, it was only reasonable that his efforts to maintain the crying child staggered to a stop. The only thing that remained was Ambrose tapping at a frenzied pitch, and even dazed on the floor, Milo could tell the effect this had on the soldiers was dramatic.

"She's dying!" one cried in a wild voice that bordered on sobbing.

"Shut up and help me!" the other snarled, and together they began hammering the padlock fastening the chains around the box with their rifle butts. Their frenzied beating became a strange counterpoint to Ambrose's knocking, then with a sharp twang, the lock sprang open. They abandoned their rifles to begin hauling the chains off of the box, casting the excess behind them.

His pulse still throbbing behind his eyes, Milo quietly began to draw the chain to himself where he lay on the floor. This wasn't the escape he'd planned, but he supposed it would have to do.

The chains were free, and he had the entire length looped between his hands when the soldiers both drew their bayonet blades from the belts. Milo, who'd begun to climb to his feet, froze where he was, his heart stopping. He was certain both were about to spring on him like patricians upon Caesar.

"Be careful," one said as he rammed his blade between the slats of wood. "We don't want to jostle something and crush her inside."

The other nodded and wedged his knife between the planks, then together they began to pry upward. The nails they'd driven in hours earlier were long and protested with hard cracks and squeaks.

"We need to hurry!" the other panted, and he grunted as the nails began to give way.

Milo crept forward, crouched to spring with the chain garotte between his hands. He was ready when the train lurched over a dip in the terrain and Milo's impromptu weapon jangled.

Both soldiers paused in their prying and turned to goggle at Milo, who sprang upon the nearest even as he turned.

Milo got the loop over the man's neck easily and pulled back hard enough that he heard bones click in his throat. He and the soldier pitched back together, the soldier unsure of which he preferred to do: breathe or beat Milo to a pulp.

The wizard twisted his body, trying to sink the chain deeper as punches were driven into his ribs and stomach. Things were, as usual, not going as planned. He'd expected to secure a tight grip and snap the man's neck, but the target was stronger and thicker-necked than he'd anticipated.

Milo looked to see what the other man was doing as a bayonet clattered to the floor and the man's feet came up. Like some putrefied revenant, Ambrose had emerged from the box and wrapped a massive paw around the man's throat.

There was a gristly crunch, and the soldier fell from Ambrose's fingers like a limp puppet. Seeing Milo grappling on the floor, Ambrose climbed out of the box as the smell of him swept through the compartment.

Eyes watering and face sweating, Milo gave a sharp grunt as he twisted and heaved himself up and onto the remaining soldier's back, chains still wrapped around his fist. The man tried to scramble free, but Milo hauled back, stopping his flight. He planted his foot on the guard's back and pulled like a long-shoreman hauling on a mooring line.

There was a strangled squealing sound from the soldier, then a resounding pop. Milo felt the man go limp under him and let the chain go with a gasp, his hands bloody and the muscles of his back and shoulders burning.

Staggering back, he slumped against the wall of the compartment.

"Not bad." Ambrose nodded and scooped up the first corpse like he was made of straw. With a soft grunt, he parked the body across the open box while the other hand reached in to peel away the false bottom.

"Thanks," Milo muttered as his chain-savaged fingers began to grope in his pockets for the key to his shackles.

"Want to take bets on what they're building out there?" Ambrose asked as he drew out his pack, then Milo's satchel. "My money's on it being like one of those mind-control organs, only on a tank or something."

"Really?" Milo laughed and then swore as the key fell from his blood-slicked fingers.

"Damn, help me out, please," he growled as he flexed his torn digits. "I'll be able to think better with these things off me."

Ambrose fetched the key from the floor and had Milo free in short order. He was still rubbing his wrists when Ambrose held out the satchel.

"You got a better idea?" he asked after Milo took the case and before holding out the fetish cane. "Let's hear it, and then you can put some money where your smart mouth is."

Milo took the cane and felt the icy thoughts of Imrah coiling across his mind.

You need to repair your hands, she instructed archly, and he could almost hear her disgusted sigh. *Why do you insist on handling problems like a ruffian?*

Because I am one, he thought and reached into his satchel for a prepared batch of healing unguent.

"A fool and his money are soon parted." Milo chuckled as he dabbed his fingers with the elixir. "You think we're lucky enough for it to be as simple as some silly vehicle we could sabotage?"

Ambrose's mouth settled into a grim line beneath his mustache.

"No." He sighed as he checked the breach of his Gewehr. "I don't suppose we are that lucky."

A flex of focus and Milo's fingers were set to mending as the unguent smoked and the smells of jasmine and formaldehyde rose to compete with Ambrose's charnel house stink.

"So, how are we making our exit again?" Ambrose said as he peeled off the befouled uniform and its gore-plastered fetishes. With two heaves and a grunt, he plopped both bodies into the box and threw the discarded uniform on top of them before replacing the lid. He looked up from fishing his clothes out of his pack to see what Milo was doing.

"We're going out with a bang," Milo said softly as he drew a vial out of his satchel. What looked like a miniature storm cloud twisted and sparked behind the glass.

"You do like blowing things up," Ambrose grumbled as he tugged on his trousers.

"Us ruffians have simple tastes." He chuckled to himself as he held the vial up to his eye. "Ready whenever you are."

THESE MISFORTUNES

The dark of the night was pierced by a rush of blue and green flame.

Less than ten miles south of Petrograd, a train rolling down the last intact railway in northern Russia saw one of its cars burst into unnatural flames. From the edge of the scorched city to the forests beyond, the burning car could be seen rumbling on like some demonic carnival attraction. For years to come, the few desperate souls clinging to survival in that desolate place would claim they saw strange, fearsome faces twisting in the bewitched fire, and they whispered that God had sent his judgment of the unholy construct being fashioned in Petrograd.

Others whispered it was because the last saint of Petrograd's blood called out for vengeance.

Those who stood guard over Petrograd and its ramshackle foundries had less fanciful theories, mostly involving spies and traitors, but soon their theories would be whispered as confusedly as those of the scavengers around their fires.

Whether it was divine judgment or bitter sabotage, all human eyes were on the flames, and none noticed the two forms darting between the trees to get clear of the wounded iron behemoth. In a stand of trees, those same forms hunkered down and waited for the last of the train to pass.

In that deepening gloom, they held their breath and then smiled as a silvery shape as pale as a ghost alighted on the branches above them.

"Enjoy the show?" The broader shadow chuckled after a glance upward.

"We don't have time for that," the silver shape hissed. "We need to move now!"

"What do you mean?" the thinner shadow asked as he stepped into the moonlight, revealing Milo's thin, scarred face. "They can't be coming after us already."

"Not the Russians," said the silver specter as it descended and became Rihyani in the moonlight beside Milo. "Hiisi are moving through the woods. I had to wind-ride higher and higher to avoid the airborne ones, but they are teeming in these woods."

Milo swore and stared between the night-blackened tree trunks. The broad shadow shuffled forward with a few choices phrases of his own, then it was Ambrose glaring out across the darkened wood.

"So, Zlydzen's got them acting as watchdogs then," Ambrose rumbled, then froze with his head cocked to one side. Milo and Rihyani froze as well, trusting the Nephilim's unnatural acuity.

"Damn, they're fast," Ambrose snarled, and he jerked his head at the railway behind them. "I can hear something—several somethings—running after that train. Only a matter of time before one of them figures out they should check back this way."

"Then we better get going," Milo murmured. He looked at Rihyani. "What is the lay of the land?"

"I spotted a road cutting through the wood parallel to the track," the fey said, pointing one long finger eastward between the trees. "If we reach that, we can follow it to a small clearing in the forest that is near the outskirts of the city."

The Hiisi will pick up your scent from the wind, Imrah told him. *Once they have it, they will find you.*

"That's not helpful," Milo growled, and he shook his head as Ambrose and Rihyani looked at him quizzically. "Come on, let's move."

Without another word, they took off through the dark.

By nature, Rihyani and Ambrose were unhindered by darkness. Milo had applied nightsight before they'd leaped from the train. Yet being able to see in the dark did not render them omniscient about all the dark-shaded forest's hazards. Roots still threatened to snare rushing feet, and branches still lashed passing faces. The promise of a horde of primal horrors on their trail did nothing to ease them, and things became even more difficult as they crashed down a slope and began slogging across wet ground.

A boggy strip of land swollen by recent rains stretched before them. Beyond it, Milo spied the break in the woods where the road lay.

"Almost there," he growled, drawing one boot out of slurping mud as he searched for something to plant it on. As he did, there was a queer reflection in a pool of standing water beside him; for a second, it was as if the entire pool blinked under the dappled moonlight.

Milo's arms and neck prickled with gooseflesh.

"Then we get to run for our lives on solid ground," Ambrose groused as he forged ahead, his heavy tread sinking him up to his knees in places. "Just lovely."

"Less talk, more walk, boys," Rihyani called from up ahead, where she stood poised on a small patch of knotted grass. With a bound and the barest flutter of her will, gentle currents bore her to a toppled tree several meters away.

Milo blinked, sweating and yet cold from the icy mud. Had he seen a dark shape slither beneath the surface of the water?

"Easy for her to say," Ambrose puffed as he tugged a foot free with a popping sound. "Damn pixie!"

Milo planted the tip of his cane in a patch of damp sod, scrambled onto the firm spot, and swept his gaze around him. He wiped sweat from his eyes, trying to press outward with his will to sense anything as he searched the inky pockets of water dotting the way to the road.

"Milo, what is it?" Rihyani called to him, and he turned, struggling to find words as his gaze kept roving.

The words died in his throat as he saw Rihyani staring at him, her back to a dripping monstrosity.

Fleshy whiskers twitched and swung to the side as its massive jaws gaped, revealing ridged gums studded with fangs. Bulging eyes glowed like ghostly lamps above a mouth wrinkled to accommodate the widening maw, turning its expression into a perverse smile. Thick webbed claws attached to swollen arms with rubbery folds stretched toward the fey as though inviting her into an embrace.

"RIHYANI!" Milo screamed, but the monster was already in motion.

Thankfully, so was she.

Talons raked the soggy tree as the huge jaws snapped shut on empty air with an audible smack. Rihyani was in the air riding willed currents, her fingers extending into dark sickles as her eyes flashed over bared fangs.

"COME TO TSAR'VODYANOY, MY SWEET!"

The sound was the chuckling of a thousand drowned throats at the bottom of a well—deep, thick, and viscous. Rihyani hissed in response but was forced to dart up to the canopy as the monster heaved its glistening bulk in a pounce. Webbed claws clapped centimeters beneath Rihyani's feet, and a hideous burbling chuckle resounded from deep in its chest.

The Gewehr barked, and Tsar'Vodyanoy slapped back down on the tree trunk with a crunch, its slimy belly opened with a black oozing wound. Ambrose worked the action on his rifle with furious speed, punching hole after hole in the creature as it turned heavily to him. Compared to the terrifying display of strength and mobility it had demonstrated, its movements were slow and clumsy now. Milo dared to hope that the bulky creature had worn itself out.

When another burble rippled out of the horror's flesh, Milo knew they had no such luck. The burble grew into a roar.

"TSAR'VODYANOY WILL HAVE YOU SOON TOO, CHUBBY LITTLE PIG!"

"Why wait?" Ambrose bellowed as he rammed another clip into his Gewehr.

Tsar'Vodyanoy's drooping facial tendrils slapped together as it shook its great head, chuckling in its water-logged voice. With a shrug of its huge sloped shoulders, it swung back to find Rihyani, but she was nowhere to be seen.

"Now, now, play fair, my sweet," the creature croaked, glowing eyes sweeping left and right in search of the fey.

Ambrose had begun firing again, and Milo decided to add his contribution.

FREEZE

Frozen darts punched into the ichor-dribbling wounds Ambrose's bullets had opened, and wherever they bit, razor-sharp crystals of black ice formed. Rubbery flesh distended and split as more spurs of ice jutted from the tears, and with a tremendous groan, Tsar'Vodyanoy rolled over on its side and slid into the muck. With a burst of plopping bubbles, it sank beneath the surface of the pool.

"Is it dead?" Milo asked as he struggled forward to get a better look around the fallen tree trunk.

"Let's make sure!" Ambrose growled and sprang atop the

trunk with his rifle still at his shoulder. The Gewehr fired twice, and the water stirred beneath the heavy rounds.

Milo scrambled over the tree as Ambrose leaped into the pool. The big man waded through ankle-deep water before his boots squelched in mud. Two stomping turns revealed nothing but muck and marsh.

"Not dead then," Milo spat, and his head began to swivel left and right.

"Not quite," came the chuckle from behind him.

He spun in time to see huge jaws about to envelop him. By reflex, he drew on the physical empowerment of his cane and made to leap back. His footing on the ichor-smeared trunk betrayed him, and his legs went out from under him as he tumbled backward. Tsar'Vodyanoy's mouth clamped down on the space he'd been in with a loud snap, but its huge bulk was already sending it churning forward.

Milo hit the pool behind the tree, and the aquatic horror's face came down on top of him. He felt something dense and knobby bounce off his back—Ambrose?—and then it drove him through the mud. More by luck than skill, his fingers gripped around the horny lip of the upper jaw and his feet planted themselves along the bony rim of the lower jaw. Necromistic magic rushed through his muscles and along every bone as he held on for dear life.

The gleaming eyes narrowed at him over a mustache of flailing feelers.

"THE SCRAWNY ONES CRUNCH SO WONDERFULLY," Tsar'Vodyanoy roared gaily as it hefted its head up and stretched its jaws wide.

Milo stretched like he was on a rack, every tendon singing a song of agony, but he held his place over the yawning mouth. If he relaxed even for the blink of an eye, he'd flop down into the maw and it would be over, but with Imrah pouring energy into his sinews, he could hold.

A hellcat's shriek sounded as Rihyani sprang from whatever illusion she'd hidden behind to fall upon the monster's head. Talons raked it, piercing rubbery flesh and puncturing the gleaming eyes, but Tsar'Vodyanoy kept burbling merrily as it threw its head from one side to the other.

"NOW THIS IS FUN!" it chortled as it spun and flailed its limbs at something Milo couldn't see. Without warning, it plopped down and rolled across the marshy ground.

Between the plunges in frigid black water and being raked through mud, Milo heard a pained scream and the sickening crunch of bones breaking. The monster whose face he was riding rose and tossed something into a nearby pool. With another shake of its head, Rihyani, who was back for another attack, was thrown aside.

The creature's head reared back as it continued to try and dislodge Milo, and he saw Ambrose's broad body floating face-down.

"ONE DOWN, AND WHAT A MEATY TREAT HE'LL BE."

The jaws yawned wide again, and for a moment Milo, enraged and trapped, stared down the gullet of the creature. The charnel stink wafting up was like the putrid gush of a hundred floating corpses in the world's foulest bog, but Milo grinned savagely into the miasma.

Dragging one hand across the jagged lip, Milo opened a gash in his palm. Tightening until his fingers ached with his other hand, he extended the hand into the mouth and sent a stream of his blood over the rows of fangs and down the undulating throat.

"HAHA! CRUNCHY, YOU ARE TEASING TSAR'VODYANOY!"

Milo managed to yank his hand back as the jaws snapped shut. Again he held on for dear life, using all his fortified strength to keep his feet and hands where they were.

At the same time, his mind, working at a frenzied, second-stretching pace, narrowed to a lethal bolt of focus and dove after the trail left by his blood. As he'd hoped, the essence-laden fluid had been sent down to the creature's belly, where a host of corpses stewed in brackish juices. His essence mingled with the slumbering deathly energies of the bones, and Milo felt the flickers of the hovering shades.

He shoved aside his fear and trepidation about the wild shades and his blood called to them, acting as a catalyst and binding agent. The energies rushed into the decrepit bodies, some only skeletal claws or grinning jaws, but all sprang to unnatural animation at Milo's command. Stoking their frenzied energies, Milo set them loose upon Tsar'Vodyanoy's innards, clawing, gnawing, and jabbing with shattered bone spurs.

The monster groaned and began to sink to the ground. Milo looked down and saw black effluence welling up from the throat.

"You are what you eat," Milo snarled into the glowing eyes. "And what you are is dead, fish-face!"

A trembling moan began in the creature's chest, but it was soon flooded and smothered by the welling blood. With a massive heave it curled up, blubberous body folding around itself. Milo heard a rattling gag inside the throat and looked down in time to see the mouth opening wide, not to consume but to expel.

Milo threw himself clear as a torrent of ichor, caustic soup, and rattling bones spewed from Tsar'Vodyanoy's gaping mouth. He danced back from the foul flood, barely keeping his feet as he slipped in the mud.

"CLEVER, CRUNCHY, VERY CLEVER," the monster moaned, still sounding amused but very weary now. "MAYBE LATER. TSAR'VODYANOY WASN'T TOO HUNGRY ANYWAY."

Tsar'Vodyanoy squirmed turgidly into a nearby pool and began to sink amidst another chorus of plopping bubbles. Milo thought of firing a parting shot at the creature, but if this was a real retreat, he wasn't going to provoke it to a second round. The cane's power had left his muscles, and he felt every single fiber shaking from the strain. If he was honest with himself, he feared he wouldn't have the strength to point the fetish without his arm trembling.

The animated corpses, their shades still intent on expending their flagging energies, plunged into the pool after their quarry. They thrashed and splashed in the mud, each effort weaker and slower, and it was a full minute before they collapsed to float in the black waters.

"Where's Ambrose?" Rihyani asked, limping toward Milo. Her leg was twisted at an odd angle, but as he watched, the phenomenal regenerative will of the fey restored her seemingly delicate bones.

Before Milo could answer, a piercing croak tore through the air above them, and Milo saw a familiar malformed silhouette pass through the moonlight above.

"Dead-Dead-Deadedy-Dead, meat-man is cold from toe to head," Lempo called in a sing-song voice as he circled between the trees overhead.

I do not like that fowl, Imrah hissed in Milo's mind, but at the moment, he didn't have the energy to reply.

He ached all over, and he felt the soul-deep drain of working blood magic on the fly.

"What's next?" Milo groaned, looking up at the corvid. "You looking for a fight, too?"

Lempo gave another shriek and then a hoarse laugh.

"No more fight for you, funny little man."

The darkness of the midnight forest was pierced by a phalanx of spotlights, and Milo had to bite his lip to keep from screaming from the pain in his suddenly abused eyes.

"Surrender now or die," came a voice over a crackling speaker.

A voice that even with the distortion, Milo couldn't help but recognize.

THESE ECHOES

Milo was dragged from the muck beneath the trees by grim figures in trench coats and elephantine gas masks.

As one, they'd advanced on Milo as silhouettes beneath the glaring lights. Their rasping breathing in time with their synchronized movements was a nightmarish spectacle.

Was his exhausted mind playing tricks on him, or was there something unnaturally sinister about them?

He could feel dozens of gunsights trained on him, but he dared a look around him. Rihyani was gone, as was Ambrose's body. There was hope in that, at least.

Looking down into the glassy-eyed masks, the magus felt something seethe uneasily in his chest. This wasn't his weary imagination acting up. Something was wrong with these creatures.

Milo pressed out with the Art as they reached for him with gloved hands and felt nothing—no will, no mind. They might as well have been filled with straw and stone for all he felt.

That wasn't good.

Milo reached out to find the essence of a shade to animate a corpse or perhaps some simulacrum of a man, but he still sensed nothing.

That was worse.

As they grabbed and twisted his arms behind his back, Milo realized with a horrible lurching in his stomach what they were —living, breathing beings with no will of their own. They were hollow creatures like the ones he'd accidentally slaughtered in Georgia with his loose shades. Men and possibly women—it was hard to tell beneath the heavy garments and concealing respirators—who'd been emptied by Zlydzen's magic and bound to a will not their own.

As they dragged him before a growling line of trucks bearing the spotlights, Milo saw the will they must have been bound to.

He was standing in the open cab of an armored truck, a microphone dangling from his tattooed fingers as he watched Milo being hauled before him. Unlike the dehumanizing garb of his minions, he was dressed to impress in a pinstriped suit of gray silk over his heroic physique, every line of him clean, powerful, and cruel. Dark, smoldering eyes watched Milo, taking in every detail but revealing nothing.

The magus, gripped between the soulless, watched a smile as cold and sharp as a blade creep across half of Roland's face.

"I couldn't believe it," Roland said in a voice even more resonant and smooth than Milo remembered. "I'm still not sure I do."

Milo wanted to say something witty or brash, but a strange and inexorable transformation had occurred. He wasn't the furious, double-fisted warlock who crushed monsters and vanquished demons, not anymore. Now he was a teenager, barely more than a child, looking up at his big brother after another escapade. He felt the corners of his mouth betraying him as a matching smile started to creep across his face. The gravity of years threatened to drag him back to old habits, old feelings of deference.

"Oh, Milo, what am I going to do with you?" Roland chuckled as he ran his fingers through his hair.

Just as the memories made him forget who he was, they sharpened his mind to recall inconsequential ingrained details. When Roland raked his fingers through his hair, he was nervous.

The spell was broken as Milo remembered.

He remembered the same motion, those same ink-marked fingers combing through his hair as the rest of the crew staggered into the room and saw the whole take laid out on the bed. He remembered how those fingers had pointed at him as that voice had heaped on accusations before Milo could say a thing.

Milo remembered it all and his rage at the memories burned away the soporific fog of nostalgia. Roland saw it happen.

For a time, neither of them said anything as the trucks idled and rumbled and the soulless wheezed through ventilated hoses. Then Roland nodded and motioned to the back of the truck.

"Load our guest in and tie him down," Roland commanded flatly as he began to climb out of the cab. "I'll square up with our friends."

For one instant, as Milo was herded to the back of the truck, he and Roland were level. Roland didn't return his gaze, but the wizard stared at his former protector and friend. Roland was still taller than he, though not by as much as before, and he was certainly stronger, but the magic Milo could wield made mere muscles almost inconsequential. Even in his weakened state, Milo could speak a word and set the man ablaze, one of many to fall before his sorcery.

I'm more than your equal now, Milo thought, nailing the words to the mast of his soul. *Even in chains, I'll be more than you. Always.*

As Milo was taken around the truck, he spied Roland stepping to the tree line and giving a sharp whistle that drew heavy wingbeats.

Then he was at the tailgate and was half-dragged, half-carried to where shackles were bolted to the bed. The ragged streaks of dried blood told him that he was not the first to be afforded those accommodations.

Milo let himself be stripped down to his shirt and trousers and then bound. He was going to bide his time.

Rihyani and Ambrose were still out there, and perhaps as Roland's prisoner, he could gain a view of the operation in Petrograd. Or perhaps they would throw him into a cell, and he would have time to recover himself enough that he could tear everything down on top of Roland's and Zlydzen's heads.

For now, his head held high, he could wait because even with iron around his wrists, he knew he was freer than he'd ever been.

They brought Milo to the edge of the city, past an old church, and then down cracked streets that ran between the husks of buildings. Some were only a few walls leaning drunkenly upon each other, while others were desolate hulks with broken-out windows like the eye sockets of a skull. As they wound their way around rubble and over refuse, Milo thought he spotted a building that might have been familiar from that night the wind was on fire, but then he'd look down another alley or side-street and realize they were all beginning to look the same.

"That part of the city might not even be standing now," Milo muttered to himself, then looked to see if the words elicited a turned head from the soulless in the bed with him. To his morose disappointment, their masked faces continued to stare through him, hands on their rifles.

He made another abortive attempt to see if his will could ferret out something from them, but again there was nothing. They were meat, bone, and various tissues, continuing to exist only because no one had told them they were dead. Even the Soviets in Georgia hadn't been this expunged from humanity.

The reality of what Zlydzen could do chilled him, not only for its effect but also the complete mystery of its means.

He'd interrogated Rihyani and Imrah on the way back from Georgia about dwarrow magic, but they were hardly more knowledgeable than he. Dwarrow magic tended to be tied to the creation of physical objects, similar in some ways to ghul necromistry, but that was the end of their understanding. Dwarrow made items or devices that worked wonders and horrors, and it seemed none knew how they worked except them.

Milo wondered if Roland, who was working with Zlydzen, could shed light on the conundrum. The thought of asking him seemed ridiculous, then Milo's wrists clinked as the truck rolled over some detritus, and he remembered his interrogation of Ezekiel Bouche. Perhaps, when he finally absconded from this place, Roland would come with them. They'd captured one warlord out from under his army, hadn't they? Why not another?

He thought of Roland bound before him as Milo conjured the images of shades to claw and scourge his flesh. The magus nursed the venomous flame of that thought until the vehicle's lurching stop drew his attention.

He looked up and saw a rusted wall nearly five meters tall looming before the truck, with coils of razor wire like fraying curls across its top. Set in the center of the wall was a gate of iron latticework, overlaid and intertwined as though someone had taken sections of wrought iron fence and welded them together. As the gate swung open and they passed through, Milo saw that was indeed what the gate was made of.

The ramshackle gate closed behind them, then the truck was rolling down a wide road of crushed rock. On either side, tin-roofed pavilions and open-sided garages were alive with bustling bodies and scattered sparks as gas-masked men and women in coveralls worked on various metal projects.

Milo's nightsight elixir was beginning to fade, but the gray of the coming dawn gave him some help, though it didn't do him much good. He couldn't for the life of him figure out what they were building. It wasn't weapons or parts for any vehicle he'd ever seen. More than anything, what he saw mostly was rods of metal being fastened together in vaguely plantlike or maybe even floral patterns. Milo shifted to try to get a better look, and the shackles gave a sharp rattle as he played out the short chain. The soulless all swung toward him, rifles coming to their shoulders.

Milo decided that the construction efforts would have to be one of the things he'd ask Roland about.

His eyes swung back to the fort, and in front of the truck, Milo saw a smooth-sided column reaching skyward. Following the stony trunk upward, he saw a plinth at the top where a one-winged angel stood with an arm upraised as though calling the earthbound mortals below to behold some miracle. The other side of the statue had been reduced to blocky broken angles with a few trailing spurs of twisted metal. Despite the mangling, something about the statue was familiar. As Milo stared up, they passed beneath its shadow, and a chill raced through him.

He felt the icy wind, that breath of the cruel winters of Northern Russia that came on so quickly. As he stared at the angelic sentinel, his mind was hurled back in time.

He was holding Momma's hand and huddling close to her against the chill.

Someone was talking to Momma, a man with a voice as cold and biting as the wind.

"And we still cling to such superstitions. Bah! Angels and crosses, and God! A real Russian doesn't believe in such foolishness as God!"

He didn't like the man. The man could sound nice when others were around, but with Momma, it was always like this. He also didn't like the man's frowning mustache and scheming dark eyes.

He pressed his face into his mother's coat.

"It is not that we don't believe in Him, Soso," Momma said softly. "It is that we hate Him—hate Him because He first hated us."

"And yet we are surrounded by all this?" the man demanded, pointing up at the angel.

His mother laughed, and it was like bells chiming through the wind, taunting and yet beautiful.

"Didn't Dostoevsky say it best? Love is not the same thing as loving. You can be in love with a woman and still hate her."

The man shrugged and turned to walk away, toward the palace.

The chill retreated, and Milo realized where they were: the Winter Palace.

A moment later, the palace hove into view over the truck as it began to slow, and he understood that he was correct, at least in part. They were at what was left of the Winter Palace. Stalin's forces had not been kind to the resplendent enclave, and in the time since then, there had been only cursory attempts to restore portions of the sprawling structure to use. The entire west wing was a bare-beamed ruin, stretching out like the blackened skeleton of a fallen giant amidst the rubble of its fossilized flesh. The central hall was in better condition. Its many broken windows had at least received the attention of boards and nails to hold them there. The east wing seemed more or less intact, but gaping windows, doors, and huge holes marred the structure like tunnels bored by beetles and worms through a corpse. In the washed-out pre-dawn light, everything seemed the sad gray or flat black of death and rot.

Roland's operation was headquartered in the corpse of Russia's old aristocracy. Somehow the irony of that reality was bitterly funny to Milo, and as the soulless moved to unload him, he was laughing quietly to himself.

They kept his hands shackled, but they separated the cuffs from the truck bed, then they hauled him down onto the ground.

He was still wearing a smile as he was dragged to the central hall, where he could see Roland standing in front of the huge black doors. They swung open and more men emerged, though these wore the khaki uniforms of the Reds and had no gas masks. On their belts were pistols and what looked like wooden truncheons studded with metal knobs.

"Take him to my suite and see that he is given clean clothes and hot water to wash with," Roland instructed without looking at Milo. "I will deal with him after I meet with the dwarf."

Without a backward glance, Roland swept inside, leaving Milo to the care of men he knew were as soulless as the creatures in the masks. Without a word, they grasped him with rough hands and dragged him inside, the great doors booming shut behind him.

Milo at first told himself he was not going avail himself of any part of Roland's hospitality, but no sooner had a basin of hot water appeared than he shed his clothes and began to wash.

The fight in the marsh with Tsar'Vodyanoy had chilled him to the bone, and he had mud and filth crusted in the most unlikely of places. Despite himself, a groan of pleasure from deep in his belly escaped his lips as he slipped into the basin. It was not large enough to do anything more than squat in it, but he savored the nearly scalding water sliding over his weary and begrimed flesh. Scooping up handfuls, he ladled the water over his shoulders, neck, and head, deep sighs humming through his chest.

For one moment he forgot about the danger, about the magically hollowed creatures standing guard over him with pistols and bludgeons, and about the fact that he was squatting naked in what amounted to Roland's bedroom.

For one moment he was enjoying a bath, savoring the feeling of shedding the filth and fatigue of violence.

The blissful amnesia lasted only a few seconds since the hot water could not stave off the chill of reality.

With one more shuddering sigh, Milo eyed his guards.

The soulless men in the Soviet khakis didn't seem to be paying him any heed, but Milo knew that could change with one wrong move from him or one word from those holding their chain. One on one, Milo thought he might have a chance even without magic, given the training Ambrose had afforded him, but there were four men standing guard over him, and he was willing to bet there were many more within easy shouting distance.

With all his magic available to him, he might have been able to fight his way out, but they'd taken the cane, the satchel, and even his greatcoat. The means to work necromistry were momentarily lost to him, and Milo didn't know if the Art could find any purchase in the soulless. The specters had worked on Stalin's men, but these soldiers seemed even more empty than the ones in Georgia. He didn't want to make a move and discover he was wrong; that could be fatal, and testing the Art would be difficult, given the one-sided way they seemed to respond to stimuli. He might not know the Art was not working until he did something to provoke them to violence, and by then, it would be too late.

No, his best option was to wait, though that didn't mean staying in the cooling water basin the whole time. Having Roland come in to see him naked and shivering was a humiliation he'd rather not endure, especially after he'd felt so empowered while staring at his erstwhile protector turned warlord earlier.

As quickly and effectively as he could, he clawed and rubbed the remaining filth off and emerged from the basin. They'd laid towels, cold but plush and clean, upon a velvet divan. Milo scuttled over and began to dry himself, looking around the room as he did so.

It was a spacious apartment with a bed at the far wall next to a large window and several pieces of furniture for reclining arranged closer to the door to the hallway. A good-sized fireplace bore a fire where a few logs crackled, but the heat wasn't nearly as much as was needed to drive out the early-morning chill or provide strong illumination in the room. The lamps in the room were dark, but the dawn had begun to fill the room with light.

In that scarlet light, Milo assessed the space.

Despite the barbaric finery of the large, ornate, and expensive-looking furnishings, it was clear the room had not originally been a bedroom but a study or drawing-room. It had built-in shelves stretching across two walls and a large desk set into the corner where they met. Other than the books being absent, there was no sign that this room had endured the violence that had swept the rest of the palace.

Given what Milo had seen from the outside, it was probably the rarity of this room's unmarred state that made it Roland's suite.

His body dry, Milo saw there were a shirt and some trousers at the other end of the divan. Throwing the towels back where they'd been, he dressed, keeping an eye on the door. He expected Roland to come in at any moment, thwarting his plans to avoid embarrassment at the last second.

Roland didn't emerge, and so it was that Milo stood in a soft linen shirt and woolen trousers, his feet bare on the cold wooden floor. Collecting his dirty clothes from the floor, he made a perfunctory attempt to get the worst of the filth off them before laying them out in front of the fire, along with his boots.

Milo stared into the flames for a second and then bent down next to the grate. Behind him, he heard the squeak of floorboards and the scuff of boots. It seemed the soulless were typically unresponsive because of disinterest rather than inattention. What did they think he was going to do, grab a burning log and hurl it at them?

Considering the option, Milo decided that if Ambrose and Rihyani weren't out there, he might have considered that action far more tempting. Still, there was something far more valuable to him right then than a hand-charring missile. Something that, even without his two companions, could afford him a chance to escape.

Hoping he wasn't taking his life in his hands, Milo scooped a pocket full of ash from the edge of the grate. Rising quickly, he dusted his hands on his pants and turned to face his guards with open hands.

The soulless had advanced several steps, their bludgeons drawn from their belts, but seeing him unarmed, they lowered their weapons and moved back to their posts.

Milo heaved a sigh and began to pick the last traces of soot on his fingers when the doors to the apartment swung open.

"Well, I've been to see the dwarf, and let me say he does not like you." Roland chuckled as he strode into the room, flanked by two more men in Soviet khaki. "And between you and me, that is putting it mildly."

At a glance, Milo could tell these men were not yet soulless since both were looking nervously between Milo and Roland.

Milo straightened, swiping his hands on his trousers distractedly as he cleared his throat.

"I tend to have that effect on megalomaniacs and monsters." He sniffed and then crossed his arms.

Roland laughed, and his eyes narrowed as he looked Milo up and down. He tried not to clamp his black-stained hands any tighter to his sides lest he give himself away, but one look told him it was too late. Roland's dark, piercing eyes darted to the fireplace, racing over Milo's dripping clothing and then back to Milo. The entire process had taken the space of a single heartbeat, and in that time, Milo's heart rose into his throat.

He was found out; he was sure of it.

Roland strode forward, his boots snapping out each step until he was looking down at Milo. It took everything he had to keep from flinching as one powerful, long-fingered hand tugged at a corner of the stained shirt.

"My God, you always make a mess of whatever I give you." Roland tutted, raising one eyebrow as he studied Milo's face. "If I gave you a little something to drink, you think you could manage not to get it all over yourself? We aren't savages here, but fresh, clean clothes like that are not easy to come by."

Milo could have collapsed with relief, but that feeling left him burning with shame. Where were his defiance and strength now?

Hating the sheepish smile spreading across his face against his will, Milo looked at Roland.

"I suppose I can try," he said, swallowing hard.

THESE GUILTS

"Milo, there are some things you need to understand," Roland began as he handed the wizard a tumbler of brandy. "Everything that happened between us from Berlin until now wasn't what I planned."

Milo ground his teeth together as he took the glass, trying to will himself back to the confidence he'd had earlier. It wasn't working, but throwing back the brandy in one hard toss served as a momentary anesthetic.

And perhaps the burn gave him a little courage.

"I'm glad to hear it," Milo snapped, biting off the words as he smiled toothily at Roland. "I'd hate to be left with the impression that when you lied to the crew that night, you intended for them to kill me, or that when Jules followed me from the workhouse to the penals, your instructions for him to kill me were literal."

Roland's eyes grew glassy, and his smile became fixed to his face like the respirators of the masked soulless. It seemed Milo could still sting him after all.

Milo savored the petty victory. Snark was no replacement for spine, but he'd take it in the process of looking for the real thing.

"To clarify," Roland said stiffly, sipping from his tumbler,

"Jules wasn't working under my instruction. I don't know if you knew, but the crew broke up after you left. You know how it is, too much success and too many secrets. Anyways, Jules was picked up a few weeks after I left the crew. He was never especially useful without someone holding his leash."

Seeing Milo's empty glass, he went to the desk and fetched the brandy

"He saw you and must have gotten the idea that he could connect himself to me if he brought your head back on a stick. You know how he was. I never encouraged that hope."

Milo rolled the last traces of amber liquor around his glass before raising his eyes to look at Roland, frowning.

"But you didn't discourage it," he said as he allowed his tumbler to be refilled. "Everyone knew he'd reached out to you."

Roland's mask threatened to come up again, but instead, he grumbled out a string of curses before taking another sip from his glass. He set the bottle down on a side table next to Milo's chair.

"No, no, I didn't," he said, staring past the magus out the window at the seething square before the palace. "To be honest, that had nothing to do with our former business and everything to do with our current impasse. I know it probably sounds trite, but coming back here was nothing like what I thought it'd be. The word from Jules came when I was neck-deep in bodies, secrets, and getting my first taste of the truth we both know about now."

Roland shuddered, and for a moment, Milo saw the creature he'd been before: fierce and clever but still fragile, still human. Then Roland shook his head and the gangster-warlord was back, every line of him sharp enough to draw blood.

"I figured Jules was small-timing and looking for a lifeline, but I didn't want to complicate my life by rejecting him. I know it doesn't help, but I hardly remember even reading your name until he was telling me you'd gone to the penals. By then, he had some sort of operation running in the workhouse, and I was using that operation to get information to a string of people who were useful to me. I'm sorry, but my hands were tied at that point."

Milo laughed bitterly and rolled the brandy around the glass once before holding it under his nose.

"Don't bother," he muttered as he drew in a breath that put the smell of the liquor at the back of his throat. "At that point, you'd done enough damage that I wasn't going to make it much longer, even without Jules dogging me."

Roland finished the last of his tumbler and placed the glass on the floor next to his chair as he sank down into it. He slouched in the high-backed seat and looked at Milo and then away several times.

Milo took a half-swallow of brandy and glared at Roland, willing him to look at him.

Slowly, incrementally, Roland's gaze slid back to him and stayed there.

"Why did you do it?" Milo asked, the words coming out slow and hard.

Roland's eyes threatened to dart away under Milo's watchful stare, but the magus wouldn't let him. He thought about using the Art, but at that moment, he decided against it. He wanted an answer from his one-time brother, and he didn't want to muddy the waters with magic.

"Which part are you talking about?" Roland asked. "Why did I lie about you stealing the money? That seems obvious, doesn't it? I panicked, and I knew it was you or me at that moment."

Milo shook his head.

"You never panicked before. Even when it was you or me, you'd proved more than once you'd take a bullet for me and me for you. You're many things, Roland, but a coward isn't one of them. Never have been."

Roland's eyes shone as he stared back at Milo, unwilling or

unable to answer for a moment. He tried to smile twice, but both times, the expression crumbled as soon as it began.

"So why, then?" Milo pressed. "Why turn on someone you'd protected from the moment we met? Why turn on the one person who trusted you most?"

"Because you turned on me!" Roland snapped, lunging to the edge of his seat, fingers clawing at the upholstery. "I'd protected you, held you, cared for you, and there I was trying to give you everything you wanted, you needed, and you pushed me away. And that look you gave me! Just like the one you are giving me now!"

Roland snarled and kicked the tumbler at his feet, sending it skittering across the floor as he threw himself back into his chair. His hands rose to his face, where they ground against his eye sockets before raking through his hair.

"I'd given you everything, and you threw it back at me." Roland sighed and sank into a slouch, elbows on the arms of his chair. "I was hurt and angry, and I wanted to hurt you, punish you for how you'd hurt me. That's why. It's not a good answer, but it's the truth."

Milo looked away, his gaze wandering to the fire as his head spun.

"You were like my brother," Milo murmured as he looked into the flames. "I trusted you, and you tried to use that trust to turn what we had into something else. Something I never asked for."

Roland made a disgusted noise in his throat, but Milo couldn't bring himself to look him in the eye.

"You didn't ask me to stay in Dresden with you," Roland said, his voice low and sharp like a knife on the whetstone. "You didn't ask me to teach you how to throw a punch. You didn't ask me to explain how to tell real jewelry from paste and cheap glass."

Milo drew in a breath, his chest feeling tight as his nails dug into the leather arms of his chair.

"What does any of that have to do with this?"

A loud, cutting laugh tore out of Roland with such force Milo couldn't keep from wincing.

"Everything," Roland spat, still laughing. "You never had to ask me to take care of you because I always did. You trusted me to give you what you needed, and that's all I was doing."

Milo sat up and turned blazing eyes on Roland.

"I didn't need that! Not from you!"

Unshed tears shone in Roland's eyes, but the smile from his laugh was still affixed to his face.

"Well, then maybe I needed that," he said with a brittle giggle, but he stopped with a sniff as he cleared his throat. "What was so wrong with me wanting something for myself for once? After everything I'd given you, would it have been so terrible to let me have that?"

Milo shook his head and stood up, leaving his tumbler on the side table.

"You say that like it was a trinket I could hand over after finding it on the ground," he growled as he stalked behind his chair. "Do you even know what a relationship is, what love is?"

Roland's hands were in his hair again, and he looked at Milo from under them.

"No." He shrugged, shaking his head. "I never had a chance to learn. I was too busy taking care of you."

The answer struck Milo like a hammer blow, and his hands fell to the back of the chair to brace himself. He looked down at the leather cushion, still deformed from where he'd been sitting, trying to figure out how they'd come to this point. Brandy on an empty stomach and long-buried emotions were threatening to send him topsy-turvy, and he needed an anchor.

"All that time keeping you alive, and then we were in Berlin, and we were rich and free," Roland continued as Milo stared down at the chair. "I could want something more, but what did I know? You. All I knew was you, so that was what I wanted more of."

Roland's open hands stretched out to Milo.

"And you didn't want me."

Milo looked up and saw that tears were now rolling freely down Roland's face.

"I'm so sorry," Roland said, his voice just above a whisper. "I didn't want this."

Milo's pale blue eyes bored into Roland's dark orbs, and something clicked into place in his mind. Roland, who was strong, clever, and fearless—everything Milo had wanted to be—had been as broken as he was all this time. He'd put on a good front, better than most could ever hope to manage, but Milo realized now Roland had needed him. Roland had needed a reason to be brave, a reason to keep fighting, something to dedicate himself to. Milo had been that for him, and in that Berlin hotel, Roland had been determined to not lose him, and it had backfired.

Milo still wasn't certain he could forgive Roland for what he'd done, but he understood it, and that was a kind of peace he'd thought was beyond his reach.

"I'm sorry too," he said, though for what he wasn't certain. They had both been broken children when their story together began, so Milo wasn't sure where culpability lay, but he couldn't keep the hatred of Roland he'd harbored for years, not now that he understood.

Maybe he could be sorry for that.

Roland leaned forward, studying Milo for some sign or indication before settling back into the chair. He wiped his tears away, and when he spoke, his voice was flat and toneless.

"It's done," he said with a nod. "And we've got bigger things to worry about than our little spat."

Milo nodded.

"Yes, I suppose we do."

Roland eyed the tumbler across the room and stifled a yawn.

"Late nights and strong drink on an empty stomach." He chuckled with a slow shake of his head. "Just like old times."

Milo nodded again, but there was no mist of nostalgia to soften his expression as he looked at Roland.

"So, what are you and Zlydzen up to?"

Roland's eyes widened a little as he looked at Milo, his expression almost pleading, but he shook his head and sat up in his seat. His shoulders squared, and the hard edge in his posture returned. The reminiscing was over; Roland had his business face on, and any evidence of old wounds and old affections had disappeared.

"That is a very important question, and one I wouldn't normally answer," he said, taking a moment to adjust the fit of his suit. "But I am willing to discuss it with you because I am interested in making you a proposition."

Milo's eyes narrowed, and it took an effort of will not to reach for the pocketful of ash.

"I can't think of any deal you could offer me that I would accept," Milo declared, his expression hardening into a scowl. "I hope that doesn't come as a shock to you, given who you've chosen to ally yourself with."

Roland didn't argue the point but rather nodded and held up his hands in acceptance.

"That is a fair accusation veiled as a reply," he replied, a small smile on his lips. "But before you light my pyre, let's be clear: the only people I've agreed to work with are sitting in this room right now. Everyone else was not my choice; they either chose me or were foisted on me by people I couldn't deny."

Milo cocked an eyebrow and nodded at the soulless at the far end of the room.

"So, you mean to tell me that working with treacherous xenophobes and bloodthirsty Bolsheviks to acquire an army of enslaved soldiers was not your plan?"

Roland shrugged.

"Believe it or not, I am as much a pawn as you in this game," he replied as he gestured at himself. "Admittedly a well-placed pawn, and infinitely better dressed, but yes, a pawn all the same."

Milo smirked and stepped around the chair to reach for his glass.

"I'd love to hear that explanation," he said before taking a sip, for the first time tasting the brandy. It wasn't bad.

"But before that, tell me what you and Zlydzen are planning," Milo said, a little breathless from the liquor. "You did promise to share that."

Roland nodded and slapped his knee before pointing at Milo. He wore a rueful smile as though remembering something.

"We can do that, but would you like a smoke first?" His hand ducked into his coat, and he drew out a cigarette tin. "I seem to recall you'd never turn one down back in the old days."

Milo eyed Roland for a moment but decided it couldn't hurt. Besides, he'd needed a smoke since leaving Sergio-Ivanoskye.

Bare feet padding on the floor, he moved forward and took the proffered cigarette and then a match. They were cheap, bitter things, and when Milo nearly choked on the bitter smoke, he realized that sharing in Ambrose's premium collection of tobacco had spoiled him. It hadn't been so long ago that he'd burnt through rubbish like this like a fiend. Milo turned to look out the window to keep Roland from seeing his watering eyes or how he was struggling to keep from coughing.

"Go ahead," he managed to rasp. "I'm listening."

The rising sun was bright and clear across the square before the palace, and below, Milo could see the full extent of the work at hand. There must have been hundreds of workers in the makeshift workshops. They'd seemed a disorderly sprawl when he'd seen them from the truck bed, but from up here, he could see that they were arranged in rough quadrants, with avenues large enough to accommodate trucks going either direction. As Roland spoke, he saw those same trucks stopping to be loaded with something before heading for the gate and disappearing into the broken city.

"We are, and I say this without a trace of exaggeration, about to end war as humanity has known it," Roland said by way of introduction as he rose and moved to the brandy on the side table. He threw back a swallow straight from the bottle and then tossed his head with an appreciative sigh before coming to stand next to Milo.

"Zlydzen, the little fiend, has found a way to enslave men's minds," Roland said and nodded at the soulless. "In a process I'm sure you understand far better than I do, he uses his infernal engines to take over men's minds so they can be controlled. It is not instantaneous, typically, but with continual exposure, even the strongest will can be broken if they don't possess proper protection."

Milo nodded eagerly. He'd thought at the outset that Roland would have nothing of value to tell him, but then the tidbit about protection sprang up. The magus had assumed there was something like that, which explained why Stalin and his subordinates had been mostly intact. He added that to the list of objectives.

"That reminds me," Roland said as though the thought had just occurred to him. "You still haven't told me how you became *De Zauber-Schwartz*, much less what you can do."

Milo frowned.

"I took a test," he muttered, not bothering to hide his irritation at the diversion. "And I already knew about the mind-control business, that street organ that Stalin was carting around. So what is he building, an army of those?"

Milo certainly hoped that was the case. Though the hellish instruments were dangerous, with proper information, the Germans and their allies could be alerted as to what to be on the lookout for.

"Oh, I heard it was quite the spectacle when you blasted that little curio to pieces," Roland offered cheerfully as he drew out another cigarette. "Is it true you can hurl hellfire like some sort of demon?"

Milo grimaced as he blew out a jet of acrid smoke and gave Roland a sidelong glance.

"Let's hope you never find out," Milo replied curtly. "Now, are you going to answer my question, or was your offer a sham?"

Roland stiffened a little, and Milo saw a hint of danger gleaming in his dark eyes. He didn't flinch away but instead turned from the window and stared at Roland. Roland resisted the urge to likewise square up, instead shaking his head and turning back to the window.

"The street organ was a crude prototype that Zlydzen has already moved past," Roland said as he puffed on his cigarette. "Now he works to create something that can reach almost anyone, anywhere in Europe. In the space of a month, we will have the means to end a war in one night that has been fought for twenty years."

Milo's stomach twisted. His mind insisted that Roland was being grandiose for effect, but the hammering of his heart told him he was far from certain.

"How—"

The doors to the suite flew open, flattening two of the soulless against the wall as something huge and snarling loped in on all fours. From its cavernous chest came a howl of rage that Milo recognized.

"I've waited long enough!" Zlydzen roared as he powered forward. "*I TOLD YOU TO KILL HIM!*"

16

THESE SCHEMES

Zlydzen was a train of meat and bone hurtling toward Milo.

Roland sprang in front of him, arms spread protectively to either side.

Milo's hand plunged into his pocket, fingers scooping up ash, but before he drew it out, the dwarrow skidded to a halt.

Muscles wider than Milo's chest stood out on each shoulder, twitching with barely restrained rage. The floorboards groaned under huge fists that ground against the wood so that it began to crack and splinter.

"Move," Zlydzen growled. Each quivering breath hissed between his clenched, snarling jaws.

Roland straightened a little and met the monster's eyes without so much as a shudder.

"No," he said, jaw set and eyes fixed. "We are doing this my way."

A low warning growl erupted from inside the dwarrow's chest, and one fist unclenched to reach out and settle with slow malevolence on Roland's shoulder. The gnarled fingers splayed across his entire broad back, while the hooked thumb stabbed into his sternum. Milo didn't doubt the dwarrow had the strength to flatten Roland's chest with one sharp squeeze, and he also didn't doubt that Roland knew that.

"I am not going to ask again," the dwarrow hissed, spittle flying out between his teeth. "Move."

Roland eyed the huge hand as though it were no more threatening than the sputum flecking the front of his suit.

"We had a deal, Zlydzen," he said, his voice calm, almost bored, as he returned the dwarrow's burning glare. "The objective and mechanisms are yours, but the operation is mine. This falls squarely under my purview."

The hand's fingers began to tighten, and Roland's not inconsiderable strength was no use against the crushing pressure. His breath became a labored gasp, and there was a series of low pops as bones shifted beneath the titanic grip. Milo's fingers curled around the ash and his focus was narrowing when Roland spoke his words clearly despite the wheeze and rattle in his voice.

"Go ahead," Roland said, sounding as though he didn't care. "Let's hope that those Reich bastards don't mind negotiating with a deformed dwarf."

Zlydzen's arm quivered, and Roland's legs buckled so he sank to his knees. Another second and Milo would launch his desperate attack, letting the chips fall where they may. It wasn't much of a chance, but he'd be damned before he stood there while the deranged dwarrow ripped him and Roland to pieces.

But Zlydzen's grip slackened and then released Roland, who fell forward, barely catching himself on his hands. The dwarrow bellowed and swatted the chair Milo had been sitting in, sending it bouncing across the floor to smash through the window by the bed.

Spit slinging from his curled lips, Zlydzen swung his gaze to Milo and began to trace one crooked finger over the layered scars on his face.

"I haven't forgotten these," he growled deep in his expanded chest. "Cut whatever deal you want with your fellow vermin, but I haven't forgotten."

Milo stared back, one hand in his pocket, but with a half-smile hitching up one side of his mouth, he let the ash slide back down. He looked the fuming dwarrow up and down as he surreptitiously hid his ash-covered hand with arms crossed over his chest.

"I haven't forgotten either," Milo drawled. "I mean, how could I? It's not every day you get to see a coward scuttle away missing half his face."

Zlydzen's fists rose and then smashed down on either side of where Milo and Roland stood, while his saliva-streaked beard flapped as he roared and bellowed in their faces.

When neither quivered or cringed, the dwarrow stood trembling for a moment, then with a nauseating slurp and crunch of distending flesh and bone, Zlydzen had returned to his shrunken form. He watched as Roland climbed to his feet and then spoke in the squeaky rasp of his reduced form. It set Milo's teeth on edge, though he refused to show it.

"Tread carefully, Roland," Zlydzen warbled as he began to waddle back the way he'd come. "I am a practical creature, but even I cannot be relied upon to always be so reasonable."

Roland straightened to his full height and cleared his throat.

"I'm glad to see our agreement still stands," he said, only a hint of a rasp remaining in his voice. "I appreciate your trust in this matter."

Zlydzen paused but did not turn around. For half a heartbeat, Milo thought he would transform back and continue what he'd started, but to his relief, the mossy head only wagged from side to side as he exited. Roland and Milo watched him amble out of the room, their silent and hateful stares following the dwarrow until he was out of sight.

"You two," Roland called to the two soulless standing at the end of the room before pointing to the two collapsed behind the doors. "Take those two downstairs to the clinic and have them looked at. Assuming they aren't dead."

The soulless bobbed their heads dutifully and sprang to the task.

A minute later, Milo and Roland were alone in the suite. The room was markedly cooler as cold air poured in from the smashed window. After a few more eternal moments of not looking at each other, their breath began to frost in front of them.

Milo shivered and spat a curse before turning to look at Roland squarely.

"Thank you," he said, the two words seeming to require a herculean effort. "If you hadn't stepped in, I'd be dead right now."

Roland smiled and then shrugged, his arm beginning to rise as he stepped toward Milo. It was the same movement he'd made all those thousands of times he'd comforted Milo, settling an arm over his shoulder. Milo didn't recoil, but something in his face, the barest curdling of his expression, stopped Roland in his tracks. A wounded look cracked his features for an instant, but he recovered as he retreated a step. The upraised arm swept to the broken window in a frustrated gesture.

"I'll have to have that boarded up before this room is habitable again," he grumbled and pointed out across the cityscape. "Well, if we are going to be cold, we might as well let you see exactly what I want you to be part of."

Without pausing to see Milo's reaction, he strode over to a trunk at the foot of his bed. After some tossed clothes and a little muffled profanity, he drew out two long fur coats, one dark marten and the other smoky-pelted Russian lynx, and advanced on Milo holding both of them.

"Take your pick," Roland said.

They were fine workmanship, probably worth more than anything Milo had ever owned in his life. Shrugging, he took the darker coat and drew it on, thankful for the insulation.

"Good choice. It looks good on you," Roland said, then seemed to regret having spoken, his cheeks flushing. Milo looked away, embarrassed, mostly because he couldn't remember Roland blushing about anything before.

Unsure of what to do, he moved to the window and looked out as Roland donned his coat.

"Not to repay what you did with disrespect," Milo began as his eyes followed a truck in the square that was moving to the gates. "But I want you to understand I'm not going to help you with whatever…"

Milo's voice trailed off as he felt a familiar intimate presence brush his will.

Can you hold out until tonight? Rihyani whispered in his mind.

Milo fought the urge to look around. She had to be close to communicate like this, but she would also be veiled by the Art. Acting oddly would alert Roland and do him no good.

"Er, whatever you are planning." Milo coughed and made a little show of blowing on his hands to warm them.

I'll manage, he replied. *What's the plan?*

"All I ask is that you come with open eyes and an open mind," Roland said, moving to stand with him at the broken window. "Now, shall we go, or are you going to keep considering an ill-advised leap to freedom?"

You stay alive and be ready to run, Rihyani replied, her will sliding slowly away from him. *We found help. We'll come tonight.*

Then she was gone, and Milo had to stifle a lonesome sigh.

"Milo?" Roland said softly, looking askance at the magus.

He forced a smile onto his face, turned from the window, and nodded at the door.

"I suppose after you saving my life, I can manage at least that," he lied. "Lead on."

"The street organ wasn't efficient enough," Roland explained as they rolled down the broken streets in an armored Rolls-Royce.

It wasn't the Rollsy, but rather a "donation," as Roland called it, from one of the White factions that had been absorbed by Roland's forces. It seemed that the Whites received support from the British in the forms of arms and materiel, so Roland could appropriate such a vehicle as a personal transport whenever he liked.

"Too easily disrupted, you see," Roland continued as they turned down a street that put them near the edge of the Neva river. "Which it sounds like you proved when you broke up Stalin's little soiree. No, we needed something that would have effects across battlefields and reach populations."

A snarl came to Milo's lips at the thought, and he was thankful that the noise of the engine hid his revulsion. He was going to have to work harder than he'd expected to stay safe until evening.

"So Zlydzen began experimenting with radio," Roland explained. "Now, it wasn't as easy as playing a magical song over the radio. No, Zlydzen made it clear that it wasn't the music or even the actual sound as much as the psychic resonance that allowed the machine to manipulate the minds of others. So he needed a means to produce psychic resonance, one for the battlefield and the other for civilian targets much further out."

Hearing the words "civilian targets" tested Milo's stomach so much he turned to the armored window to hide his disgust.

The Neva River was a gray ribbon, still obstructed in spots where the wreckage of buildings and vehicles jutted into the river, creating snarled strands of refuse. Speckling the gray, turgid waters eddying around these spots were smaller collections of refuse. When he pressed against the slotted window of the armored vehicle, Milo could see that several of these collections included bobbing bodies.

"Were the bodies down there part of the experiments?" Milo

asked, his mouth suddenly tasting like the ash which still sat in his pocket. "Or did you add them for decor?"

Roland spared a glance at the Neva and shook his head as though dismissing the sight before it could even register.

"Not directly," he said, trying to sound as eager as before but failing. "The battlefield application is, as you might expect, messier. Zlydzen is still fine-tuning it, but there have been errors, and errors make bodies. Simple as that."

Milo decided the window offered no relief from his growing nausea, so he stared at the floor. Roland thankfully lapsed into silence, leaving Milo in peace.

After a few minutes, there was a dull thump-thump as the road under them changed. Milo saw they were crossing the Neva, heading for an island cradled in the arms of the river. Looming from the center of the island was a strange cyclopean structure, its dimensions and proportions reminiscent of ancient temples in antique lands. From its roofs and spires, dozens or maybe hundreds of metallic antennae extended. As they rolled across the bridge, skirting the scorched remnants of barricades and overturned hulks, Milo saw they weren't antennae but the metallic branches he had seen being forged in front of the palace.

His mouth went dry as they drew closer to the bristling monument. In Milo's mind, it seemed like some shelled parasite with its head burrowed in the flesh of the earth until it rose, swollen to bursting. With a surge of righteous hate, Milo wanted the thing destroyed. He didn't need the abomination explained, but Roland, his eyes shining with pride, seemed determined to share it.

"The Resonator is quite the sight, isn't she?" He chuckled and glanced at Milo, who had barely enough time to contort his face enough to hide his true feelings. "We've only turned her on a few times, but you've already seen her handiwork."

Milo stared blankly at him for a second and then remembered

the barren streets in front of the train station and a dark hotel bar.

"Gzhatsk," Milo muttered. His words were barely audible over the engine, but Roland nodded all the same.

"Yes, one of our first successes," Roland said, beaming. "Nearly eight hundred kilometers away, and at a quarter of our signal's potency, we had the entire town under our sway in less than a week. At a little over half-power, we could target Berlin, and at full strength, Paris or even London is not out of reach."

They'd left the bridge and begun to prowl around the open space, which must have been a park before it became the birthplace of a doomsday monstrosity. Up close, Milo could see that what had once looked like a single massive structure was more like a central infestation from which had sprung radiating protrusions of metallic corruption. The bulky core of the horrific edifice had been built with whatever was at hand, its exterior riveted together from scored and rusting hunks of scrap. The spired colonies radiating from the central pod were of fresher and more purposefully crafted materials.

Milo wasn't sure he could speak without betraying his utter horror, but somehow he forced the words out of his mouth.

"Why would the Reich be helping you with all this?" Milo asked, tearing his eyes away from the Armageddon spectacle. "I mean, do they not understand, or do you have something over them that they'd channel these kinds of resources your way?"

Roland swung the car around for another pass by the Resonator, a toothy grin spreading across his face. Milo recognized the look from the night he'd shared the news of the great weapons heist that was going to set them free.

"A little bit of both and more besides," Roland said and winked as he leaned into the accelerator. "They've fully bought into their own 'superior' nonsense. We have them convinced it only works on the brains of subhumans. The fact that we managed to covertly enslave some of their members and pump them for information has also ensured that they understand failure to cooperate could leave them exposed. They are convinced this is an attempt to restore the Russian Empire and will continue to assist if we guarantee to turn it upon their enemies on the Western Front."

It seemed a fool's bargain, but Milo imagined the likes of the Reich were the kind of arrogant, vicious fools who would go along with it. He also imagined they had plans to betray Roland and Zlydzen at the first opportunity.

Monstrous bullies of their caliber suffered no rivals if they didn't have to.

"I'm sure they plan to try and take it by force as soon as they think they can work it," Roland said as though reading Milo's mind. "But by the time they learn that's impossible, they'll be dancing to our tune."

Milo nodded and sank back into his seat, his heart thundering in his ears.

This was much bigger and much worse than anything he could have dreamed of. His head swirled with images of entire cities shuffling out of their homes, joining a stream of soulless marching eastward to answer the call of their masters. An entire continent, every man, woman, and child hollowed out to accept the psychic strings of a hopeless living marionette.

Milo held his head in his hands and stared at the floorboards.

His soul scrambling against the abyssal despair settling over him, Milo affixed his mind on a question emerging from what Roland had said.

"Why would it be impossible?" he asked, looking up to see Roland staring at him with obvious concern. "I mean, why couldn't they figure it out?"

Roland reached out and squeezed Milo's shoulder, and it took everything in him not to squirm away.

"Well, because it's magic, obviously," Roland said with another wink as he looked appraisingly at Milo. "And that's where you come in, little brother. But for now, you don't look so good. A little food and some sleep are called for, I think."

"How about a lot of food?" Milo asked with a weak smile.

"I think we can manage that." Roland laughed and gunned the engine as he swung back to the bridge that would take them off that wretched island.

17

THESE ASHES

Milo ate until he was full and then had another two helpings. He had a feeling he'd need every single calorie soon.

It was late morning by the time he and Roland returned to the suite, and they found the room much warmer, with a fire burning and the broken window thoroughly boarded up. The heat, combined with fatigue and the burdensome food in his belly, sapped whatever energy Milo possessed, and he staggered across the room to the divan, shedding his borrowed coat as he went. He'd very nearly thrown himself down on the velvet-covered couch when Roland wrapped an arm around him and began marching him to the bed.

Even in his current state of near-exhaustion, Milo found the strength to arch his back and start to pull away.

"Stop it, Milo. It's not like that," Roland snapped without letting go of him. "You need proper rest. Can't get that on a couch."

Milo's brain rejected the placation, demanding he rise and throw off Roland's grip, but his body was plummeting onto the plush bed by the time it got the message. By then, it was too late. He was swimming in silken sheets, nestling in as his body remembered every bump and bruise of his time on the train and every danger since then. The bed seemed to swallow him, and with it came the oblivious embrace of sleep.

He vaguely felt someone tug his boots off as his feet dangled at the end of the bed, and then he was gone.

The hibernation of exhausted sleep was fractured for brief instances, but Milo was determined to fight off the distractions. Sometimes his eyes fluttered, and he got an unfocused glimpse of a long and sinewy figure stretched out beside him, not touching but desperately close. Other times his eyes didn't even open as he felt the whisper of a breath across the back of his neck. The depths of exhaustion always won, and he was drowned anew by sleep.

When he finally emerged, it was by degrees, and that extended awakening time was a slippery and pernicious thing.

Milo felt as though he were ascending to the surface from slumber at the bottom of some black ocean. As he rose, he heard voices, muffled but insistent, and something that sounded like a snarled whisper. Then he became aware of bronze light through his eyelids, and it changed to red as it faded. After that, his eyes finally opened, but it took some time for him to remember where he was and what was going on.

He beheld Roland's suite, melancholy and imperial, in the dying light of the sky outside and the fire within. He shivered at the sudden realization that it had become cold again and drew the sheets around him as he scanned the room with gummed, blinking eyes. He thought for a second that he was alone, then he saw Roland's legs dangling from the end of the divan.

I wouldn't have gotten much sleep on that, he thought, and just like that, he remembered everything. Heart leaping into his throat, his hand snaked down to his pocket and found it nearly empty. Licking dry lips, he checked to make sure Roland was not stirring and drew back the heaped sheets as quietly as he could.

Smeared across the folds of the sheets were several broad strokes of ash.

Cursing silently, he folded and piled the sheets to one side, glancing at Roland from time to time. The man didn't stir, but Milo knew that could change in an instant. He'd always been able to spring from sleep to desperate action in an instant in their youth, and he couldn't risk hoping things had changed.

Milo's eyes slid to the fire, where his clothes were still laid out, though on closer examination, someone had done a far better job than he had of cleaning them in his absence. The ash he'd spilled around the fireplace this morning had been cleaned up and fresh wood added, though that must have been some time ago since there was a fresh layer of ash glowing under the grate. Checking one last time that Roland still wasn't stirring, Milo slid out of bed and padded silently over to the fireplace.

With his breath sounding thunderous in his ears, Milo somehow made it to the fireplace without waking Roland. Crouching by the grate, he twisted around and could now see Roland lying stretched out on the divan, his face crushed into the velvet cushion as his back gently rose and fell with his steady breathing. There wouldn't be a better time than this.

Milo scooped up a handful of the ash from the fireplace, being as careful as he could not to spill a mote of it. It was uncomfortably hot in his hand, and as he drew his arm back, fingers tightening, he discovered there was still a live cinder within. He didn't dare drop the ash, dousing it instead in the smothering flesh of his hand, but he couldn't avoid allowing a sharp hiss of pain to escape his lips.

"Milo?" Roland called from his couch, "What are you doing?"

He was caught, but then he spied his trousers at hand. Snatching them up, he slipped the ash-filled hand into his pocket while the other hand stretched them wide. He turned and held them to Roland

"Checking to see if my clothes were dry," Milo said, fighting with every syllable to keep his voice steady. "Seems they were laundered at some point and then put back here to dry."

Roland was still stretched out on the divan, but he'd raised himself on his elbows to look at Milo. He blinked once, squinted at the uplifted trousers, then managed a sleepy smile.

"One of the advantages of being the leader of an army." He chuckled as he rolled his head from one side to the other. "Never a shortage of hands to do the laundry."

Milo gave a little laugh in reply that sounded nervous in his ears, then rose as he gathered the rest of his clothes.

"I'd like to change back into my uniform," Milo said, unsure of which part of the whole situation made him uncomfortable. "To maintain discipline if nothing else."

Roland curled and stretched like some great feline on the couch and then settled into a seated position.

"Go ahead." He shrugged with a yawn.

Milo stared back as his chin lowered and his eyebrows rose. Roland blinked again, then flushed red.

"Oh!" he said, a sheepish smile forcing its way across his face. "Of course."

He rose to his feet so sharply that the divan scooted back a few inches, and he turned to scowl at the furniture before look backing at Milo apologetically. When he said nothing, he darkened to a shade Milo might not have thought possible and turned to leave the room.

"Let me know when you're done," he called from the door. "We still need to finish that conversation."

Milo nodded and waited for the door to shut behind Roland before he dared to breathe easily.

Gingerly he drew his hand from his trousers, still careful not to spill any of the precious ash. The blistered flesh of his hand wasn't pretty, but he'd survive. Flexing his fingers, Milo looked at the dying light of day and wondered if when the time came, he could bring himself to do what was necessary to his former brother. Milo knew he had every reason to hate him, but seeing him again and glimpsing his twisted but sincere motivations, Milo struggled to stoke his rage to its previous level.

Neither of them was who they once were, to the world or to each other, but there was so much history between them, it was almost impossible for Milo to think of it ending.

Then Milo remembered the abomination on the island in the Neva river, and dread sharpened something as dangerous as hate in him. Where anger might no longer burn hot enough, the icy grip of fear might be enough to harden his heart to do the job.

He supposed he wouldn't know until the moment came, and with a heavy sigh, he set about changing back into his uniform.

The sky was turning purple above them as they rolled down the crumbling streets, entourage in tow.

Roland had explained that sometimes things grew more "interesting" in Petrograd at night when the smaller bandit bands attempted to scavenge or steal supplies. As a result, along with the Rolls Royce, they were accompanied by a truck full of soulless soldiers. Roland had explained as they'd left the gates of the palace that they'd been attempting to clean out the few remaining parasites hanging about the city, but some of them were proving remarkably resilient.

"I suspect once we start using the Resonator to acquire aircraft, we can try an aerial application," he'd muttered as they began weaving between the sloughing assembly of buildings. "Not an efficient use of hollow gas, but once things begin, we'll need to guarantee the area is secure."

Milo looked at Roland, barely able to see him after staring out over the pools of light created by the vehicle's headlights.

"Aerial application?" he asked, trying and failing to sound interested in only the most academic senses. "Hollow gas?"

"Yes, we never talked about that, did we?" Roland asked. "The Resonator can enslave entire cities, but it is targeted, and even under optimum conditions, it would take at least a day or two. The hollow gas is another creation of Zlydzen's to accelerate the process."

Milo knew he wasn't going to like where this was going, but he nodded along as Roland spoke, hoping to squeeze out every last detail before his escape. He fought the urge to look around to see where Rihyani and Ambrose might be coming from. They would arrive when they would arrive, and until then, he was keeping a hand near his ash-filled pocket.

"Not sure how it works, of course, and I can't say I like it," Roland said, shaking his head. "But the basic fact is that the gas kills something in the targets, so even a quick burst of resonance can enslave the meat that's left. They start breaking down after a time, but that takes weeks, sometimes months, and as it gets colder, they seem to last longer."

Roland punched Milo in the arm and smiled with a flash of teeth in the deepening shadow.

"Good thing for us winter is coming, eh?"

Milo only nodded and turned back to the street.

It was well and truly night when they finally came to a stop in a part of the city where the scorched facades of what had once been homes stood side by side. They were in various states of ruin, some little more than a few bricks leaning against blackened spars, while others had one or two walls still standing.

"Here we are," Roland said and opened his door.

"What are we doing here?" Milo asked, narrowed eyes darting between the houses and Roland.

"Finishing that conversation," Roland said as he clambered down and walked into the light cast by Rolls Royce's headlights.

Milo saw that their escort had parked behind them and the soldiers were disembarking to maintain a perimeter.

Swearing quietly to himself, Milo got out of the vehicle and walked toward Roland, their shadows stretching long under the headlights' glare. Roland looked up and down the street, his breath rolling out in plumes of white that glittered in the electric light.

"Do you recognize it?" Roland asked, nodding at the street, a small smile playing on his lips.

Milo looked around and shook his head. He'd already decided one stretch of ruin looked much the same as any other, and his mind was on more important questions than what wrecked street they were on.

"This is the street where you were almost run down," Roland said, hands sweeping in a wide gesture at the road in front of them. "This is where I saved your life, the first time anyway."

Milo looked down at the indicated ground and then around them. It could have been, but so could a dozen other streets he'd seen in the city. He looked at Roland, who was waiting for a reaction, but Milo felt certain their time was growing short. If something was going to happen, he was certain it would happen soon.

"Okay." Milo shrugged, the sable fur of his borrowed coat tickling his jaw.

Roland's smile faltered for a second, then he pointed to a gap between two buildings where shattered bricks and a few charred beams lay in a pile.

"That's the alley where we first met." He nodded eagerly. "That's where you took my hand and trusted me to take care of you."

Milo stared at the alley, which could hardly be called that, given the state of the buildings around it. Roland was expecting a great surge of emotion at the revelation, but Milo found he couldn't even pretend he was moved. Anxiety about the coming escape and gnawing dread at what he'd discovered had eaten up whatever emotional capital he had left.

"Why are we here, Roland?" he asked, having to raise his voice as the wind picked up. It smelled of ash, sulfur, and old earth.

Roland's face fell, and for a second, beneath the tattoos, scars, and roguish good looks, Milo saw the friend and protector he remembered: fierce and strong and dangerous, but still so young and so afraid. Milo pressed a finger into the stinging wound on his hand to try to shake off the enchantment of the moment. Being drawn in now could have dire consequences, and not just for him.

"I wanted to make my offer to you here," Roland said, stepping closer and lowering his voice. Milo resisted the urge to recoil. "Here, where I saved you, I wanted to ask you to save me."

Milo, who'd been avoiding Roland's gaze by looking at the alley, whipped his head around to stare at him. That wasn't the offer he'd been expecting.

"I know Zlydzen is using me, and it is only a matter of time before I'm not useful," Roland continued. "It could be tomorrow or five years from now, but the reality is that inevitably I'm going to join them."

His thumb hooked over his shoulder at the soldiers fanned out across the street. Milo felt a shiver that had nothing to do with the cold as he glimpsed their cold, flat eyes.

"I can't walk away either because he'll hunt me down," Roland added quickly as though trying to preempt the suggestion from Milo. "Those things he's struck a bargain with have tracked targets across oceans when properly motivated, and if I run, I won't know a moment's peace until one of them rips my throat out one night."

Milo could only nod as another shiver wracked his body. He imagined Borjikhan's eyes watching him from a dark alley, Tsar'Vodyanoy's smile inside a sewer drain, or Lempo's shadow passing overhead. He'd only faced the Hiisi one on one, and with all his magic, it had always been a near thing. Someone like Roland wouldn't stand a chance against a host of them.

"So then, what's the plan?" Milo asked, hoping against hope that things weren't going to go as he feared.

Roland moved half a step closer and was so near that even whispering, Milo could hear him over the wind and rumbling engines.

"Help me while you work with us," Roland said, the white gusts of his breath breaking on the side of Milo's face. "You're powerful, and Zlydzen, even with how much he hates you, will see you could be useful. That will give you a chance and an opportunity to figure out what magic he uses. Once you've puzzled it out, we can turn the tables and dispose of that warped monster."

For a second Milo imagined it, his mind racing as he thought about Rihyani and Ambrose creeping through the rubble even as he stood there. What if this was another way? What if Roland was offering him a better way to take down Zlydzen, a way that didn't involve destroying the oldest friend and only family he'd ever had?

There was one nagging detail that caught in Milo's mind like a barbed hook.

"And then what?" he asked, the words coming out almost before he'd had time to formulate the thought.

Roland blinked several times and raked a hand through his hair.

"What do you mean, 'and then what'?" he asked in an almost-laugh that became a snort.

Milo skewered Roland's eyes with his own.

"Say your plan works. I take control of the Resonator, and we kill Zlydzen," Milo rattled off, his voice beginning to buzz with growing anger. "What happens next, Roland? We make the big score, and then what?"

Roland took a step back, neck arching and face twisting as though he'd been slapped.

"Whatever the hell we want!" he snapped, baring his teeth in a savage mockery of a grin. "We'll have an army and means to conquer all of Europe, perhaps without firing a shot, if we can figure it out before Zlydzen's campaign starts. Think of it, Milo! We could not only end the war, but we could bring about a new order."

The fire raging in Roland's eyes withered Milo's heart in his chest. He wished it didn't hurt as much as it did, but by God, he'd hoped he was wrong.

"What if I wanted to destroy the Resonator?" Milo asked wearily. "If I refused to use the power we'd stolen from Zlydzen?"

Roland's burning stare searched Milo's face.

"Why would you do anything so stupid?"

Milo shook his head. Could he even explain the horror of what that techno-magical construct was? Would it even matter?

"It is evil, Roland," he said, every word heavy. "It doesn't just make them do what you want, it hollows them out. You didn't just trick or bully those people in Gzhatsk; you scraped their souls out!"

Somewhere in the darkness rubble shifted, sending bricks slithering down over each other. Roland's eyes darted through the darkness as he motioned some of his soldiers over to the side of the street where the disturbance had come from.

Milo held his breath as four men trudged over, rifles on their shoulders, but they picked among the ruined buildings without incident. They emerged after a minute and settled in as sentries along the street half a dozen strides from Roland and Milo.

"Souls and evil?" Roland snorted after another minute of listening to nothing but wind and combustion engines. "Did you become religious or something in the last few years?"

Milo opened his mouth to retort, but his tongue didn't coop-erate as a rush of tangled thoughts bounced around his mind. What was he talking about? By what right did he talk about souls and evil? He could have talked about stripping one's will, but he knew with a deep certainty it was more than that.

"I'm not religious," he murmured. "But seeing these things, doing these things, performing magic? It's opened my mind to a world that isn't only what I can see or touch. There are realities besides the physical; I know that now, and knowing means I can see there is such a thing as evil."

Roland's fingers raked through his hair with such ferocity and frequency, Milo expected blood to start trickling from his hairline.

"You aren't making sense!" Roland snarled. "You'll throw away a chance to end the war and right every wrong we've suffered because it's *evil*? You, *De Zauber-Schwartz*, don't have the stomach for it after everything you've done?"

Milo felt pressure building in the back of his mind; the familiarity of the situation was not lost on him. He'd held a bag containing the bones of an infant in his hand.

"We've all got to draw the line somewhere, Roland," Milo said, meeting the accusing glare with a sad smile. "I'll help you destroy Zlydzen, but I won't stop until all his works burn with him."

Roland nodded slowly, then looked up from under his brows with a fell light that made Milo's stomach twist.

With a bestial howl, Roland sprang at Milo, his hands curled into claws that gripped the marten fur in two great clumps. With a hard yank, he drew Milo to him so they were nose to nose.

"No! You don't get to do that, not after everything!" Roland snarled as he ground his forehead against Milo's. "I gave you everything I had in a world that gave me nothing! You won't take away my chance to balance the scales! You can't do that to me!"

Milo felt Roland's fists pressing into his throat.

"I can," Milo gulped, his fingers digging for purchase on the silky furs. "I can, and I will."

A roar tore from Roland's throat, and he threw Milo down to the ground. The magus managed to keep his head from bouncing off the broken cobbles, but his elbow struck the ground hard enough to rob him of all feeling from the joint down. That happened to be on the side his ash-filled pocket was on.

Roland loomed over him, the four soldiers now flanking him with their guns leveled at Milo.

"You are so selfish!" Roland spat, a pistol appearing in his hand, not yet aimed at Milo but hanging at his side. "Everything you have is because of me! Every breath you took from that night I saved you on was only because I was there, and you have the arrogance to defy me?"

As he lay looking up at Roland and four sets of cold eyes above rifle barrels, Milo slid his nerveless fingers into his pocket. Roland glared down at him, his eyes bulging with rage as the hand holding the pistol quivered and began to rise toward him, then stopped. Milo met his furious gaze, tears rising in his eyes as he did, though that was as much from his teeth crunching through the inside of his lip as from the emotion of the moment. Milo began drawing his hand out of his pocket as slowly as possible, hoping there was enough ash between his tingling fingers.

The pistol nearly leveled with Milo, then Roland sobbed and let his arm hang at his side, the pistol loose in his fingers.

"Don't make me do this," he pleaded, fingers dragging across his scalp and stopping to grip a hand full of hair. "Please, for the love of everything we once had, don't make me kill you."

Blood had begun to stream from Milo's mouth so that as he spoke, it spattered the ash-filled hand he raised to his lips.

"You won't have to," Milo muttered thickly and opened his hand.

RISE

His focused mind thrumming to the tune of his blood flecking the ash, Milo felt as much as saw the bloody darts rise into the air. The red projectiles trailed streamers of ash as they hurtled toward the four soulless. Chasing each of those streamers were ripples of gloaming light, hungry shades that keened as they closed on their quarry. The gory shards struck the four soulless simultaneously with the slap of fluid striking a hard surface as the contrails of ash crumbled. The wailing lights, scenting the bait, dove in without hesitation.

All that happened so quickly that Milo's eyes barely had time to register everything, and by the time they did, he was distracted by the eruption of essence his mind felt emanating from the soulless soldiers. Their bodies rocked and quivered, the rifles tumbling from their grasp as every joint twisted in a different direction.

Roland looked at the soldiers spasming on either side of him, then swung his gaze to Milo and raised his pistol.

OBEY

The four soulless pounced, seizing on the arm holding the weapon while the others grabbed whatever part of Roland was handy. The pistol barked twice, one shot whining off the cobbles beside Milo the other rocketing straight overhead. Roland roared and cursed, but as strong as he was, four full-grown men couldn't be thrown off so easily.

"Petrograd is seething with unsettled shades," Milo growled as he sat up. "That's the thing when you hollow people out. There's nothing to keep them from being filled with something else."

The pistol fell from Roland's grip, but only so that he could strain at Milo with hands intent on strangling him.

"Traitor!" he howled between a slew of blistering, venomous curses as he struggled. "Ungrateful whoreson! Liar! Traitor!"

Milo would have thought the words would slide off him, but they stung deeply as he tried to clamber to his feet. He thought to say something, to rebut or maybe even explain, but several things happened in quick succession.

The other soulless opened fire and a trio of shots sailed past Milo's bent back, while others hammered into the flesh of the shade-possessed soulless. Milo felt a shade's wail of frustration as its host succumbed to its injuries, but before he could redirect it to the soldiers firing on them, Roland lunged forward and grabbed him by the throat with his free hand. Milo gasped and pried at the fingers crushing his windpipe as the three remaining servitors pulled on Roland's arms.

Then a wild, whooping cry tore through the night from the opposite end of the street.

Through his hazy, black-spotted vision, Milo saw a nightmare from the past barreling toward them. A gaunt figure riding a skeletal charger was bearing down on them, a crackling wheel of fire spinning around his head.

18

THESE INSANITIES

Milo didn't have the breath to curse, but if he had, it would have been a good one. Something poetic, with metaphor and symbolism, but as things stood, he only managed a gargle. Roland seemed determined to keep strangling Milo singlehandedly, despite three soldiers contesting the point.

Instead, he saved his breath for a final heave at Roland's throttling grip, and the investment paid off as the hand came free and air poured through his bruised throat.

Roland surged forward with a scream, but Milo slipped past the clawing hand and drove an elbow across his jaw. He felt the jaw crack under the blow, the reverberations traveling up his arm, and Roland collapsed to the ground under the shade-dominated assailants.

Milo looked up in time to see the rider charging at him, screaming like a burning demon, as the wheel of fire spun over his head. This close, he could see that the steed was none other than the Qareen mount he'd made in Georgia, but that was not what made the bottom drop out of Milo's stomach. Astride the necromistry-powered horse was none other than Ezekiel

Bouche, looking filthier and more ragged than Milo had ever seen him, yet smiling as wide as ever.

"YEEHAW!" he shrieked and then threw back his head to laugh with wicked mania.

Milo gaped. He was as vulnerable as he'd been that night when the city burned, but this time, the rider rode right past him without a sideways glance. Ezekiel hammered his heels into the unfeeling flanks of the unliving horse and made a beeline for a collection of soulless huddling against their truck. Round after round from their rifles sent up puffs and thin splatters of dark blood from the wild cowboy's chest, but he rode on, laughing all the while.

A stone's throw from the truck, Ezekiel launched his wheel of flame, and Milo realized for the first time that the flame was an incendiary device spinning frantically on a length of rope.

The wheel became a crackling star that struck the truck and exploded in a shower of broken glass and burning fuel.

"Burn, haha! Warm right up, darlin'!"

As if in answer, the fire expanded with an oxygen-slurping *whoosh*, sending waves of flame in every direction. The truck bore the incendiary attack stoutly, the men around it less so. They might have been soulless, but their flesh still felt pain, and the lizard-brain response to the gnawing flames was as hard-wired as breathing. Screams rose in concert with the crackle of flames. A few managed to fire a handful of shots, but even with Ezekiel cackling half a dozen yards from them, their shots sailed into the night before they surrendered to the flames.

Those less fortunate were put out of their misery a second later, crumpling to smolder on the ground as the throaty call of the Gewehr sounded from the ruins.

"Let's not linger here, if you please," came a crisp voice in American English at Milo's shoulders before someone began to draw him out of the street. "Mr. Bouche and your man seem to have things well in hand, but it would be a shame to lose the world's first wizard to a stray bullet."

Blinking but not resisting, Milo looked over and saw he was being led away by Percy Astor in a navy suit and a fedora.

"You!" Milo exclaimed as he followed. "What? How?"

"A moment," Percy said as he half-led, half-dragged Milo behind a freestanding section of brick wall. "Yes, now, where were we? Oh, yes, what and how? Are particulars important at the moment, or can I summarize?"

A shot whined off a brick a few inches from Percy's shoulders, spraying jagged fragments as the American lurched back. Milo spied a few soldiers moving through the ruins, whether flanking or making a fighting retreat, he wasn't quite sure. No sooner had he spotted them than he was flattening himself against the bricks as more bullets hissed and zipped through the air.

Milo heard the clop of hooves on cobbles and then another scream, and he poked his head out to see Ezekiel riding down the soldiers. The pale light in the eye sockets of the unliving horse danced and flared as it ran men down. In the muzzle flares and the flicker of the Qareen's eyes, Milo watched men die screaming in defiance as a hurtling body began what a hard hoof finished.

"He certainly has his uses." Percy chuckled as he stepped away from the wall and brushed vainly at the brick dust staining his outfit. "Crude tools can still be effective, as I'm sure you understand. Sometimes all you need is a hammer, am I right?"

The grin the American gave Milo seemed to suggest they were sharing an inside joke, but Milo squashed the moment with a tremendous frown and responded with a question of his own.

"What the hell are you two doing here?" he asked hoarsely, raising a hand to his throat.

Percy drew back, looking affronted, but he gave a little bow as he swept his hat from his head. The man's pate was noticeably balder than the last time they'd met.

"Oh, you are quite welcome for the rescue. It's nothing," he cooed, then gave a tart smile. "No trouble at all. Don't worry about thanking us."

Milo massaged his throat, wincing at the swelling and when he found places where Roland's nails had cut his neck.

"You're not answering the question," he said, his voice rasping like a file over stone.

Percy raised an eyebrow before replacing his fedora.

"And you're being very rude," he replied archly. "Now, are we going to stand here making asinine observations about the obvious, or do you plan to reunite with your compatriots? Makes no difference to me."

Milo spat at the man's feet, then looked up the ruined street and saw no further sign of the soulless soldiers. His gaze swung back to where the confrontation with Roland had taken place and he loosed a stream of invectives.

The three shade-powered humans lay in a broken heap, but Roland was nowhere to be seen.

At that moment, Ezekiel trotted up from the other end of the street, still mounted on the unliving steed. This close, Milo could see that Ezekiel wasn't just ragged but rotten. The flesh of his face and chest were pocked with gangrenous holes, while his hands were nearly black with dried blood around tattered skin through which the dirty ivory of tarnished bone showed. The wind shifted, and despite the cold, Milo could smell putrid meat.

"Dear God." He coughed. "What happened?"

"I've been set free!" Ezekiel crowed, then threw back his head to loose a wild, undulating howl.

Milo frowned, trying to reconcile the nightmare before him with the broken man he'd left chained in the Marquis's dovecote. Uneasiness stole over him as he stared at the cowboy's eyes, still bulging from their sockets, yet without the malicious gleam. Milo had given Ezekiel the means to escape his curse and embrace death, which was the freedom Milo might have expected. Staring at the maniacal display, he wasn't sure what new sort of freedom the scalp hunter had found.

As he stood staring at Ezekiel, Milo eased his will outward to probe the edges of the man.

"We should be going," Percy pressed, stepping to Milo's shoulder. "I believe there is stolen property to return to y—"

A rending scream cut Mr. Astor off, and it was half a heartbeat before Milo realized he was the source of the sound.

It was like nothing he'd ever felt.

Typical souls pressed back with their wills at varying strengths against the Art, defining themselves by their resistance. Practitioners of the Art like fey or Milo were dynamic, resisting but also moving, pushing back. The soulless were chilling in that they were absent, sometimes giving the bare sense of a depression or indent where a will might have been, and sometimes not even that.

This was different. It wasn't resistance and it wasn't absence; it was anguish.

Where a will should have been was a gaping cleft, threatening to swallow anything that came too close while bleeding pain and oozing oppression. It was an infected wound, yawning in the psychic space where Ezekiel Bouche should have been.

Milo's eyes began to slide back into focus, but in that space between, he saw an alien light shining and twisting like a halo around Ezekiel's head, forming strange shapes.

The symbols were writing, and as before, Milo could read them if he wished. If he dared.

With a blink, the physical world resolved before his eyes, only the barest after-image remaining. Through that fading panoply of dread, Milo saw the thing that had been Ezekiel smiling down at him.

"I see you too, little man," it purred with a thick, liquid voice the cowboy could have never produced.

Milo blinked again, then looked at Percy Astor, who appeared

AARON D. SCHNEIDER & MICHAEL ANDERLE

to be extremely uncomfortable. The pieces, half-realized and hardly understood, began to click together in Milo's mind, and in some primal instinct, his hands shot out. Percy was thrown back by the sudden assault, but instead of anger, there was only deeper discomfort in his face.

Shame, Milo realized. He was ashamed.

"What did you do?" Milo cried, his throat tightening as his voice shrank to a horrified whisper. "What did you do?"

The inhabited shell of Ezekiel heaved a great crowing laugh, and God help him, Milo was too scared to even look at the thing. His hands tightened into fists, and he felt a sudden, desperate need to beat Percy Astor to quivering pulp. From the look Percy still wore, he might have let Milo do it without protest.

"Milo!" called a strong voice that cut through red fog settling over his mind. "Milo, look at me!"

Milo turned, his body rigid and his movements ungainly, and saw Ambrose coming through the ruins.

"Ambrose," Milo wheezed, his chest tight and his mouth dry. "Do you realize what's happened? What he's done?"

Ambrose nodded and raised his eyes to look at Ezekiel.

"Better than most." He sighed, and where Milo had expected to see righteous wrath, he saw only a weary sadness. The gravity of the melancholy look was almost unbearable as it turned to Percy.

"I don't envy you, young man," he rumbled, shaking his head slowly before he turned back to Milo. "But right now, we've got other things to worry about."

Milo nodded and forced himself to focus. The tumult of the last few moments threatened to overwhelm him, but he needed to shake it off. He had much to tell his companions and even more to ask of them.

But they weren't all together.

"Where is Rihyani?" he asked, looking around, though he realized if she wanted to be seen, she would have appeared.

"Right here," came a silken voice from above. Milo saw the fey descend from the dark sky, silver skin aglow.

Her feet hadn't yet reached the ground before Milo scooped her up in a fierce embrace. She returned it and then pressed kisses upon his neck and cheek until she found his mouth. Her lips, warm and soft, sent a current through him as their bodies pressed and formed together.

"Well, that was refreshing if a bit primal." Rihyani smiled as she drew back from the kiss, Milo's blood on her dark lips.

"Magic can get messy," Milo said with a wink and kissed the vitae from her lips.

Not satisfied with that, she gripped the back of his head and pressed him for a deeper kiss. Milo felt his unsteady hold on his composure tighten into a fearsome grip.

He was Milo the Magus, *De Zauber-Schwartz*, and he had a job to do.

Reluctantly but firmly, Milo broke the kiss and turned so he could see both Ambrose and Percy. He still wasn't ready to acknowledge the giggling horror behind him, but all things in good time.

"Looks like I've got another suicide mission for you," Milo said grimly, nodding at Ambrose before looking at Percy. "And if you're here, you might as well help out."

Ambrose nodded grimly while Percy fiddled with the cuffs of his coat.

"You know my answer, Magus," the big man said, then cocked his head to one side. "But we need to get clear of this spot before a patrol comes sniffing around. Follow me."

With that, they all loped off into the cold darkness of the ruined city.

"What exactly is required for this suicide mission?" Percy asked as they huddled in a gutted home.

They were in another residential area across one of the branches of the Neva from where they'd reunited. Ambrose had taken up watch in the fractured second story of the home, while not-Ezekiel and the Qareen waited in the backyard. Milo, Rihyani, and Percy stood in what might have been a living room that was one wall short, creating an open path to the back of the house.

"Besides the prerequisite acceptance of certain death, of course," the American added with a sniff.

Milo smiled and then winced as he felt fresh blood pool in his mouth. In the moment, he hadn't hesitated to do what was necessary, but now he was wondering if next time there wasn't a better way to tap into the essence of his blood.

"You and that thing," Milo began as he raised a hand to his mouth and jerked his head in the direction of not-Ezekiel. "Gather as much as you can from anything that looks like a home."

Percy opened his mouth to say something, then stopped and frowned at Milo

"I'm sorry," he said with a fair attempt at a jovial chuckle. "What are we gathering? Ash?"

Milo nodded as he swiped at his mouth with his furry sleeve again. He hated to waste so much of his precious fluid, but he didn't seem to have an option at the moment.

"Especially if it might have come from around a fireplace," he said, trying not to choke on the blood. "But we'll take anything that's burnt to powder. Quantity has a quality all its own, after all."

Percy Astor raised his eyebrows and then bowed his head, clearly at a loss.

"Very well." He shrugged and turned to go.

"And get that thing off my horse," Milo said, punctuating the command by spitting a gobbet of blood at the American's feet.

Mr. Astor went off to see an un-man about an undead horse while Milo turned back to his love, shaking his head.

"How did they even get their hands on that thing?" he growled under his breath, blood flecking his lips. "And how did they get it to work?"

He raised his eyes to see Rihyani smiling and hold out her hands.

"I might have had something to do with that," she said, and with a flick of her wrists, there appeared Imrah's cane and his hardened satchel in one hand and his long coat in the other.

"What?" Milo gawked, and with almost childish haste, shuffled out of his soiled furs and into his ensorcelled coat. "How?"

Rihyani laughed as she handed over the cane and satchel.

"I spoke very tenderly to a lock." She smiled, showing her gleaming teeth. "And then I whispered sweet nothings to a safe. I hope you aren't jealous."

I'm sure you understand it was far more complicated than that, Imrah's icy voice droned in Milo's head. *But not nearly as complicated as using that tainted fool Astor to awaken your Qareen.*

Milo's heart leaped into his throat, and his grip on the cane tightened until his fingers popped as he turned the bird skull to face him.

"You taught him magic?" he demanded, his former confidence threatening to topple like a house of cards.

I couldn't if I wanted to, Imrah replied with a psychic impression of a disgruntled huff. *You're still the only human magus, so stop your fretting.*

"Then how did you do it?' Milo demanded, scowling suspiciously at the faintly glowing sockets of the skull.

I channeled some of my power through him, almost like a shade possessing a dead body, the ghul explained. *It was difficult, short-lived, and extremely painful for Astor, but we managed all the same.*

Milo wasn't sure how he felt about the disclosure that Imrah could at least temporarily take over a human body, but even more, he couldn't understand why she would go to all that trouble. The Qareen was useful in a pinch as accelerated transportation, especially when wind-riding wasn't an option, but it wasn't necessary for the rescue. Theatrical certainly, but not worth the difficulties they seemed to have gone through.

Milo expressed his confusion, but before either Rihyani or Imrah could answer, Percy returned with the Qareen's black sack in his hand.

"Because someone had to get word to your forces in Sergio-Ivanoskye to come north," the American said, holding the sack out to Milo, bones clicking softly inside. "And your fairy lover seemed unwilling to make the journey."

Milo looked at Rihyani, who squared her shoulders and raised her chin.

"I wasn't about to leave you unguarded with that lecherous brute," she replied archly, giving Percy an acidic sidelong glance.

"So, Lokkemand is coming here?" Milo asked, trying desperately to not get his hopes up as his gaze swiveled between the two of them. "How long before he arrives?"

Rihyani's gaze sharpened on Percy, who glared back defiantly.

"It's not my fault," he protested, crossing his arms. "If you were so worried about it going well, you might have gone yourself instead of fretting over your darling here."

The fey bared leonine fangs and leaned toward Percy, but Milo held up a hand, and they stilled.

"So, Lokkemand isn't coming?" he demanded.

Rihyani's fangs vanished as she shrugged.

"We don't know," she said, looking at Milo. "He said he would 'see what he could do' and then sent this fool on his way."

"He threatened to shoot me if I didn't get out of his sight," Percy announced with his chin in the air. "Hardly the behavior of an officer."

"Welcome to the German Army," Milo remarked dryly, then leveled a scowl at the American. "Didn't you and your pet abomination have a job to do?"

Percy turned on his heel and began to walk back outside, muttering as he went.

"Typical. Ingrates. That's what I get for taking another operation on this damned continent."

Milo watched him go as Imrah's frosty whisper rose in his mind.

Don't mistake that one for a dandy or a fool, she warned. *I've touched his soul, and besides the corruption, I know none of this was an accident. He's too clever to just happen to be here.*

"But what does he want?" Milo muttered.

The ghul did not answer.

"What's this plan, then?" Rihyani asked, drawing his attention to the immediate concern.

"Our enemy has an army of stolen slaves," Milo said, feeling his skin prickle into gooseflesh even as he spoke. "And we're going to steal them back."

19

THESE SACRIFICES

From above, the city of Petrograd seethed like a disturbed ant nest, roused in the dark of night to defend the colony. Entire companies of soldiers were marshaled, and with electric torches, lanterns, and even armed trucks with spotlights, they swept over the city. The sounds of battle on the wind had alerted sentries that the nest was under attack, but the violence had been too brief to guarantee the location of the assailants. So the barracks, the palace, and even the square within the scrap-metal walls were all emptied.

In places where the buildings were fairly intact, they formed rivers of probing light, flowing down streets as individual lights groped aimlessly at whatever they passed. Occasionally, tributaries and eddies were formed in the blind streams as they found breaks, ruptures, or preexisting pockets in the city's winding streets.

In places where the city was so devastated that a rubble-strewn street was indistinguishable from a collapsed building, the soldiers moved in waves. They lapped over the urban wasteland, slowly but inexorably washing over vast stretches of the city.

For all this incredible, unrelenting effort, none seemed to

think it worthwhile to look above the broken crowns of fire-gnawed buildings. If any had bothered to let their lights stray above those jagged tusks of timber and stone, they might have caught a flash of silver twisting in a ripple of black.

Rihyani rode the cold, howling wind, hardly aware of the smell of sooty snow in the air. Her dark eyes darted across the city, trying to guess the number of soldiers the roving lights suggested. Each time she thought she had the troubling figure, more lights emerged to scour another corner of Petrograd.

There were so many. Too many.

None yet had worked their way to the edge of the city where Milo and Ambrose had hunkered down in an abandoned building, but it was only a matter of time before the tide reached them. As inevitable as the ocean, they would come.

Rihyani checked their rate of advance and swallowed a despairing cry, then cut across the wailing air currents. She came within sight of the leaning, cross-topped building at the city's edge as gray snow began to fall.

"It occurs to me only now," Ambrose grunted as he heaved a pair of trunks commandeered from the ruins, "that this plan involves magic that has a better than fair chance of killing you."

Milo looked up from his preparations, his face paler than usual; his skin looked like the translucent belly of a fish. Given the bowl of churning blood and the perpendicular slashes on his wrists, it would be natural to assume blood loss was responsible for his condition, but that was the least of it. Milo's vital fluid might be roiling about in the bowl, but it was the subsequent essence he'd drawn with the blood that rendered him so corpse-like. The red liquid was only the token of what he was sacrificing to the formula, and not only that, but until the time was right, he had to keep the essence active, or it might diffuse and become useless. If that happened, his plan was shot; he knew a second attempt would kill him before he'd gotten halfway through the preparations.

Despite all this, he still managed to smile at the big man over the bowl of his swirling blood.

"With Imrah's help, I'm much more likely to succeed," he said, doing his best to keep his focus even as he tried to encourage Ambrose. The distraction wasn't welcome, but the bodyguard doing something foolish to thwart him at this stage would be disastrous.

You are being disgustingly optimistic, Imrah grumbled in his mind.

No one asked you, Milo shot back without letting his smile flicker.

"Success is not as important as your survival," Ambrose growled as he laid the trunks down in front of Milo's impromptu workstation. "I mean, besides me not wanting you to die, have you thought about what will happen if you die pulling this off?"

Milo had, several times, but saying that didn't seem likely to shorten this conversation or reassure Ambrose.

"I appreciate the concern, all of it," he said, not having any attention to waste on being irritated. "But this is our only hope for stopping Zlydzen, the Hiisi, and that device he's made."

Ambrose's brows knit together in consternation as he bent and unclasped the trunks. With a frustrated flick, he flipped them open to reveal ash that filled them to the brim.

"Well, these have all been sifted," Ambrose rumbled, crossing his arms. "I've got the American and his pet sifting the rest of what we could gather, but it's not going to amount to much more than half of one of these."

Ambrose scowled down at the trunks, chewing his lip beneath his mustache before raising his gaze to give Milo a pained look.

"Is this going to be enough?"

Milo looked at the two trunks, guessed their dimensions, and tried to do the calculation of how much ash was there, but quickly abandoned the attempt. Even if his attention hadn't been so divided, it wouldn't have done him much good. This was magic, and magic was as much art as science. He had a lot of ash, and he had to believe it would be enough because that belief would be more valuable than more cubic centimeters of material.

"Absolutely," he said, realizing his voice sounded very tired.

This is no way to start the struggle to save all of Europe, he thought idly.

It certainly doesn't bode well for this scheme, Imrah replied to the wayward thought.

You were the one who told me we could pull it off, Milo shot back.

There was silence for a moment, then an icy whisper prickled at his thoughts.

I said we might be able to accomplish it, not that it was a good idea.

Milo shook his head and realized that during his internalized conversation, Ambrose had begun to stare at him.

"What?" Milo asked, an edge forming at the cusp of his voice.

"Are you sure you are okay with what this is going to do?" Ambrose said softly, his green eyes searching Milo's face. "After how you took it in Berlin, I don't want to win a battle just to lose you, and I'm not talking about dying."

Milo had thought a good deal about that point since they hoofed it across the city, and he didn't have a good answer. As they'd run down the streets, he'd had the conversation with himself, his thoughts chasing themselves around his head. He'd settled on the uneasy idea that those he would be offering to the shades were already gone, and they were going to be used to keep a similar fate happening to others. He was certain there was a flaw in the logic, but for the moment, he'd resigned himself to facing whatever regrets and recriminations would come once he wasn't in the thick of things.

For now, there was nothing to be done except to do it.

The wind keened sharply outside, and no one seemed particularly surprised when Rihyani slid through the front door, a flurry of ashen snowflakes chasing her.

"As you expected, Zlydzen's turned most of his soldiers loose," she declared as she moved between the rough benches toward Milo. "I haven't seen any sign of the Hiisi, but they won't come from the woods or the river unless the situation is dire."

Things couldn't have gone better than if he'd planned it this way from the start, but that only sharpened Milo's suspicions. He licked his lips and felt an awful thirst clawing his throat.

Focus! Imrah snarled, and Milo realized with a start he'd allowed himself to let the blood slip from the center of his mind.

His gaze whipped to the blood, where the last of the ripples were racing to the edge of the bowl. He hammered down and sent a needle of his intellect to pierce the settling energies, setting the fluid to roiling again.

"What is it?" the fey asked as Ambrose stepped closer, arms out as though to catch him.

Milo didn't trust himself to speak for half a minute as he stared at the seething blood.

"Lost my focus for a second," he muttered, then looked at Ambrose. "I'm fine, Simon. It's okay."

Ambrose lowered his arms but he kept his place half a stride from Milo. His mustache quivered beneath glistening eyes, but he didn't say anything.

"It's fine," Milo said, looking from the Nephilim to Rihyani and back again, his smile weaker than ever. "It's going to be fine."

You can't keep this up much longer, Imrah warned.

Milo wanted to argue, but he knew she wasn't wrong.

"We need to get that bait together," Milo said to Ambrose, doing his best to sound officerial despite the quaver creeping into his voice. "Please, get Percy and the Ezekiel-thing to help you set that up. This will be enough ash."

Ambrose met his eyes, and for once, Milo didn't feel the gathering pressure attempting to force him to look away. The big man stared at Milo, then with a grim nod, headed out. If Milo hadn't turned to watch him go, he might have missed the look that passed between Rihyani and the big man.

Were they about to try something well-intentioned and foolish to stop him?

Milo found himself grinding his teeth before Ambrose had closed the door behind him.

Rihyani's golden pupils glittered as her eyes narrowed. Milo felt the temptation to start a preemptive argument, but a hiss from Imrah drew his attention back to the blood. Rihyani used the distraction to advance, coming to stand before the trunks, hands held out to the offering of ash.

"Why are you doing this?" she murmured.

Milo shook his head as though the question were a bothersome insect at his ear.

"The ash and its connection to the hearth act as a beacon to the shades," he began distractedly, reciting a section of *Spectral Ruminations* he'd long since committed to memory. "The ash when catalyzed by essence—in this case, my blood—will draw them like moths to the flame. After that—"

"Not what I'm asking," Rihyani said, cutting him off. "I'm asking you why you are choosing this? Why this desperate attack when you could as easily go back to Berlin and make your report?"

Milo felt cold sweat beading on his brow as he felt his mind might split in half, torn between two fronts.

"If I do that, Zlydzen could get the Resonator working at full capacity," Milo said, not bothering to keep the hot edge out of his voice. "He could scoop up thousands before the Germans pulled it together, and that doesn't take into account what roadblocks the Reich might throw up."

"So, it's for expedience, then?" the fey asked, her narrowed gazed threatening to skewer him. "It has to happen fast, and this is the only way? Even if it costs you your life?"

"Yes," Milo said, and he saw a dangerous light flash through Rihyani's eyes. "I don't know. Yes, that's part of it, but I don't have the words. I've got to keep the essence dynamic."

Rihyani pursed her lips and Milo felt her will brush his, an intimate caress flesh could only try to imitate.

Then don't tell me. She sighed as though resting her head against his soul. *Show me.*

So he did.

He allowed the vision that had overwhelmed him in the presence of the Resonator spill out to her. She opened herself to the experience, letting it wash over her. On a level separate from the mental strain of keeping the blood mobile, he felt her will tremble and eventually push back against the vision he'd unleashed. She'd seen enough; she understood. He sealed the vision like a barkeep turning off the tap on a particularly venomous vintage.

It took her a moment to compose herself, but he waited, comforted because she didn't shield herself from him. He felt the raw chaos of her vibrant inhuman emotions rushing past him like unfamiliar winds. When things finally settled, he felt the closeness of her resting against him.

I suppose for a man, there are few better ways to see it done, she whispered. He could taste the smile on her lips.

So I'm dead already, am I?

Rihyani's will stroked his, as melancholy and sweet as the keening of a violin echoing over a moor.

Since the day I met you, my love, she breathed on his soul. *It is the fate of every son of Adam I've ever loved. You are suns born to consume yourself on this cursed earth.*

Milo couldn't hide the roil of emotions that rose in him at the intimations of her heart, but she didn't withdraw even as waves of jealousy and shock lashed her.

I'm older than you can imagine, my love, but my heart, the will of what I am, is still a young lover. I will not love you any less for the parting that will come between us and may love you even more for it. It will break my heart if you spurn me for what I am, but in time, long after you are gone, I will find another to love. Such is my way, and I would have you know it if we go to face the end together. Can you love me still?

The ache in his heart was real, the wild emotions rampant and fierce, but the answer came up from the depths of him all the same.

Yes, he replied, then reached out to touch her with both will and flesh.

She pressed against him, and once again, it seemed that they were made to fit together, every contour melding seamlessly into a glorious whole.

"Then let's go and die well, my love."

The wind was on fire.

Or at least it seemed that it might kindle at any moment as the heaped bonfires' flames licked up and out over a plain of leveled buildings. Tongues of fire lapped the falling snowflakes as they fell, a defiant dragon's breath raised against the descending snowstorm. Milo watched the twists and writhing of the flames and felt a shudder pass through him that had nothing to do with the cold.

He lowered his gaze, dismissing the old memories as he stared over the wasteland.

The first of the lights were coming into sight, at first in small fireteams, but then in whole platoons accompanied by vehicles sporting headlamps. Milo smiled as he watched more and more of them come.

Zlydzen might have been a diabolical schemer, but he was not a creature with military experience, or perhaps he had panicked when Milo escaped. He was using a sledgehammer to swat a fly, and for his trouble, Milo was going to pry that sledgehammer from his hand and use it to smash all his little toys.

"On your word," Percy muttered from where he stood a short way out of the firelight. There was a brass-chafed Very pistol in one hand, prepared to signal some enticing light resistance. They couldn't have the soldiers advancing unopposed and expect someone somewhere not to grow suspicious.

"A little closer," Milo muttered as he stepped next to the trough that had been built to hold the ash. The bowl of blood was in his hands, still churning, with little tendrils of steam emerging as it roiled.

The lights had grown to a wall, a wave of illumination rising out of the cityscape. There were so many.

"Now," Milo said firmly, determined to set things in motion before he lost his nerve.

Percy raised the flare gun and launched a star into the icy wind. The boreal gusts dragged the flare hard to the east, creating a slash of phosphorescent light across the black heavens. As the star became a comet in the howling gale, the sounds of gunfire rose in sharp pops. The deeper, throatier thundercracks of the Gewehr beat out a steady rhythm, while the snapping barks of pistol fire played a wilder tune.

Before Milo's eyes, some of the lights winked out, and he held his breath.

For a moment, the wave of lights slowed, threatening to stall as the foremost points clustered together. Milo's heart sank as he watched the entire advance grind to a halt, trying to take stock of who was shooting at them from the dark.

Had he guessed wrong? Had he thwarted himself?

Then there was a scream like a wildcat insane with rage, and he could make out a silvery flash darting from cover toward a knot of lights. Rifles barked from the huddled points of illumination as men shouted and howled, and then Milo saw the silver streak dart back to where he stood.

The Gewehr and the pistols barked again, but Rihyani's wild charge and retreat had been the ticket. Like a vast beast awoken by having its nose pinched, the army of soulless surged forth, some advancing so quickly they had to be bounding over the broken, rubble-strewn ground like hounds on the chase.

"They're coming," Percy said, face pale and eyes wide as he glanced at Milo. "Can you do it? That many of them?"

Mil stepped to one end of the trough, bowl upraised.

"We're about to find out."

He tilted the bowl, and dribbles of blood fell on the ash with a hiss like new-forged steel being quenched. Milo moved along the length of the trough, letting the blood slide slowly free of its container. As the bowl lightened, he let go with one hand to take up Imrah's cane, which was clenched in the crook of his arm. He leaned on the cane like an old man as he shuffled the last steps of the trough, exhausted in body and soul.

It wasn't a liter and a half of his blood that had drained him but his very essence, his soul. That, combined with the focus he'd had to exert over the last few hours, had left him exhausted and ready to crumple if not for the energies he'd begun to draw from the cane to fortify himself.

Quickly, Imrah urged, a note of anxiety in her voice Milo wasn't sure he'd ever heard before.

From inside his coat, Milo drew out two vials, and with a trembling hand, tore the wax seals off before drinking them together. The taste of sweet onions combined with a cold that numbed him from the inside out brought a surge of twisted and uncomfortable feelings, but the magus shoved them aside as he felt fresh strength and energy pressing through him.

"Now comes the hard part," Milo whispered as he held both his hands over the hissing, roiling pit and let the world of mere physical realities slide off to the side.

Milo's arcane sense opened wide, wider than he ever would have dared, and what he saw filled him with horror. With a clarity beyond sight, he perceived the raging beacon he'd created, the likes of which made the blazing bonfire behind him seem like a child's campfire. Yet for all the furious light his expanded mind perceived, it was only a tiny dot piercing a vast expanse of utter darkness.

And that darkness was hungry.

Seething around the point of light, he could feel the attention of a thousand upon a thousand shades gazing hungrily at the beacon he'd lit. Slithering over each other in such numbers that it was impossible to tell where they ended and the void began, they crept forward with long teeth wetted by lamprey tongues.

They let out a collective rasping snarl no ear could perceive.

Time to play follow the leader, Milo whispered to the dark.

You keep teasing them and they'll rip us both apart, Imrah warned.

Milo turned and beheld her, no longer the disembodied voice in the cane, but her ghulish figure hunched at his side. Her clawed fingers gripped his hand, and for an instant, he felt a gentle strength in the grasp he'd never known when she was alive.

Are you ready for this? he asked, knowing it wasn't just his soul on the line.

It is a poor penance, she replied, bowing her head. *But it is better than I deserve.*

You and me both, he said, and for perhaps the last time, they shared a smile.

Together, they threw their combined magical might into the beacon, fracturing it into a roiling cloud of burning sparks. The horde of shades moaned and clamored, rushing forward, but the sparks were already racing out.

Milo's eyes opened to see that the trough had erupted in a billowing rush of smoke filled with traceries of green lightning and blue fire. The vast cloud rolled out like a poisonous bank of fog to meet the soulless army charging at them.

There were flashes of unearthly brilliance as the sparks and cinders of magically driven ash fell upon hollowed soldiers, and in an instant, shades plunged into the cavities where men had once lived. First tens, then hundreds, and then thousands of hungry echoes chased the beacons into the empty flesh and there nestled in with relish as they turned stolen eyes upon the world.

And with each one that did so, Milo felt them pulling, each shade seeking to snap the cords of blood and soul that bound them to him. He bore down with his mind and heart, refusing to let one strand part as they tugged and snarled. It was like thousands of strings had been tied to individual nerves, and now each was pulling at a different angle and intensity, but all with the intent of breaking him or breaking free. Imrah's strength poured into him, every ounce of her subsumed by him as the struggle grew desperate.

With a scream that rose with an intensity that made his throat strain and tear, Milo roared his command across all boundaries of existence.

OBEY

For a second, it seemed to be too little, too feeble, but he held on, and little by little, the cords went slack. With agonizing slowness that would not let him rest until all surrendered, the shades ceased their struggle.

Milo, blood trickling from his nose and mouth, saw Zlydzen's army turn and look at him. Thousands upon thousands of shades, their pale gleams showing in those dead eyes, watched and waited for their master's command.

Milo began to smile but paused to cough up blood. Wiping his mouth, he bared red-stained teeth to his new army and leveled a finger in the direction of the Neva River.

"Let's get to work."

THESE ALLIES

It soon became apparent that not all of the soulless had been swept up in Milo's incantation as he turned the tide of soldiers back upon itself. The crackle of rifle fire and the scream of men dying bore testament to those who for whatever vagaries of fate had escaped his grasp, but they quickly fell under boot and bayonet. The onslaught was an avalanche in reverse, and within moments it was clear he wouldn't be able to keep up.

"Come up here with me," Rihyani crowed over him as she swept down on a howling gale.

Milo, his heart thrilling at the idea, was about to spring upward when he heard Percy Astor stumbling over the debris-covered ground. He turned and saw the posh American staggering from a snarl of wire, cursing as he glared at fresh holes in the leg of his trousers. Percy must have felt Milo's gaze on him, and he returned Milo's scrutinizing stare, looking abashed.

"Don't stop on my account," he called with a flap of his hand. "I'm not cut from the same rugged, adventurous cloth, but I'll be along as soon as I'm able."

Milo, to his surprise, felt a pang of sympathy for the man, but as he watched the American and felt watched in turn, he began to wonder. What had Percy and not-Ezekiel been sent here for? Milo still didn't know why they'd been in Georgia, and now here they were again, conveniently present to aid them despite previous hostilities. Could "the enemy of my enemy" truly apply here? And now once more, Percy Astor seemed ready to fade into the background of events as he had in Georgia, quietly departing to see to whatever his real business was?

"Go ahead, and let me know when you spot the Hiisi," Milo shouted to Rihyani as he waved her on. "We'll be joining you at the front shortly."

The black bag holding the bones of the Qareen steed hung from Milo's belt, and with a tug, it was in his hand.

"No, no, you go ahead," Percy cried, slowing to a shuffle. "I'm catching my breath, and besides, I prefer not to be at the front of anything."

I don't expect that you do, Milo thought as he ignored Percy and began to undo the bag's drawstrings.

You could shoot him now, Imrah said in a frosty mental wheeze. She sounded so weak he felt a flutter of concern quicken his heart.

Not yet, he replied, though he had to admit the idea had merit. He might be the only check on the abomination he brought with him.

Milo bid the enchanted remains form as he poured them out, setting bones and dried viscera to dance about.

"Really, I would prefer to amble along at my own pace," Percy pressed, beginning to look more nervous than he ought in Milo's estimation. "There's no need to bring me into danger, where I'll be more of a burden than anything."

Milo didn't deign to respond as he watched the unliving construct form.

Fair enough. Imrah sighed. *I suppose you still have to interrogate him to find out how he managed to stuff a corpse like that.*

That hadn't been the top of Milo's priority list, but it was in the upper echelons for certain.

Is that another kind of magic?

Not really, no. More like ritualized communication, at least from what I understand from what Zlydzen taught. Almost likely courtly protocol involving blood sacrifices.

Milo supposed he should be relieved, but as the Qareen finished forming and a pale light kindled in its sockets, he felt nothing so sweet as relief.

At a thought from him, the Qareen knelt before Milo, and he hopped on. With another impulse, it cantered over to Percy, who stood scowling up at Milo.

"Get on," Milo instructed as he held out a hand, his other hand holding the cane so the eyes were surreptitiously facing the American.

Percy's jaw ground back and forth, but finally, he reached out and took Milo's offer with a hand that seemed to be missing a few fingers. The grip, even sans fingers, was hard and clear in its intention. This wasn't over.

With friends like these, Milo thought as he spurred his mount after his charging army.

The advancing shade-bound soldiers met little resistance as they crossed the city. There were outbreaks of gunfire and even grenades erupting, but whenever one of the bodies was too broken to carry on, the shade simply possessed one of its attackers. As a result, even the worst pockets of resistance did nothing to rob Milo's forces of their strength as they marched inexorably to the river.

Mounted on his tireless steed, Milo, with Percy clinging to his back, rode at the head of the loping horde. The Qareen's hooves clattered over cobbles and hunks of rubble as it galloped through streets that were even more hellish than before. Bullet casings scattered in their wake, some rolling through pools of blood seeping from broken bodies. In a few places, small fires somehow found fuel to sputter and crackle. Flashes of his protean memories from the first night he saw Petrograd burn played in Milo's head, but he shook them off with a snarl.

FORWARD

His command played like a spider's tune across the thousands of ethereal strands that bound his army to him. The strain of keeping so many shades mastered was more than he'd feared, but having something at which to direct their violent nature kept him one step ahead of losing control. At this point, it was not so much commanding as channeling the hateful animus, and though he felt a brutal, grinding pain behind his eyes, he pressed on.

They were so close now. At this rate, they would swing wide of the Winter Palace and whatever force remained there and make for the bridges. Once they crossed, Milo could utterly expend his force in destroying the Resonator. Locating and eliminating Zlydzen was secondary, but Milo was almost certain the dwarrow would be with his beloved machine.

That suspicion was confirmed in the worst possible way when Milo reached the street leading to the bridge Roland had taken to the Resonator's island.

The vanguard of his forces, mounted on various vehicles, had begun to cross the bridge, while the bulk of the army on foot formed a packed throng behind the outriders. Small-arms fire from buildings across the river peppered the shade-bound, but flesh wounds were of little concern to the bloodthirsty creatures. Return fire from Milo's forces was sporadic and unorganized, but he didn't bother to change that. They needed to cross and get to the machine.

As the undead horse cantered around the edge of the massed soldiers making their way onto the bridge, Milo stared across the length of the bridge and saw a trio of squarish shapes sidling over to block it. Astride one of the crawling behemoths was a squat figure that could have only been dwarrow.

"They gave him tanks," Milo muttered in surprise before a trio of 5.7-centimeter Maxim-Nordenfelt cannons bellowed. The forwardmost vehicles on the bridge came apart in eruptions of broken men and twisted metal. One shot lanced through one truck, only to plow into a car before cratering a section of the bridge. The fractured remains of automobiles and bodies hadn't even finished falling to the deck and the river below when machine guns began to chatter. Heavy 7.92-millimeter rounds filled the air, perforating the light vehicles and the frontrunners of the forces on foot. The bodies of men crumpled, only to be trampled under the press of shade-bound still clamoring to charge.

The cannons fired again, and the few remaining members of the automotive vanguard crashed into and over the mangled remains of their comrades.

"Those are German tanks!" Percy shouted in alarm, his fingers tightening painfully on Milo's shoulder as the other hand pointed at the mobile bulwarks. "They're German, aren't they?"

"Yes, A7Vs," Milo growled, then freed his shoulder with a savage twist. "Now shut up unless you have something useful to say."

The shades sprang free of bullet-chewed hosts, but there weren't any spare bodies near at hand. Like salmon swimming upstream, the specters tried to rush across the bridge, but even those who didn't expend themselves crossing the distance discovered that they found few hosts. It seemed whoever or whatever was guarding the bridge were not soulless.

Some of the freed shades attempted to burrow into the occupied bodies around them, and those that weren't immediately rebuffed set the bodies to tearing themselves apart. In the space of a few seconds, hundreds had fallen, and the advance stalled.

WITHDRAW

SEEK COVER

RETURN FIRE

The commands rippled out, and the shade-driven struggled to comply. They were packed together, and the limits of flesh were an ill-understood frustration to them. Nearly as many fell in the floundering withdrawal as in the initial onslaught, as Zlydzen's forces continued to gnaw at his stumbling army. The shade-driven hunkered in whatever cover they could find and opened fire in sporadic pockets with no coordination and little precision. Their shots rattled off the tank armor or kicked up brick dust in the occupied buildings, and Milo was uncertain it would have made any difference.

Looking beyond the tanks, Milo saw the Resonator looming like an ugly mountain glittering with malice. So close, so very close.

"Milo!" cried a voice above him. He was thrown bodily to the ground, Percy coming down on top of him. As the breath was driven from his lungs by the American's weight, Milo spied the flash of silver-white hair. A second later, a 5.7-centimeter shell blasted through the Qareen horse as though it were offal in a paper sack. Milo raised an arm over his head as gobs of dry, chunked flesh and splinters of old bone rained down around him.

"Get off," Milo wheezed as he attempted to free his arms from under Percy's bulk.

"Sorry about that," Percy replied with a nervous, almost manic chuckle as he clambered off Milo, but he kept low to the ground. A glance showed they'd fallen behind what might have once been a decorative wall. They were screened from lighter arms, but if the tanks shelled the spot, they'd be paste in seconds.

"Move!" Milo snarled as he twisted onto his belly and began to crawl along the wall toward an embankment of debris that must have been the home or business the wall had been attached to. Percy followed, muttering something about his suit as his belly dragged over the cracked and jagged ground.

They reached the pile of apocalyptic detritus as two more cannon shots plowed furrows where they'd lain seconds earlier.

"Keep moving," Milo shouted over his shoulder as he rose to his feet and ran doubled over to a building that still stood a few feet away.

Machine guns chugged, sending up stinging splashes of broken plaster and stone around them, but somehow Milo and Percy staggered into what looked like the storeroom of a shop. Kicking over broken crates and knocking over shelves, they found another door that opened to the storefront, where they leaped over a counter and hunkered down.

Cannons boomed and machine guns flung a hail of shots at them, but nothing seemed to be striking too close for comfort. Chests heaving and soaked in sweat, both men lay against the store's counter and caught their breath.

Percy began to inspect his thoroughly ravaged vest, jacket, and slacks, while Milo stretched his mind to his dwindling army.

Between enemy fire and the shades attacking each other, he'd lost nearly a fifth of his forces in the space of a minute, maybe two. Worse, he wasn't sure he had a way forward with the forces he had left. If he tried to press across the bridge, he'd lose more, and those lost would see their shades inflicting greater casualties.

And the Hiisi hadn't even come into play yet.

There was the crunch of broken glass under boots, and Milo saw not-Ezekiel stride into the shop through the broken front door. It sported several new wounds across its body and one side of the face had been rent, now just flaps of sickly gray flesh hanging off discolored bone. The exposed teeth made the manic smile even larger and more horrific than before.

"Found you," it called in a thick, syrupy voice, and Milo noticed that something had punctured the body's throat, from which dark, almost tarry blood now ran.

"Yes, you did," Percy said, sounding quite put out as he made a feeble and futile attempt to smooth his jacket. "Wasn't the plan for you to help with the distraction and then return to me?"

The un-man spread his gnawed hands wide and gestured expansively at Percy and then the shop.

"I'm here now, aren't I?"

Percy made a disgusted sound in the back of his throat and shook his head.

There was another crunch of glass outside and Ambrose came jogging into the store, shouldering roughly past not-Ezekiel, who only giggled.

"We need to do something about those tanks," he rumbled with a nod at the far wall, beyond which the sounds of battle were evident. "And I think I've got an idea."

Milo looked up at him from his place on the floor, trying not to wince every time he felt a shade abandon its body to the wraith and expire. If things kept up at this rate, it wouldn't be long before half of his forces were gone.

"I'm all ears," Milo muttered.

"We'll need Rihyani and the killer sand," Ambrose began.

"Si'lat," Milo replied, but Ambrose waved off the correction.

"Whatever. You're going to give one to me and one to this thing," the big man continued, tilting his head at the un-man. "You'll need to be ready to set them loose as soon as we pop them into the tanks, but once inside, they should make quick work of the men. That should give us a chance of making it across that bridge."

Milo started shaking his head before Ambrose finished speaking.

"I've only got two si'lat," Milo protested. "You've got three tanks."

"Let me worry about that," Ambrose growled. "I'm giving you a chance to get your army across the bridge, and you're going to whine to me about arithmetic?"

Milo met the big man's eyes and remembered the first thing

he'd learned about his bodyguard: Simon Ambrose didn't need to lie. If he said he could take care of the tanks, then by Heaven and Hell, he would.

"All right." Milo groaned as he struggled to his feet. "But where's Rihyani?"

In answer, a feline yowl overlaid across a corvid squawk somewhere above the street outside. Milo and Ambrose rushed to the exploded display window as a thrashing comet came hurtling out of the dark, snow-strewn sky.

Milo had the fleeting impression of enormous black wings and something that was a blur of fangs and talons. The plunging spectacle struck the street with a chorus of crunching bones and an eruption of black feathers. Shrieking black birds of every shape and size rocketed out of the dark cloud, leaving the fey to spin and rake her claws at empty air.

"COWARD!" she screamed after the fleeing corvids, then whirled around to fix Milo with a savage stare.

"The Hiisi are coming."

Milo looked at Ambrose, who nodded and stepped to Rihyani.

"I'm going to need you to make a little storm for me, *mon chéri*."

"This is going to be fun," the un-man burbled in the back of its ruined throat.

Ambrose growled as he adjusted his grip around the creature's narrow waist.

"One more word and I'll be doing this by myself," Ambrose growled.

Not one to miss out on such suicidally violent antics, the thing that had been Ezekiel Bouche settled for a gurgling titter of laughter before holding out a bony hand to Milo.

"I'm still not sure how this is going to work." The magus

sighed as he handed over an orb while doing his best not to touch the ravaged fingers. "But we don't have time for another plan."

"Your confidence in me is inspiring." Ambrose chuckled as he reached out to take his orb.

They all turned to Rihyani, who'd spent the last few minutes communing with the winds through the Art. High overhead, dark clouds had begun to gather, though not a snowflake had fallen since she'd stepped aside to begin her efforts.

"You two should get inside." She nodded at Milo and Percy. "This isn't going to be gentle."

Not needing a second warning, both men darted into the store as the winds began to pick up once more.

Milo watched from inside, feeling the deteriorating state of the shade-driven like a rough file scraping at the back of his mind. If this didn't work, they would be caught between the Hiisi and the Zlydzen's armored praetorians. That would be the end of this push and the beginning of the end for Europe.

Flurries began to descend in spiraling patterns around the three standing in the middle of the street. The howl of the wind grew until the sounds of the battle were drowned out by its keening. Occasionally, gunfire from a street over intruded with a stray shot zipping past into the night, but soon even those were washed out in rushing torrent of sound that accompanied a descending cyclone of cloud and snow. Milo couldn't hear anything besides the eardrum-throb of the changing air pressure, but he saw the un-man's head thrown back in maniacal laughter before the cyclone swallowed the three remaining in the street.

Milo hammered a fist on Percy's shoulder and shouted words neither of them could hear.

"Come on!"

Together they rushed back to the storeroom, punctured and battered as it was, then crept to the edge of the back doorway to watch the scene at the bridge.

The crackle of rifles and machine guns was a barely perceptible background to the howl of the unnatural weather that seethed overhead. Occasionally the roar of a cannon would punch through, but even that was only a dull, crunching boom. A second later, all of it was muted as the cyclone descended, spraying snow in every direction. For a second, Milo thought the storm had the force to sweep the tanks aside like children's toys, but the low-slung war machines bore the tearing gales with impunity. One of the walls left standing beside the rightmost behemoth teetered and fell, though it didn't have the decency to fall on the armored giant.

As quickly as it had descended, the enchanted storm began to rise and dissipate, leaving the far side of the bridge crusted in snow and two of the A7Vs bearing new passengers.

Milo watched as Ambrose scrambled across the snow-slicked surface of the tank. One leg dragged, evidence that his descent had not been gentle, but he managed to reach the access hatch. With an ease that belied the terrifying strength on display, Ambrose tore the door loose and threw the orb in.

At the same time, out of the corner of his eye, Milo saw that the un-man had taken a different approach. Limbs moving like a poorly controlled marionette's, the abomination crawled spider-like along the side of the tank until it reached a machine-gun port. With a wild cackle, it pushed the chattering weapon aside, not caring how the barrel scorched its ruined hands, and shoved the orb inside.

With both orbs delivered, Milo drove forth a spike of focus to release the si'lat. He'd intended to do as he'd done before, asserting control as he set them loose, but this time, he found he couldn't. His vision blurred and blood gushed from his nose, and it took every ounce of mental energy he could muster to keep control of the shade-driven.

The si'lat were set free, and he could only watch and dare to hope as the tanks began to rock and shiver. Two of the cannons and several machine guns fell silent, but in their absence, a new sound rose on the wind. To the south, Milo heard guttural howls and screams. The Hiisi were coming.

"Now or never." Milo coughed, tasting more blood.

His eyes fixed on the looming Resonator, Milo wove together the strands of his remaining army around a single lightning rod of a command.

DESTROY

Milo hurled the command with all the entwined cords of control like a thunderbolt at the Resonator. The sudden release of the crushing pressure he'd borne took his breath away, and with a cry that was both pain and ecstatic relief, he sank to his knees.

With a keening moan no human throat could have uttered, the shade-driven sprang up and rushed across the bridge. Their frustration and confusion at being held at bay gave their strides preternatural speed, and though one tank still poured its fury across their flank, the tide could not be stemmed. Like hounds catching the scent, wraiths wearing the skins of men hurtled over the broken and the dead to their target. They reached the quivering tanks and didn't slow, scuttling over and around them even as one burst into flames

The Resonator would fall; this Milo knew. Now it was a matter of getting out of here alive.

"Fetch your pet," Milo called over his shoulder to Percy. "I'm going to get my friend."

He made it two strides before he realized no response had come from the American.

The wizard whirled and found himself alone. Once more, Percy Astor had slipped into the dark. Milo swore savagely and contemplated searching for signs of the slippery provocateur when the bark of a Gewehr drew his attention back to the bridge.

He looked up in time to see Ambrose hurled bodily off the remaining A7V while Zlydzen in his ogre form loomed over the tank, which had begun to smoke and shudder. Zlydzen didn't seem to notice the tank's distress as one massive hand hefted a hammer as tall as a man. His enraged glare was fixed on Ambrose as he shakily rose to his knees.

Milo was moving before he realized what was happening, summoning witchfire through the cane as he leaped over the mounded dead.

We don't have the strength for this, Imrah protested.

"We don't have a choice." Milo panted as he leaned into the biting wind, his eyes fixed on the dwarrow's hammer, which rose for a smashing strike.

Milo punched out with the cane, launching a spear of emerald fire. After arcing through the air, it struck the dwarrow in the shoulder and raced over his uplifted arm. Bellowing like a wounded bull, Zlydzen let the hammer tumble from his grip as he threw himself on the ground. The snow hissed and a cloud of steam rose, but the fire was quenched. Zlydzen heaved himself to his feet with a snarl.

Milo had used the reprieve to reach Ambrose, who was staggering to his feet. He threw an arm under the big man in time for them to race for cover as the smoldering A7V brought a pair of machine guns to bear. A hail of bullets chewed up the ground at their heels as they dove for the shelter behind piled remains of the wall that had collapsed during the storm.

"You all right?" Milo shouted over the hammering of the automatic fire.

Ambrose's green eyes struggled to focus for a second, but then his gaze locked onto Milo's face. A smile spread beneath his mustache, and he nodded as he chambered another round in his rifle.

"Never better," he shouted back and spared a glance over his shoulder. "Give it a minute."

Between ripping bullets and fragments of masonry flying in every direction, Milo saw the dwarrow's back receding behind the smoke-belching tank. Zlydzen seemed to think he could still save his creation. Milo couldn't risk that he was right.

"We don't have a minute," Milo called and looked across the bridge.

Was it his imagination, or were those hungry red eyes moving between the buildings across the river?

The tank behind them gave a series of heavy clanks, then its engine stalled and its guns fell silent. Its hatch blew open with a screaming eruption of flame and shrapnel. Ammunition cooked off in a series of staggered detonations that forced both men to hunker down to avoid the discharging shells and bullets that flew in all directions.

"You young folks." Ambrose chuckled as he lurched to his feet. "Always in a hurry."

Shaking his head, Milo joined Ambrose on his feet, and they skirted around the burning wreck. Expecting to race after the retreating dwarrow, both staggered to stop when they saw that Zlydzen had not been so lucky when the tank exploded. Pitched over on his side, Zlydzen leaked his brazen blood from a dozen bullet wounds across his broad back, while one leg must have taken a cannon shell. The foot was still attached but only just, most of the calf having been reduced to a dangling curtain of shredded meat.

One hand clawed for the hammer he'd dropped, but swooping down like a bird of prey, Rihyani raked talons across his outstretched hand. The dwarrow swatted at her, but the fey easily dodged the clumsy swing.

"I'll crush you," he raved and swung again.

He missed again, but he twisted as he did and fell flat on his stomach, his head turned to Milo and Ambrose as they advanced.

"It's over, Zlydzen," Milo called, letting witchfire play across the head of his cane. "The Resonator is being reduced to scrap as we speak, and what's left of your army is mine."

"Nothing's over," the dwarrow snarled, trying to raise himself before collapsing onto his side with a groan.

"You don't look so good," Ambrose remarked dryly as he sighted down his Gewehr.

"I'm not done," Zlydzen growled, hands curling into frustrated claws.

"Yes, you are," Milo said and raised his cane as an ear-sundering howl rent the air.

Milo reeled, his concentration shivering to pieces as he raised his hands to his ears.

He staggered a step back as the sound receded, looking around dazedly, ears ringing.

A pair of huge red eyes set in long lupine face shone from the shadow of a collapsing alley.

"No, I'm not," the dwarrow chuckled. "You aren't the only one with friends."

THESE WOUNDS

Borjikhan had come, and he hadn't come alone.

The city seethed with Hiisi in various bestial forms, each more awful than the last. Turning in place, Milo saw a coal-black horse walking on two legs with a mane of blue flame and tusk-filled jaws opposite the monstrous wolf. Continuing to rotate, he saw behind him crawling onto the bridge the slippery bulk of Tsar'Vodyanoy, as hale and openly grinning as before. In juxtaposition to its lumbering, a serpentine horror with a head resembling a woman who'd traded her jaws for those of a pike gracefully slithered. Overhead something with huge leathery wings swooped by, and Milo had the impression of a batlike snout filled with teeth over a scaly body.

Second by second, more nightmares crept and slithered and loped into view. Some were the size of large dogs, some bigger than the defunct tanks that sat sizzling in the snow.

"You got closer than anyone has ever come." Zlydzen chuckled as he slowly dragged himself into a sitting position, his wounded leg stretched out before him. "But I've been planning this for too long and sacrificed too much to let even an oddity like you spoil this."

"Our fight is with the dwarrow," Rihyani snarled as she swept her gaze across the circle of glowing, hungry eyes. "The Hiisi have always stayed out of the fighting between Shepherds and the Guardians. Coming to his side will be a declaration of war."

A chorus of hissing, screeching, and snarling rose in mocking answer to the fey's warning.

"Not if none ever find you, pretty pixie," the pike-mouthed serpent cooed, lank hair hanging about her sallow face. "I have a perfect spot in my garden where I'll keep you safe and drowned."

The upright horse snorted and tossed its head.

"Not if I take her first," it slavered, bilious spittle dripping from its fangs as it thrust its hips forward with a grunt. "I'll beget a handsome crop of bastards on her before she finally breaks."

The monsters chortled gleefully at the proposition, all except the woman-headed snake, which clapped its jaws together angrily.

They're not an army, Milo realized. *Just a band of thugs.*

And bound to their old ways, Imrah mumbled in his mind, the effort of communication being a strain. *Remember, these are creatures of the First Wood who see themselves as gods.*

So, archaic ideas of honor and shame might mean something to them, Milo thought, his mind racing as he turned to glare at Borjikhan.

Imrah did not answer, but a sense of affirmation radiated from the cane that went beyond words.

Milo stepped toward the monsters, looking at each of them as he lifted his voice.

"Gods of the First Wood," he shouted, drawing every baleful eye to him. "Before we come to blows, may I humbly ask to be heard?"

There was tittering and jabbering at the request, the great wolf laughing the loudest.

"Begging for your life now, witch child?" Borjikhan chuckled in the back of its throat. "How disappointing."

Milo couldn't have asked for a better setup.

Forcing back a smile, he whirled and shot a furious glare, undaunted and shining with indignation, at the wolf.

"I will fight and die as is fitting, but I ask this," Milo roared and pointed a condemning finger at the huge lupine. "Do not allow that unworthy cur to gnaw my bones! If I fall, it is in sacrifice to gods, not as a carcass for some cringing scavenger!"

The host of monsters fell silent, several of them blinking at Milo while a few turned their glowing gazes on Borjikhan.

A rumble like a building volcanic eruption shook inside the shadow-wrapped Hiisi as it glared at Milo.

"You dare!" it snarled. "You *DARE!*"

Milo threw back his head and laughed. The sound was forced and harsh, but he managed it with a leering smile.

"At least the mighty Tsar'Vodyanoy was brave enough to do battle with me," Milo taunted, sweeping his hand at the blubbery monster. "Not only me but my allies as well. You slunk away like a whipped dog before me, and I expect you'll let these true Hiisi bring me down before you come and nip at my heels this time."

"LIAR!" Borjikhan roared, the sound rising to an ear-shredding level once more. "I'll eat your heart for such blasphemy, such deception."

From a broken window, a familiar croaking laugh sounded.

"No lies, Borji, no lies," Lempo squawked as it rocked on the windowsill in the shape of a huge malformed raven. "Magus chased you away, he did, he did, and the Heart Eater ran, ran with tail between his legs."

Borjikhan snarled to contest the mocking raven, but the words were lost in a howling chorus of laughter from dozens of monstrous throats. The great wolf turned its toothsome snarl this way and that, but all met it with derision and more jeering laughter. Doubt and rage twisted its features until with a venomous glare at Milo, it threw back its head and howled with mind-shattering potency.

"I CHALLENGE THE MAGUS!"

It took Milo a moment to realize that the silence which followed was not because of his ringing ears. Every Hiisi again alternated between staring at Milo and Borjikhan.

"A challenge has been called!" they wailed in unison, a horrible blood-curdling sound. "A challenge will be answered!"

Every inhuman eye fell on Milo. For a second, he fumbled for something to say and settled for a pugnacious sniff and a toss of his head at the huge wolf.

"About time."

The gathered Hiisi screeched their approval and fell back several paces. It seemed the challenge was imminent.

"We don't have time for this!" Zlydzen bellowed, struggling to his stand on his good leg. "Kill these fools and be done with it."

The Hiisi growled and hissed at the injured dwarrow.

"You swore an oath!" he spat, but that was the wrong thing to say.

Every Hiisi turned unfriendly eyes on him, seething.

"We do things our way," the standing horse growled as it pawed the ground with one jagged hoof, sending up sparks from the cobbles. "We are allies, not slaves, dwarrow."

Tsar'Vodyanoy gave a resounding belch that filled the air with a charnel stink.

"And last I smelled, your store of offerings was greatly diminished," the blubbery monster grumbled. "It seems you will be taking this service on credit."

The dwarrow, undaunted by the host of unfriendly faces, flapped a huge bleeding hand at the bodies strewn across the bridge.

"There is flesh a-plenty. Eat your fill," he growled, shifting his weight uneasily.

Every Hiisi visibly recoiled at the suggestion.

"The hollow stuff you offer is poor enough," the pike-mouth

rasped. "But shade-tainted meat? Is this how Zlydzen the Engineer treats his friends?"

The ogre looked around and saw the dangerous gleam in the eyes of the assembled congregation of horrors. With a heavy sigh, he took up his hammer, and with a sickening series of slurping pops, shrank to his stunted form, the hammer shrinking with him. He leaned on the stout-hafted hammer like a crutch and gave a slow nod of acquiescence.

"Fine." He glared from underneath his eyebrows at Milo. "Have your pageantry, but make it quick. Who knows when reinforcements might be coming?"

The assembled Hiisi gave a monstrous cheer and turned to watch the spectacle.

Borjikhan padded forward, dragging the shadows with him like a cloak.

"I will make your death scream echo through the ages!"

The triumph Milo felt at challenging Borjikhan evaporated the instant the challenge began.

He'd managed to bluff the lupine Hiisi into retreat, but now he wasn't sure how that had happened. The beast's night-wrapped shoulder was as tall as a horse, and the long body padding forward seemed even more massive. It was as though someone had taken a wolf and decided the lean frame would be better served if an additional layer was applied. Despite the obvious mass, the creature's steps didn't make a sound, and its clawed paws left no imprint upon the fresh snow.

As the great wolf began to stalk in a wide circle, Milo mirrored the movement and sent an urgent thought out to both Imrah and Rihyani.

All right, somebody tell me something useful.

Don't get eaten, Imrah offered. *And don't be afraid. Hiisi savor the emotions of their quarry.*

Borjikhan's lips peeled back in a smile, revealing gleaming fangs. Milo fumbled a step as he considered the serious question of why every evil thing and its brother seemed to have teeth like knives. Being eaten would be unpleasant, he was sure, but why did they all seem to have dentistry that made such things so likely?

Don't try to run away or even reposition outside of this circle, Rihyani whispered. *Hiisi are notoriously picky, and even floating could provoke them all to attack.*

Borjikhan's damson tongue traced lasciviously across its fangs.

I am hearing a whole lot of what not to do! Milo snapped across the psychic channel even as he fought to keep a sanguine exterior. *What I need is some advice on what I should do!*

LOOK OUT!

Acting on raw instinct, he threw himself to the left. Milo drew on the cane for strength, and though he didn't get as much as he'd expected, he managed to clear a pair of snapping jaws made of raw shadow that emerged at his feet. He was still dancing across the snow-slicked ground when the beast vaulted toward him, claws and jaws stretched wide.

Fighting the instinct to backpedal, Milo launched, aiming to pass beneath the gaping maw. His unstable footing betrayed him, though, and with an undignified shout, he lurched into a shallow dive.

He felt streamers of hot spittle slap his ducking face as teeth filled his vision. A surge of hope erupted inside of him at the realization the fangs had missed him, which vanished the instant he realized they had missed his head and hooked the back of his high collared coat. His flight was arrested, and his body snapped back with bone-popping force. Milo tried to free his pistol from his belt, but he only managed to have it tumble from his grip as Borjikhan shook him like a slipper.

The world became a discombobulating pinwheel where the street and the sky exchanged places with terrifying alacrity. Milo drew on the cane to fortify his bones and joints against the violent movements, knowing that without it, he would be shaken to jelly.

He had just enough awareness to sense the incredible hatred radiating from the Hiisi, transmitted to his will like heat radiating from forge-heated iron. His skin prickled with the intensity of it, and he had an idea despite the brutal knockabout he was receiving.

Unfortunately, the second after that thought, he was sent flying through the air by a sharp toss of Borjikhan's head.

Milo would have liked to think the scream that escaped his lips was one of challenge and not terror as he sailed through the air, but the hard landing knocked all breath and any illusions clean out of him. The enchanted coat protected him from the worst of the impact, but despite everything, he was slow to get up. Gasping and wheezing, he managed to make it onto one knee as the spectating monsters hooted and jeered.

"And you doubted me!" Borjikhan bayed, swinging his burning eyes around the circle. "You thought some capering ape could stand before me! Me, the Moon Hunter, Chorusmaster of World's End."

Milo saw the great wolf's back exposed as it defied its fellows, and, his germ of a plan momentarily forgotten, lashed out with a volley of witchfire.

Borjikhan didn't leap out of the way so much as melt into a ripple of shadow that slid away from the sorcerous blast as quick as thought. The standing horse gave a bestial snort as he ducked the bolt meant for the wolf.

"Careful, Czernoboch." Borjikhan laughed, waving his

shadow-wreathed tail like a teasing pennant. "I'll protect you from the nasty little witch."

Milo saw the shadows slithering along the ground toward him this time and fortunately remembered his plan before they reached him.

Shadowy jaws, umbral imitations of slavering canine fangs, rushed up from the ground and plunged into boots.

"Nowhere to run this time," Borjikhan snarled as it sprang forward, jaws wide since the captive human possessing no ready means of escape. Milo's belligerent yell became an agonized scream as fangs longer than men's hands finger to wrist punched through fabric, tore meat, and cracked bones. With a sickening, slurping crunch, the jaws met, and everything below the waist fell to the snow with a sloppy thud.

Borjikhan, drunk on its victory, danced around the bloody circle holding the gory trophy high for all to see.

"Who doubts now?" it called despite a mouth full of broken meat and bone.

The other Hiisi stood mute, their gaze fixed not on Borjikhan, but on a space several strides away by the defunct tanks.

Milo, desperate for any arcane strength he could muster, released the illusion as he reached out to the unbound si'lat lurking within. The shades infusing the constructs, glutted on the massacre of the crews, were sluggish in responding. He needed them now, but they seemed obstinately opposed to being yoked to his mind once more.

"The coward fled!" Borjikhan snarled as the jeering of his fellow Hiisi needled him.

"Chase your tail, silly dog," the pike-mouth called with a warbling laugh. "Maybe then you'll find him."

Czernoboch neighed savagely as its tusks raked the air.

"Your quarry eludes you, Moon Hunter!"

Milo knew he had less than two heartbeats before Borjikhan's fangs sank into his neck for real, so he bent entirely toward taming the si'lat.

His eyes watered and his tongue tasted blood in the back of his throat, which he used as fuel as he drove the hammer of his mind down on a spike of focus.

OBEY

There was the press of resistance, but then the spike drove through and burst into a thousand barbed shards all bound inexorably to him.

They were his.

His howl of rage and lethal intent matched the great wolf's as he whirled to meet the beast's lunging charge. Milo saw the huge teeth lining the hideously stretched maw but didn't shrink away as the shade-driven sand rushed past him and into the waiting jaws of death. For all its weight and momentum, Borjikhan was thrown back as though its charge had been checked by a hammer blow.

As the great wolf struck the ground, the shadows scattered like shards of pottery fleeing the scene of a dropped vase. In their absence, the freakishly muscled lupine form was laid bare, along with its mangled patches of fur and knotted whorls of scar tissue.

Milo didn't give the creature a chance to gather itself but wielded the si'lat in sweeping waves that sent sheaves of fur and flesh flying into the air like wheat chaff before a thresher.

"I am Borjikhan," it panted as it struggled to climb to its feet. "I bring the Dark. I am the fear behind the howl... I...I am..."

"Dead," Milo said, the word hard and flat as he drove the si'lat, condensed into titanic spears, through the Hiisi's body.

Borjikhan gave a choked whine as it was dragged off its feet by the rising skewers. Milo's outstretched hand curled into a fist, and with a chorus of grinding pops, the spears tore free. What was left of Borjikhan fell to the ground with four bloody splats.

Milo didn't bother to look at the other gaping Hiisi as he turned a lethal glare on Zlydzen.

"Now," he said icily, "where were we?"

The dwarrow stood leaning on his hammer, smirking at Milo.

"Come at me with all you have, Magus." Zlydzen chuckled, sweeping one huge hand over his person. "If you are so powerful, reach out and strike me down."

His blood up and adrenaline coursing through him, Milo nearly complied, but Imrah's thoughts, barely a whispered impression, played across his mind.

Beware, she murmured. *Beware.*

Milo squinted at the leering dwarrow, then reached out with his will, the nape of his neck prickling with the premonition of something unseen.

His will felt that opaque wall he'd first experienced in Georgia, the warding that was proof against magic. Was Zlydzen hoping to make a show of blocking Milo's magic for the benefit of the Hiisi, rallying them to attack once more? And were the wards as invulnerable as they believed?

As Milo flexed his will against them, he was certain he felt a subtle aetheric movement.

"What are you waiting for?" Zlydzen snapped, slapping a hand against his chest. "Finish it and prove yourself the victor. I would gladly give my life for the Guardians, so strike!"

Milo did not strike, but he leaned hard into the wards with his will, a sort of psychic shove, sensing something he was certain was the dwarrow on the other side. With a breathless curse, he learned he was wrong.

These were not the same wards, but something far more insidious.

If his will had been a ripple, the retaliatory magic was a tidal wave ripping across the space between them. Milo sensed it coming, but it was as though he was watching his hand turn against him. The rebounded and amplified echo of his will crashed upon his psyche, and he screamed as his senses exploded.

It was freezing cold and searing heat, crushing silence and

shredding shrieks. Every synapse, fooled and fouled by the Art, experienced the extreme of every sensation. Milo reeled, dropping the fetish cane and gripping his head as the agony crested, echoing and reverberating through him.

He knew it wasn't real, wasn't happening, his will was telling him it was so, and his body seemed unable to believe it wasn't true.

He felt a terrible psychic tremor growing inside him like some sort of eldritch feedback screech. Milo felt it shivering along the connections binding the si'lat to him and even the shade empowering his coat. The feedback grew and the magical links began to tremble violently, bleeding essence.

Milo threw back his head and screamed both physically and metaphysically as the feedback exploded out of him. Snow, dust, and the remains of Borjikhan flew away from him as a pressure wave of detonating magic ripped through his frame.

The si'lat sank to the street, inert sand to be blown around by the chill winds of Petrograd.

Milo's blackcoat hung about him once more, nothing more than a piece of cloth, its pockets filled with the dust of that which once filled its extra-dimensional pockets.

The magus sank to the ground and retched, then raised his head at the sound of Zlydzen's grating cackle.

"Behold the mighty magus, bright hope of humanity," the dwarrow squawked triumphantly as he turned to the gaping Hiisi. "See with what poise and power he claims his victory."

Milo spat out a curse along with more bile, which made the shrunken monster titter all the louder.

"So genteel, too." Zlydzen snorted, his eyes gleaming with delight.

"My brothers-in-arms," the dwarrow said with a raised voice. "I hope this renews your faith in our cause. True, the Resonator has been damaged beyond use by this fool and his pawns, but there's no reason we cannot build again. Everything lies within my notes for an even grander design and one less dependent."

The incredulous looks of the Hiisi obviously chafed him.

"Yes, the Guardians have faced a setback, but our greatest enemy lies at your feet, doesn't he?"

Zlydzen turned back to Milo and gave a disdainful flick of his overlarge hand.

"Devour him if you like, but let us quit this place. We have so much work to do."

Zlydzen gave one last sneering look at Milo and turned his back.

"These humans won't exterminate themselves."

The dwarrow pitched forward, his head coming apart in a spray of copper blood.

The cranial explosion occurred as the Gewehr's throaty roar echoed through the streets of Petrograd.

Ambrose lowered the rifle from his shoulder and spat into the snow.

"Exterminate this, Armageddon that," Ambrose muttered. "Why can't we murder each other without all the delusions of grandeur?"

Rihyani was at Milo's side as soon as the dwarrow's body hit the street, drawing him to his feet. Milo felt as though every bone in his body was broken, and he leaned without shame or pretense on her shoulder.

Despite his fatigue, he felt the tension in her svelte form, and he saw that the hand not holding him was splayed, talons exposed. His eyes traveled up to her face, and he saw her fangs bared as her dark eyes swept left to right and back again. He followed her gaze and saw the Hiisi leaning in hungrily.

"Thank you for removing that little fool." Czernoboch snorted, his eyes settling on Rihyani. "Things were growing stale with him anyway."

"Very much appreciated, yes," the serpentine creature warbled in her watery voice. "But now that all that's settled, we still have to decide what to do with you."

"Couldn't say you owe us one and leave it at that?" Ambrose grunted as he raised his rifle back to his shoulder.

The Hiisi hissed as they leaned forward, teeth dripping.

"Now, where's the fun in that?" rumbled Tsar'Vodyanoy.

The numbness of Zlydzen's attack was beginning to dissipate, but Milo knew that by the time he recovered, it would be too late. He'd be dead or very much wishing he was. Looking at the gaping maw of Tsar'Vodyanoy, he thought about the skeletons formerly moldering in the beast's vast stomach.

It was almost hilarious that he'd emptied the creature's belly, only to be one of those about to fill it.

Ambrose shrugged and looked at Milo and Rihyani.

"Been a pleasure," he said with a warm smile, then took aim.

"GET DOWN!" roared a voice so strong and clear it demanded to be obeyed.

Reflexively Milo and Ambrose dropped, Rihyani's inhuman agility allowing her to make up the difference. It was just as well since the world erupted with the crackling fire of over a hundred rifles and the chattering thunder of several machine guns. The air over the trio's head was infested with hissing metal that ripped through it at lacerating speed.

The Hiisi, ancient and evil creatures, their very skin worked with fell charms, were not easily harmed, but the sheer volume of firepower that poured on them began to tell instantly. The smaller of their number suffered the worst, shrieking and yowling as they sought to vanish into the shadows. The larger ones, kings and queens among their godlike kindred, took a few abortive steps at the three cowering on the ground, but each Hiisi that fled meant the fury of the manmade storm focused on those that remained. Less than thirty seconds later, the largest of the monsters decided to beat a retreat.

"One day," Tsar'Vodyanoy roared. It was the last creature to vanish, heaving its bulk in a ponderous dive into the Neva.

The chiming music of shell casings striking wet cement had ceased echoing when Milo, Ambrose, and Rihyani raised their heads and beheld their rescuers.

Captain Lokkemand stood at the foot of the bridge, black coat whipping around him, arms clasped behind his back. Were he not surrounded by an entire company of soldiers, he might have seemed like a thoughtful man taking in the scenery.

"SECURE FORWARD POSITION," he pronounced in that same indefatigable bellow, and after a chorus of acknowledgment from his junior officers, the soldiers rushed to obey.

Milo and his compatriots climbed unsteadily to their feet, hardly daring to believe what they saw as soldiers crossed the bridge and filed past them.

Lokkemand approached them at a far more leisurely pace, hands still clasped behind him. He looked around languidly, seeming like a man at complete ease despite his men having to unleash hell on a host of monsters only moments ago.

"I could see you had the situation well in hand," the captain remarked dryly, then nodded. "Still, I didn't want the men to feel they came all the way here for nothing. Sorry if that stole the show a bit. I know how you three like to be stupidly heroic."

Milo and Ambrose exchanged looks, and Rihyani, seeing their faces, could only roll her eyes.

"Simon," Milo said with a wry grin, "I do believe the captain called us heroes."

Simon Ambrose grunted and nodded sagely.

"About damned time."

2 2

THESE PIECES

Milo was back in Berlin and within the general staff building, sitting at a table, staring at General Erich Ludendorff with sweat threatening to pool where he sat.

"My apologies," Colonel Jorge muttered as he crept from the door to the table, an office folder in hand. "I wasn't informed this meeting had been moved up to today until thirty minutes ago."

Ludendorff made a disgruntled noise in the back of his fleshy throat, the sound malignant with tumorous warbles.

"Sit down, Sebastian," the old man grunted impatiently, then coughed into a sodden handkerchief. When the cloth came away, there was a smudge of blood clinging to the general's lip.

Jorge's hand gripped the back of the chair next to Milo, fingers clamped tight for support, but he did not sit down.

"I'm known at this point for arriving when I will," the colonel continued as though Ludendorff hadn't spoken. "But this is not one of those cases. Rather, it seems as though someone was once again trying to hold official yet confidential proceedings concerning one of my subordinates without me being present."

A small man with a hatchet of a face and round spectacles

AARON D. SCHNEIDER & MICHAEL ANDERLE

spoke up in the sort of officious nasal voice that begged for the speaker to be punched squarely in the nose.

"The general is under no obligation to—"

"Oh, shut up, Heinrich!" Ludendorff snarled thickly before turning a baleful eye on Jorge. "Sit down, Jorge, for God's sake."

Jorge shuffled into his seat, giving Milo a surreptitious wink.

With the colonel by his side, he realized the only ones missing were Karl Mayr and his cronies. Milo allowed himself a grim smile at the realization, even though he was quite certain that was the reason he was here. The murder of superior officers could not be condoned, no matter how much they deserved it.

"I suppose you both think quite highly of yourselves, hmmm?" the general remarked acidly. "Perhaps you think your efforts deserve some sort of medal?"

Milo stared back blankly, unsure of what the old man was talking about. He'd come to this meeting hoping to avoid a firing squad, not to have a bauble pinned to his chest.

"I've already received more than my fair share of such things," Jorge said, waving the suggestion away as though it was on a dish in front of him. "Though I can't speak for Volkohne. Perhaps he would find the novelty of the experience worthwhile, though I must tell you, my boy, it grows tedious very quickly."

Jorge gave Milo another wink and turned his knowing smile on the general, who continued to watch them both with blatant irritation. Milo felt as though they were sharing some joke he had not been let in on.

"I'm afraid the magus will have to wait for another day to receive his commendations," Ludendorff remarked dryly, shuffling a few pieces of paper in front of him. "For obvious reasons, we would like to keep this whole business as quiet as possible. With peace talks underway, the last thing we need is the truth getting out and spoiling everything."

"We certainly wouldn't want that," Jorge agreed, nodding sagely.

Milo looked from the colonel to the general and back, gripping the table as though the floor might fall out from underneath him. There was a rushing noise in his ears, and something that was not exhilaration or terror but both at the same time seized him.

Peace talks?

Ludendorff read Milo's face at a glance, and something that might have been pity raced across the old man's features.

"It seems your man was not aware of the recent developments."

Jorge nodded slowly, his eyes fixed on the general.

"What else could be expected when he has been sequestered in Spandau this past month? He could hardly be expected to be aware of the situation when his treatment has been that of a prisoner of war rather than the savior of our Empire."

Ludendorff shifted in his seat at the final proclamation, looking almost as uncomfortable as Milo felt.

"Fine." The old man grunted, and his mouth puckered as though expecting something uncomfortably sour. With a sigh, he turned to look at Milo squarely and began in a tone that left little doubt he wanted this to be over as quickly as possible.

"It seems that word reached the Americans of all people that there was some experimental weapons testing being conducted in Russian territory. When the former Russian warlords and their forces disappeared, notice was taken. Then Captain Lokkemand of Nicht-KAT mobilized his forces into Russian lands. Word made its way around the circles of military intelligence, and before long, the French reached out, willing to talk peace."

"Which was just as well," Jorge put in when Ludendorff paused. "One determined offensive and the entire Western Front would have rolled up like a rug."

The news was too much for Milo's mind to digest. He slumped in his chair, raising a hand to rub his aching head. The war couldn't be over, could it?

"Regardless," Ludendorff rumbled, drawing Milo's attention back to the fore, "we would like to keep the knowledge of the 'experimental weapon' to ourselves, lest the entire world feel the need to throw itself off another cliff."

Milo cleared his throat, and every eye in the room turned to him.

For a second, he froze.

He understood the power of lies, their allure and sweet promises, and with so much at stake, he couldn't fault men like General Ludendorff and Colonel Jorge for seizing the opportunity for peace. But could a premise as hollow as this tremendous lie support something as monumental as the end of the war? And what would happen when it all came crashing down again?

"I understand that an end to the war would be best for the Empire," Milo began, picking his words very carefully. A firing squad might still be in his future if he didn't tread lightly.

"But what is going to happen when everyone discovers that you don't have the weapon because I destroyed it?"

Ludendorff stared at Milo for a moment, then blinked several times before turning to Jorge.

"Sebastian, see to your man," he ordered before a fit of coughing broke up his words.

Milo looked at Jorge, doing his best to hide the violent twisting of his stomach. Was even that too much?

"Milo, you didn't destroy the weapon," Jorge said softly, one hand settling on the magus' shoulder. "You *are* the weapon."

"To the experimental weapon!" Ambrose cheered before throwing back another stein of lager. "May the fear of him forever keep the peace."

Milo didn't return the toast. He looked out over the Alster river and watched the snowfall.

Jorge had arranged for Milo's and Ambrose's release from the Spandau prisoner of war camp and sent them to the Wellingsbüttel Manor, a fine estate north of Hamburg. Jorge had explained that the owners of the estate had fallen on hard times during the war and had been forced to sell it for pennies to the German Army, which used it as a recovery hospital for officers injured on the Western Front. As the war ground to a stalemate and officer casualties were reduced, the manor had been reduced to a skeleton staff, and then recently to a small family to keep the house and tend the grounds. Now that the war was coming to an end, the German Army was soon to auction the place off as it went about preparing for the next war.

As a result, Milo and Ambrose had the run of the manor, eating, drinking, and smoking in expansive dining halls or sitting in solariums like the one they were in now that overlooked the Alster river. A few days after their arrival, Rihyani rejoined them, and after a few nights of pure revelry, she'd decided now was the time to tell him what she'd been about since Petrograd.

"I couldn't find it," she'd whispered to him between Ambrose's raucous toasts. "I couldn't find a scrap of the notes, and Astor's trail went cold almost as soon as I found it."

Her breath smelled of apples and her lips looked even sweeter, but for all that, Milo could barely stir himself to take her hand.

"It's all right," he said, squeezing it softly. "It's going to be all right."

He felt her dark eyes staring at the side of his face, but he kept watching the snowfall. It had to be getting close to Christmas, didn't it? Perhaps he'd go ask the housekeeper to find something to decorate the manor, something festive for the season. It would give him and Ambrose something to do besides drink and stuff their faces.

Why won't you look at me? Rihyani asked. *Are you angry with me, or is it something else?*

No, I'm not angry, Milo assured her. *I don't want you to see how afraid I am.*

Rihyani's hand brushed his cheek, but Milo still refused to look away from the snow.

"You know, I heard somefin'," Ambrose slurred as he staggered over to the keg to refill his stein. "Heard it when you were talkin' to Jorge on that new contraption they had wired up in the hall. What did they call it again, Magus?"

"A telephone," Milo said without bothering to look up.

"Telephone," Ambrose intoned as though the word was the start of an incantation. "As much magic as anything our boy can do, eh, *mon chéri?*"

Hardly, Rihyani whispered and leaned her head against Milo's shoulder.

"You were saying you heard something, Simon," she cooed. "Don't be such a tease and tell me already."

Ambrose turned from the keg and wove his way back to his seat, fighting a fit of giggles as he did.

"I heard you talking about the Reich. Sounds like Jorge, the wily ol' cat, has been usin' 'is time to chase those bastards down. Isn't that what I heard you two talkin' about?"

Milo nodded absently and felt Rihyani nudge him with her elbow. With a grunt, he craned his neck to look over her head at Ambrose as he cleared his throat.

"Yes," Milo said, trying and failing to sound as exuberant as Ambrose looked. "It seems that after Mayr reached Berlin, the rest of the rodents got the hint and went into hiding. Resignations, retirements, and plain disappearances happened very suddenly across several branches of the Empire's military and governmental offices."

"Suppose havin' your boss sent back in a box will do that." Ambrose chuckled into his beer. "Didn't sound like Jorge was goin' to let us in on the fun, was he?"

Milo shook his head, striking his best frown for Ambrose's drunken benefit, the look coming much more naturally to him.

"Not at the moment," the wizard said. "But I imagine by New Year, he might have something to throw our way in the matter of 'cleaning house.' At least, he intimated as much when we talked."

Ambrose drained the stein, belched, and sank a little deeper into his chair. As a Nephilim, it took an ungodly amount of alcohol to get him drunk, but like any mortal, he was prone to sudden collapse when his limit had been reached.

"I sure would've liked to roast some o' those pricks wi' my chestnuts," he muttered, his eyelids fluttering as the stein slid from his hand to clang on the floor. "But I suppose there's no finer way to start the new year."

"A year of peace," Rihyani said, watching Milo from where she rested her head on his shoulder.

"I'll drink to that." Ambrose yawned and sank a little lower in his chair. A moment later, content but bellowing snores resounded as his mammoth chest rose and fell rhythmically.

On a whim, Milo's fingers found the handle of his untouched stein. Smiling at his slumbering friend, he raised it.

"I'll drink to that too," he said, and without too much trouble, drained the stein in one go.

Rihyani sat up and watched him for a moment, golden pupils dancing in the light of the hearth's fire.

"You don't seem so afraid to me," she said softly, leaning forward so her lips brushed his cheek. "Or are you getting better at hiding it?"

Milo chuckled and, borrowing a little of the strength in the cane resting against his knee, he swept her up in his arms and drew her into his lap.

"I've nothing to hide from you," he said, drawing her close for a fierce, crushing kiss. Lips and tongue danced together to a voiceless song of desire. When they parted, their breath was coming heavy and hot.

"When I'm with you, I know there's nothing I need to be afraid of," he declared, a throaty, needful growl in the back of his throat.

As Rihyani plunged back into his hungry embrace, he felt an icy thought prickle at the corner of his mind.

Liar, Imrah chided, her presence still weak but growing stronger with each day.

With a shift of his knee, Milo let the cane tumble to the floor, then scooted it beneath the table. He didn't need an audience for what came next.

EPILOGUE: MEMENTO MORI

Cold water splashed across his chest, and then he was being hauled to his feet.

The sack they'd thrown over his head collected water from the rude awakening, and he started choking and coughing as he struggled to breathe through the damp cloth. He doubled over to retch, but the hands gripping his arms refused to let go. Instead, his body curled with a painful seizure of muscles. He gagged as a thin stream of bile squirted up his tightening throat, fouling the sack, but nothing else came.

He had nothing else to give; it had been days since he'd eaten.

With staggering steps, he was half-marched, half-dragged under a series of pale yellow lights he could make out through the weave of the sack. He could hear the tramping steps of the men dragging him echoing off of a hard surface.

Was he in a hallway or corridor of some sort?

He told himself he should count the steps from where he was being kept to where they were taking him, but at the moment, breathing took serious effort. More than once, the world took on the sub-aquatic quality of the unconscious, and with a start, he realized the lights overhead were a glaring orange-white. With a grunt and a guttural curse, he was deposited in a chair, then he felt the sharp chill of steel against his wrists binding him to the legs.

Mercifully, the sack came off, and Percy Astor was left sucking in breaths with a single, bare bulb burning overhead.

He heard a door close with a metallic squeal and then a thunk as it latched.

For a few moments, Percy seemed to be alone, seated in a wooden chair on a concrete floor in a pool of electric light. Everything beyond that pool was dark, though as his breathing steadied, he thought he heard the thrumming whine of heavy machinery somewhere over his head.

He tested his bonds half-heartedly and was unsurprised that they were secure. He didn't suppose he could be that lucky. In fact, upon reflection, he wasn't certain the opposite wasn't true— that he had been singularly unlucky, especially of late. It was bad enough he'd been forced to perform that unseemly ritual after Zeke had the temerity to die on him, but then after all his efforts to shepherd the Passenger in its borrowed flesh, it had abandoned him.

"The Kingdom will be served better under their hands than mine," it had intoned as they'd made their way to the train that was to get him out of goddamned Russia.

"What Kingdom?" Percy had asked, not expecting a coherent answer. "And who are you talking about?"

He'd learned not to expect the un-man to make much sense.

"The Kingdom of Noise," it had answered as though he were being obtuse. "To which I now return. Thank you, Percy Astor. I will see you soon."

Then Ezekiel Bouche's body had collapsed, all animation banished. Percy was still cursing and kicking the ravaged cadaver when they'd come and taken him. It had turned out "they" were Germans dressed as Russian peasants. They'd surrounded him as he was venting his frustration, and they'd seized him, stripped the Package from him, and then escorted him to a waiting truck.

His time since then had been one of regular mistreatment and deprivation, none of which was as distressing to him as the fact that the Passenger had so obviously used him.

He knew it was irrational, but for the hundredth time, he swore an oath that when he escaped, he would drag that same Passenger back into a vessel to express his acute displeasure. He just had to make it through this latest ordeal in one piece.

Several unfeasible ideas rose to mind for escape as he waited so that when he heard the door behind him open, he almost growled for them to leave and give him more time. Was it so much to ask that he have a little time to plan his escape?

There was the rap of hard soles on the floor, coming to stand a stride or two from where Percy sat. The American held very still. The footsteps did not sound familiar, but he'd learned that even shuffling about to look over his shoulder could provoke violent reactions.

He assured himself it was not that he was afraid of their fists or bludgeons, but further battering would compromise his ability to escape.

The newcomer did not speak for some time, but Percy could hear thick parchment pages being turned. He knew what the sound signified.

"I'm told your German is passable," said a sharp male voice in Percy's least favorite of the Old World languages. He would have struggled to explain it, but he'd always thought it was a curdled mongrel tongue.

"Passable, yes," Percy replied, glad the questioner couldn't see his sour face.

The pages ruffled again, then there was the slap of the leather binding being shut abruptly and a soft clink-click as the brass clasps were rebound on what was perhaps the most dangerous item in the world. It took everything in Percy to keep from looking over his shoulder.

"I hope your last few days have been instructive as to how earnest we are," the voice said behind him. "If you require further convincing it can be provided, but if this continues, I'm afraid your use to us may be compromised."

They couldn't have started by asking? These Old Worlders, for all their pretentious airs, were just as savage as the heathen wandering jungles and deserts.

"I am convinced," Percy replied steadily. "And I would be more than willing to cooperate if I knew exactly what you wanted."

Percy reminded himself it was not treachery if it was done to preserve his life. He was no use to anyone if he was dead, no matter which flag they flew.

"This book, these diagrams, symbols, and notes," the voice said, each word mounting in pressure and intensity. "They are the keys to saving my country and my people from themselves. You will help decipher them to ensure they can be put to use for such a purpose. You will join the tide of history that prepares to carry us to a new and glorious day."

Percy squirmed in his seat a little, the man's messianic tone approaching mania.

He'd been afraid that was what would be asked of him, and of his many talents, this arena was the one he least preferred.

"I'm a very talented and useful sort," he stated matter-of-factly, doing his level best to hide his unease, "but what makes you think I have the slightest idea how to translate what's in that volume?"

The owner of the voice stalked around to stand alongside Percy, stopping at the edge of his peripheral vision. He made out a man of average aspect standing there not in a black coat, but the uniform of a common soldier of the German Empire. As best Percy could tell, he would have seemed rather an ordinary sight on any battlefield in Europe, yet the way the man talked made it clear he was anything but a typical German soldier.

"Do not toy with me, Mr. Astor," the man growled, his voice sinking lower yet keeping the same fevered urgency. "The Reich has tolerated your interference thus far because it was inconvenient to do otherwise. Now, though, we have every reason to make you either a valued ally or one more of the voiceless dead. The choice is yours."

"Well, when you put it like that," Percy said, trying to sound jocular but only managing to seem wheedling, "when do we begin?"

The man stepped around to stand in front of Percy. He *was* rather average, though older than a soldier of the line typically would be, with a bit of jowl about the collar. His dark eyes were intent, threatening to pierce him with their stare, while the brows were so sparse that as he glowered, they disappeared into the lines of his face. Perhaps the most peculiar effect was the mustache he wore, which seemed bound within the parallels of his nostrils above, refusing to touch the corners of his mouth.

"We begin immediately," he remarked in that hot, almost breathless tone, leaning forward. "The rest of the world talks of peace, but I want the means to win the last war ever fought before the end of next year. The Endless Reich has been delayed for too long!"

Again, Percy squirmed back but found he could not look away.

"That will be difficult," he muttered. "So many things to do, you know, and there will be obstacles to overcome, other interested parties and the like."

The man tilted back, a smile curling the bare corners of his mouth.

"Obstacles do not exist to be surrendered to," he remarked, his cadence making the words sound like a recitation. "Only to be overcome."

AUTHOR NOTES - AARON SCHNEIDER

Dear Reader,

As you finished this third book, I hope, as ever, that you found something in here to your liking. I'm not silly enough to believe it will please everyone on all points, but I hope there was something here, at the closing of one chapter of Milo's journey, that you found illuminating and worthwhile.

Maybe, even worthy enough for you to demand more, eh?

If you call loud enough, LMBPN might even hear you.

In the meantime, I'll be working on another series to start coming out next year along with a few other projects. So far I've been blessed repeatedly to not just get to work with some great people in LMBPN but also hear from some of my readers. Some responses were encouraging, some challenging, but all were welcome and appreciated, because, as I've mentioned, they gave of their time, our most precious resource.

As I'm writing this it is an election in the (not so) ol' US of A, and as the election cycle which seems to devour more and more time in our lives I do wonder at how we humans spend our time. I wonder at our preoccupation with pasts and futures, and our neglectful attitude of the present and in doing so we become more squanderous of our little time in this world and therefore all the more preoccupied with what we do with what little we have left.

As the Grand Carpenter told us, no one adds to his time with worry.

So what are we to do then with our time? Well, I think we are to do what many good and great people far wiser than I have suggested. Say that bit of encouragement even if it seems awkward, hold out that hand to help even if it will be slapped away. Buy those roses, walk into that church, play with your children, call that parent. Do right this day, this moment: be kind, be wise, seek truth, love well, love fierce, and refuse to surrender to fear and dark.

Whatever lies ahead I appreciate you walking with my dear reader, and hope to see you soon.

Regards,
Aaron D. Schneider

AUTHOR NOTES - MICHAEL ANDERLE

First, THANK YOU for not only reading through this story but these *Author Notes* as well!

"Be good to each other, because sometimes that is all we can afford to provide, and frankly it is the most precious gift you might purchase." – MA, if not one else has already said it ;-)

I'm done with all the BS, Trolls, Jerks, Jackoffs, and Jackasses.

These *Author Notes* will be short.

I refuse to allow my doom-scrolling desires to overtake my productive days for the next week.

I will continue to work on stories that carry this company forward, relieve the monotony of a crap year for my fans, and discuss the better part of human nature that is more exciting, more liberating, and more loving.

There are more exciting things to learn about that are manifestations of realities humanity is just learning (or re-learning, depending on your view regarding history). Nothing has to deter you or me from deciding that today is a fantastic day.

Should I get frustrated with the news, I will take that frustration and use it for kindling to create a bonfire of stories to regale those who have decided that we won't be manipulated to morbidity.

Read on, and may our reality dictate a better future, no matter what manipulations others try.

Ad Aeternitatem,

Michael Anderle

ACKNOWLEDGMENTS

As with the two books before, there are so many to acknowledge that have made this book possible. Friends, family, and the many wonderful people working at LMBPN all contributed, and all were a great blessing to me.

But at this moment, I want to thank my readers.

You've given me your money, but more importantly your time, something so precious you can never get it back. It has been a privilege and an honor to serve you, and by God's good grace, I hope to continue to do so.

You guys are awesome. Thank you.

CONNECT WITH THE AUTHORS

Connect with Bradford Bates

Facebook:
https://www.facebook.com/authoraarondschneider/

Amazon:
https://www.amazon.com/Aaron-D-Schneider/e/B07H8WZ2HT/

Connect with Michael Anderle and sign up for his email list here:

Website: http://lmbpn.com

Email List: http://lmbpn.com/email/

Facebook:
https://www.facebook.com/LMBPNPublishing

Twitter:
https://twitter.com/MichaelAnderle

OTHER LMBPN PUBLISHING BOOKS

To be notified of new releases and special promotions from LMBPN publishing, please join our email list:

http://lmbpn.com/email/